PORT JACKSON, ALABAMA

Teresa's house

Balboa St.

Sister Hanks
Verastine Johnson

Dauphin St.

Cecelia Joachim

Barron Rinaud

Alley

Columbus Ave.

Warehouse

Eugenie Wallace
Durinda Talmadge

Hope St.

Teresa's office

Government St.

Talmadge Mansion

Davis Circle

All underlined places are fictitious.

ALABAMA

Port Jackson
Fairhope
Pensacola
Florida

Mobile Bay

Gulf of Mexico

CAST OF CHARACTERS

Teresa Worth—This P.I. nursed a private hurt, but was intent on solving every case.

Wells Talmadge—The heir apparent to a powerful Southern clan, but his family's secrets could be his undoing.

Barron Rinaud—The clever bachelor was everybody's favorite . . . and nobody's fool.

Eugenie Talmadge—The well-bred spinster carried a torch.

Jordan and Tal Morrisette—This brother and sister shared many things, but was murder one of them?

Raoul and Cecelia Joachim—This brother and sister were on the run . . . and headed for trouble.

Dubois Beaulieu—Teresa's ex-husband has disappeared . . . but with whose help?

Teresa was in a cramped, dark space....

When she regained consciousness, she couldn't move. Was she in a closet? Some kind of bin?

Her wrists and ankles were bound tight. And the floor was wet! She could feel water seeping in from somewhere ... perhaps from the slashing rains of the storm. Outside, she could hear the wind howling and the sea pounding mercilessly against rocks.

Light shone through a crack in the ceiling.

Who was above her? Was it the person who'd locked her inside the damp, enclosed space ... or someone else? Her breath caught in her throat.

Then suddenly she heard footsteps. And footsteps that were moving closer.

ABOUT THE AUTHOR

A lover of romantic-suspense reading, native Californian M.L. Gamble followed the "itch to write it herself" and began her fiction-writing career about six years ago in Alabama where *Dead Magnolias* takes place. The author continues to write in her favorite genre, now from her new home in Maryland, where she resides with her husband and two children.

Books by M.L. Gamble

HARLEQUIN INTRIGUE
110–STRANGER THAN FICTION
146–DIAMOND OF DECEIT
153–WHEN MURDER CALLS
172–IF LOOKS COULD KILL

Dead Magnolias

M.L. Gamble

Harlequin Books

TORONTO • NEW YORK • LONDON
AMSTERDAM • PARIS • SYDNEY • HAMBURG
STOCKHOLM • ATHENS • TOKYO • MILAN
MADRID • WARSAW • BUDAPEST • AUCKLAND

For Alice and David Rowlands, Roberta Eckert,
Mary Zurales, Rebecca Meggison, Carrie McCord
and Frank and Nancy Madison. Friends found in
Mobile who will remain forever dear.

Harlequin Intrigue edition published May 1993

ISBN 0-373-22226-2

DEAD MAGNOLIAS

Chapter One

Teresa Worth took another breath and stared down at the smooth features of Verastine Johnson.

Years of training kept Teresa from visibly reacting to the pain she felt over the fact she was, indeed, looking at her friend's dead face. For several moments her mind recoiled from accepting that it really was Verastine. The Verastine Teresa knew was a distinctive-looking woman, expansive in girth and spirit, with more energy than any three other people in town. In all the five years Teresa had known her, she'd never seen her still.

In constant motion, Verastine had moved around Teresa's small house dusting, cleaning, scrubbing, cooking, moving...always moving. She rarely stopped to chitchat or gossip but concentrated her total attention on whatever task was at hand.

The only time Verastine slipped out of her work mode was if Teresa asked about one of her eight children. Suddenly Teresa could hear the woman's voice in her mind, soft and proud, describing her older son's acceptance at the state university. Verastine had a remarkable voice. Teresa had heard her firm alto—singing the hymns she'd learned as a child—when she walked down Balboa Street in Port Jackson, Alabama, each morning at precisely five minutes to seven.

Blinking away sudden tears, Teresa realized it was Verastine's stillness that made her death at last sink in. Teresa also knew her tears were not just for Verastine, but for herself. Verastine had been a rock in the stormy sea of her own life, and now she was gone.

Teresa took another deep breath and stared at the motionless form, heavier in death than in life, the quick eyes forever closed. With the soul and breath and personality gone from her body, Verastine Johnson was gone, too. Her corpse, dressed and made up in Sunday finery, seemed at best an impostor of the woman loved by those crowding the Taylor Baptist Funeral Home this sweltering August evening.

Verastine's green silk dress was too bright against the pale yellow lining of her coffin, her black hair too glossy against the white satin pillow. Her brown hands, so capable in life, sported red-painted nails that were as foreign to the live woman as the high heels covering her feet under the discreet casket blanket. Verastine hated shoes, and Teresa pictured the worn terry-cloth slippers the older woman had slipped on whenever she worked.

The only thing familiar to Teresa was the worn leather Bible tucked beside Verastine. She'd had it with her always, in her huge pocketbook or weighing down one pocket in her apron. Teresa had never actually seen her reading it, but would have risked big money that she had.

Sprays of yellow roses flanked Verastine's coffin, the petals turgid with scent and unfolding almost before Teresa's eyes in the summer-evening heat. Teresa reached down and touched the cold body. Vividly she recalled Verastine bending low over the ironing board, making perfect pleats in a tiny pink dress. The thought brought more pain and made her feel shallow and helpless, so she finally moved on.

Around her the funeral home was teeming with people. All of the dead woman's eight children were there. Verastine's church friends sat in hushed, weeping groups of four and five, female heads bent, hat brims touching in sorrow. Several men, mostly elderly, wearing dark suits and yellow rose boutonnieres, policed the crowds. Every once in a while they would beckon solemnly to a white-dressed matron, volunteer nurses clutching boxes of tissue, and send them in the direction of those most prostrate with grief.

Verastine's pastor, Odell Williams, and his wife hosted the wake and greeted Teresa as she turned away from the viewing.

"The family appreciates your coming."

Teresa shook the reverend's strong, dry hand and nodded feebly. "I was planning on coming later, to pay my respects privately, but Vergel Glenn called and asked me to attend. Is he here?" An echo of Verastine's oldest boy's voice buzzed in Teresa's brain. He had telephoned two days before at midnight to tell her his mother had been killed by a hit-and-run driver.

Odell Williams and his wife exchanged glances and the pastor spoke. "He's here with some of his family in the other room."

"I'm sure he called because he knew how close you were to his mama," Mrs. Williams added, a shade of doubt in her voice.

Teresa kept on her impassive police-trained face; she'd found it was helpful to wear it when emotions ran high around her. "He called me because he wants me to look into Verastine's death."

"Look into? You don't mean . . ." The look on the pastor's face changed to apprehension.

"It's not uncommon for people to call me if someone in their family dies. Especially if violence is involved. They think a private detective can and will give them answers the police don't or won't," Teresa said softly.

"I don't know why that boy is acting this way. The police of this town are decent and hardworking. Vergel doesn't

need to be doing this." Reverend Williams folded his arms
portentously and his forehead creased. "That family has
enough grief as it is, Miss Worth."

"I think Vergel's the best judge of what he needs right
now, Reverend."

"I'm sure you're right," Mrs. Williams broke in, laying
a hand on her husband's arm. "You let us know if there's
anything we can do."

Teresa nodded and turned away from the couple, annoyed that her presence in an official capacity put even the
most law-abiding people on the defensive. She told herself
the reverend was just watching out for his flock. But his cool
look had hurt her, probably because she felt the loss of
Verastine as much as he and knew with a part of her heart
that investigating at a wake was right on the edge of good
manners.

Teresa continued down the aisle, her mind churning.
Verastine's son had said he wanted her to find the person
who had killed his mama. He didn't expect the police to put
much effort into running down the murderer of a forty-four-
year-old black maid.

From what Teresa knew of the police in Port Jackson,
Vergel was wrong, but she understood his need to get more
help. As the victim herself of a crime whose result was sim-
ilar in emotional devastation, Teresa knew firsthand that it
would help Vergel to feel he was personally doing something. Vergel's decision to hire her was his something.

Teresa took a seat beside Valerie and Velma, Verastine's
twin sixteen-year-old girls, and looked discreetly through the
sea of sad faces for Vergel. Her glance didn't find Vergel,
but she noted two women with bowed heads who looked
self-conscious and out of place.

While there were several white people in the hall full of
black families, these two women had an air of not belong-
ing. Both were blond, dressed expensively and sedately in

pale linen suits and hats with veils. They sat across from her, near the side exit. Teresa couldn't place them but thought she had seen one of them before. Verastine worked exclusively for the families on Balboa Street, and Teresa knew all her employers. Occasionally she helped a friend who did catering in other neighborhoods, however, so Teresa decided maybe that was who they were.

Furtively she studied the pale profile of the woman closest to her. She was the older of the two, shorter by several inches, prettier, with a sharp, small nose and tiny ears. Under the veil flowing from her hat, diamond earrings sparkled.

As Teresa watched, the woman closed her eyes and sighed sharply. One of the nurses knelt in the aisle between where she and Teresa sat and hissed, "Are you fixing to fall out?"

The woman shook her head and her companion sent the nurse away. Before Teresa could get a better look at the second woman, a man standing just outside the door took a step into the church. He was tall and broad shouldered, with a well-formed head full of blond hair. He wore dark, mirrored sunglasses and a navy suit and dark tie that somehow looked like a costume. The man balanced forward slightly on the balls of his feet. An athlete, Teresa found herself thinking. The man was staring at someone behind her and appeared to be concentrating on something other than the wake.

Teresa felt a trickle of perspiration run between her shoulder blades and twitched it away. She'd always been a people watcher. It was one of the characteristics that had made her a good cop and now helped her be a successful private detective. She could size people up accurately, particularly those with a problem they wanted to keep from sight. Something about this good-looking man told her he'd be more comfortable dressed in tennis clothes and that he didn't want to be here today.

Why? her mind asked. From his stance, hunched and tense and somehow defensive, he appeared to be a man with a serious worry.

Teresa let a faint smile touch her face and crossed her legs at the knee. Maybe he would prove a future client, she thought. Maybe he'd come to her and ask her to get the goods on an errant wife.

Although anyone who'd cheat on a hunk like that... Teresa snapped her gaze back to the man, embarrassed by her thought, but he was gone. Disappointment chewed at her, and the emotion caught her by surprise. In the three years since her divorce she'd lived an emotionally detached life that had not allowed any new men to spark attraction in her.

Today must be different, she thought, tuning back in to the sorrowful crowd around her. Today, in the presence of death, she'd subconsciously craved some kind of comfort and had naturally reached out to life. She put the blond stranger out of her mind.

"Miss Worth?" a young male voice whispered behind her.

Teresa turned and found Vergel Glenn Johnson, the older of Verastine's two sons, leaning over the back of the pew.

"Can you come talk for a minute?"

She nodded and slipped quietly out of her seat. Following him outside, Teresa took long strides, relieved to be moving away from the overt display of misery that made her private demons bubble up in her gut.

"How are you holding up, Vergel?" Teresa squeezed his arm and kept her voice neutral, pushing the smiling face of a young girl down into her memory.

"I'm doing all right, Miss Worth."

"Who's staying with the younger children?"

"My sister Vontel came down from New Orleans to stay with them. The twins are with Mama Pearl. It's just Vernon and the baby that are a problem, really. That's why I'm thinking of dropping out of the university to help with them." Vergel's face caved in suddenly, and he looked years younger than the nineteen he had lived.

"I'm so sorry, Vergel." Teresa put her arm around his slim shoulders and the two of them walked toward the magnolia trees shading the walkway. Verastine's husband, Claudell, had died last year of a stroke. This grown boy looked like a man, but Teresa knew he felt like any orphan, alone and scared. "Do you want to tell me what happened now or would you rather wait? I can get a police report—"

"No. It's best we do it now. Can you start today? Working for me, I mean?"

She nodded briskly. "It's nearly seven-thirty at night, Vergel. How about if we wait until tomorrow, okay?"

That made him smile sadly. Fresh tears brimmed in his eyes and he looked away, toward the crowded parking lot. The sky was still brilliantly light and would be for another hour or so. Vergel shook his head as if something amazed him, then turned back to Teresa. "Mama shouldn't have been out there. Had no business going back out. It was money, she was always worrying about the money, now that Daddy died."

Teresa waited for him to explain, but he only pressed his lips together and stared at her. "You mean she went back out to earn more money?" she finally prompted. Her voice sounded cold to her ears, but she pushed on. "What do you mean, Vergel? Why did Verastine go out?"

"She got a telephone call next door at Sister Hanks's house. Sister yelled through our front door that Mama had to go back to Miss Wallace's 'cause she couldn't find something Mama had ironed. Mama didn't understand what it could be, but she went, anyway. It was past nine o'clock when that happened."

"Miss Wallace? Who is that?"

"That shut-in lady who lives over by the flower shop," Vergel answered.

"Why did she call Sister Hanks's house? Your mama had a phone." Teresa was puzzled at this small mystery, and the first warning light of inconsistency blinked on in her brain.

"I don't know. But when Sister called, Mama didn't ask any questions. She was already dressed for bed, but she put her uniform back on, got her purse and went out the door."

"Was her purse returned?"

"Yes, ma'am. It had over two hundred dollars of her pay still in it when the police gave it back to us. Mama always hid that purse when it was full of money, till she could get to the bank. Don't know why she'd take it out to go to Miss Wallace's."

Teresa agreed silently that this was odd behavior, but didn't ask any more about it. "I don't know, either, Vergel. But I'm glad you got it returned."

Vergel shook his head fiercely, his large eyes filling with tears. "I can't believe she's not coming back, Miss Worth."

Teresa pictured Verastine in her mind, wearing her starched white uniform that was the preferred dress of household help in Port Jackson. Verastine should have been easy to see in that outfit. The thought made Teresa's heart beat faster, and she patted Vergel's arm. She wished she hadn't when his face contorted with fresh pain. "What were you doing at your mama's?"

"Came to do my laundry. She didn't want me messing with those machines over at the dorm anymore. Said they weren't getting things clean."

"I'm glad you got to see her that night."

"I should have stopped her," Vergel said suddenly. "I told her not to go, to wait till the next day. But she wouldn't listen. She told me to stay and make sure Vernon was asleep, that she would be back in an hour or so and to stay put."

But she never came back.

The unspoken words hung in the heavy air between them. Teresa brushed off three pairs of red-spotted black love-bugs that lighted on her arm and wished for a cigarette. "When did the police come?"

"About ten-thirty. I had just called Violet and told her to come mind the children 'cause I was going to walk over and get Mama. I was standing at the door, looking down the street, when I saw them. Two police in the car. Said Mama was run over in the driveway of that abandoned grocery warehouse on Columbus. Said it was a damn shame there weren't any streetlights on Columbus."

It was a dangerous shortcut for Verastine to have taken, Teresa thought. But not an unlikely one. Columbus was a block over from Balboa, but an alley cut across that part of the residential section and linked it to the main street, Hope Avenue. She must have been headed for that.

"Did the police say if there were any witnesses?" Teresa asked. She had already talked to Betts Vaut, the investigating officer, but she was curious to see what they had told Vergel.

"No," he answered. "Said nobody heard anything until some white man drove by and found Mama lying there. Dead."

Dead. The word settled heavily in the middle of Teresa's brain. "I'll get a copy of the report tomorrow, Vergel, and call and let you know what I think. I'm not real sure how much I can do...."

He stuck his hand in his navy-blue jacket and pulled out some bills. "I don't know how much you usually charge, Miss Worth, but here's some money toward it. You know I'm good for the rest."

She accepted the cash, for to turn it down would hurt his pride and undercut his control. Teresa remembered how important control was when your whole life lay in pieces around your feet. "Don't worry about the fee, Vergel. We'll arrange something."

From behind them a deep male voice called out. "Vergel?"

They turned toward the funeral home. Reverend Williams was standing at the door. He beckoned Vergel and gave Teresa a look that told her she didn't need to come back in. "We need you in here, son."

"I'll be over to see you, Vergel," Teresa murmured.

"Thanks, Miss Worth. I know my mama and you were friends."

His sweet words made her eyes ache again. They had been friends, even though Verastine had worked for her. They had been through a lot and had respected one another. She watched as Vergel hurried back to the wake.

Just then Teresa heard a car start in the parking lot and glanced over in time to see a silver Mercedes back up sharply. With a scrape it ripped into the side of a red, hubcapless Oldsmobile and screeched out of the lot without stopping. The blond man Teresa had noticed earlier in the church rushed from the shadows of the magnolias.

"Sissy!" he yelled, waving his arms.

The car continued down the side street, ran a stop sign and turned out of sight.

"Damn it to hell!" the man swore, then looked at Teresa, hands on his hips. He shook his head and turned and glared in the direction the Mercedes had taken. "My grandmother should not be allowed to drive," the man announced in an aggravated tone.

"Your grandmother should not have left the scene of an accident," Teresa replied.

"What?"

"She hit that car," Teresa said, pointing to the damaged door panel. "The law in Alabama requires you to leave your name, phone number and insurance information if you do any damage to an unoccupied vehicle.''

The man stared at her for a moment. "Are you a cop?"

"No. But I do know the law."

He removed his sunglasses as if to get a better look at her, then surprised her by walking toward her with his hand outstretched. "My name is Wells Talmadge," he said. "You are?"

"Teresa Worth." She shook his hand, trying to match his firm grip with one of her own but was a bit overwhelmed by how big the guy was now that she was next to him. He was well over six feet, and had the sure, confident demeanor of someone who was used to being in charge of a situation. His next words confirmed that opinion.

"I'll leave the necessary information on the car and will see to it personally that the repairs are made. You're absolutely right, Miss Worth. My grandmother should not have left. I hope you'll understand how upset she was, and accept my word that Talmadge family members do not make it a habit to be so careless or lawless."

She couldn't see why he'd really care what a stranger thought of him, but it was no time to be irritable. "I'm sure your grandmother and the owner of that car will appreciate that, Mr. Talmadge." Teresa turned to leave but Wells reached out a hand and stopped her.

"Thanks for bringing me back to earth. It was kind of you."

"You're welcome," she replied.

He dropped his hand and slipped the sunglasses back on. "Well, have a good evening, Miss Worth. I hope to see you again under more pleasant circumstances."

Her expression must have revealed some flash of doubt about his sincerity, for he smiled and touched his hand to her elbow a second time. "I mean that, Miss Worth."

"Port Jackson's a small town, Mr. Talmadge."

"That's a fact, Miss Worth. But sometimes that isn't all bad. You'll find that out once you've been here as long as I have."

Despite feeling the slightest bit manipulated by the man's more than abundant charm, Teresa smiled and nodded her head in agreement. "Good evening," she said. She turned and walked toward her car, wondering if the man had pegged her as an outsider because of her lack of an accent.

His own was cultured Port Jackson, but not as broad and rich as most natives. She'd bet he wasn't born on the gulf coast, despite the fact that the family he had spoken about was most likely one of the fifty who ran the civic and social affairs of the small town.

Talmadge? Had she met any of them? No one came to mind, although it seemed to her that an ex-mayor was named that. Settling behind the wheel of her car, Teresa glanced over in time to see Wells Talmadge slip a business card under the windshield wiper of the red Olds. He then headed in the opposite direction, toward the historic garden district.

She could give him a lift and see where he lived, Teresa thought to herself, glancing quickly in the mirror to see how much of her face the evening's humidity had melted off so far. She looked okay. Tired, but okay. With that self-appraisal Teresa turned the ignition on and pulled out of the space, aware of a small flutter of anticipation in her stomach.

This is just good business, she told herself. After all, anyone at the wake might know something about Verastine's last night. Besides, it was perfectly proper. Wells Talmadge hadn't had on a wedding ring.

"Honestly," Teresa said aloud inside her hot, sticky car, amused nonetheless by her rising spirits. At the exit she glanced in the direction Wells had taken, just in time to see a dark blue Cadillac with tinted windows and Florida license plates stop and pick him up.

As she watched the car roar off, Teresa's cheeks warmed. She let up on the gas and the car stalled. Aggravated, she slapped at the steering wheel, feeling foolish and exposed as she restarted the car.

Suddenly she thought of Verastine and Vergel Glenn, and how you couldn't count on anything in life staying the same for even a blink of an eye. Somber once again, she turned in the opposite direction and went home.

EARLY THE NEXT MORNING, while Teresa dressed for work, she mentally planned what she'd do first for Vergel Glenn. She'd call around and find out more about this Miss Wallace, then verify she'd called Verastine and try to find out why she'd called Sister Hanks's house. It was a small discrepancy, but Teresa knew from her three years of investigative work that it was the tiny knots of oddness that often untied the big mysteries.

One just had to approach things slowly and not alarm folks by making them defensive. Defensive people rarely told you more than what you asked, and getting people to talk and reveal something they didn't realize was important was the key skill in her work as she saw it.

And her work was made more difficult in this town due to the fact that she hadn't been born here. People in Port Jackson, Alabama, didn't take to strangers very well, especially those from the wilds of L.A., Teresa had found. A few had made an exception for her, a native Californian, when she and her husband and young daughter had arrived five years before, but that was primarily because her ex-husband, DuBois "Doobie" Gaillard Beaulieu, *was* a native son, and the scion of one of the oldest Port Jackson families. His family didn't have much money, but since they'd settled here in 1711 with the French, they had social clout matched by few others.

As in any town in America, money and birth connection moved the wheels of society, and the Beaulieu name ensured that Teresa had been invited to her share of card parties and teas. They, of course, had invitations to the most prestigious balls every Mardi Gras season.

The fact that Teresa was an ex-LAPD policewoman and that she insisted on opening a private investigation office made her of great interest to Port Jackson natives. When she and Doobie divorced shortly after their arrival in town, most of the invitations dried up, though Teresa was pleasantly surprised that her new work as a P.I. was successful. She felt this was due to the fact that she got the town's sympathy vote. Even though DuBois Beaulieu was one of their own, he was not the most popular man in Port Jackson.

Teresa had learned through intuition and the grapevine that most of Port Jackson's elite found DuBois Beaulieu lazy, rude and ruthless. There were few in Port Jackson who hadn't been burned by him at one time or another when he'd started a land investment firm in the eighties, and those financial wounds were very slow to heal.

Teresa still felt their animosity toward her ex when she was hired by members of the ruling class for work on divorce cases or when she was out and about, doing background checks for Ivy Inge Insurance, the firm whose retainer paid most of her living expenses.

It was ironic, Teresa had realized more than once, that the single biggest reason she was able to make a living in Port Jackson was that people disapproved of her ex-husband. The fact that he'd kidnapped their daughter and disappeared from sight eight months ago had turned that disapproval into out-and-out condemnation. So despite her outsider status Teresa had found herself at home in Port

Jackson, accepting and accepted, at least until she got her child back.

As she opened her car door she remembered what Betts Vaut had said to her when she'd reported her husband's crime at the police station. "There's no love lost for Du-Bois in this town, honey. You're the one folks care about."

Simple words of comfort. Of course, Betts Vaut had a sticker on his police car that read "American by birth, Southern by the grace of God," so she'd do well to remember to tread lightly with this Miss Wallace, especially until she found out who she was related to.

When Teresa had readied herself for work, she went out to her car and turned on the ignition. Nothing happened. She pumped the car's gas pedal and turned the key again. Nothing. Inside the car, moisture dripped down the center of the windshield and a fire ant skittered across the dashboard. She slapped the ant, slapped the steering wheel and got out. She lifted the car hood and began tinkering, but nothing brought the car to life.

Her forehead was blistering from the fifteen minutes she'd spent in the sun trying to fix her car; she returned to the house to call a tow truck and the Port Jackson police station. Betts wasn't in and the cop on the desk told her curtly that she wouldn't be able to pick up the accident report on Verastine's death until after two o'clock. When she pressed him, he would give no information as to what the holdup was.

But his attitude said it was none of her business. Wearily she waited for the towing service. The man got the car running but warned that she'd have to take it in for major work or risk having it die on her again.

She mentally ran through her budget on the drive to work, trying to figure out how she was ever going to afford a new car. She wasn't. Deflated, Teresa stepped out of the antique elevator in her office building at ten after ten. Instead

of the usual empty alcove in front of her office, she found
two Port Jackson natives draped over the green Naugahyde
sofa that served as her client waiting area.

Teresa rented the alcove and one small room in the Jef-
ferson building on Government Street, smack in the middle
of the antebellum mansion district. The furniture was tacky
but the marble floors and cornices were artworks. Besides,
it was within walking distance of the courthouse, jail and an
incredible luncheonette known as Mama's.

From the early days in town when she'd been invited into
their homes, Teresa had seen the rich gentry that lived in the
area close up. Now, she pegged this man and woman to be
members of that tribe. The pair of them looked like Vanity
Fair Goes Southern. The woman was dressed in the palest
pink. She wore stockings, flat leather shoes, a filmy geor-
gette dress and a picture brim hat. She carried no purse.

Teresa quickly compared her own looks to her visitor's
and grinned over how easily she came up the loser. Teresa
was slight and unremarkable looking. She had nice brown
hair and hazel eyes. Good smile, too strong a chin. The visitor's eyes were blue, but not just blue. They were a shade
Teresa had seen in a Cartier catalog described as lapis. Her
hair was thick and blond, but not just blond. White blond.
Platinum blond. Madonna-eat-your-heart-out blond.

"Hi," Teresa offered, tamping down her unusual feelings of envy. "May I help you?"

"I'm looking for Teresa Worth," the woman replied, then
gracefully stood.

At least five foot ten, the woman held herself as if the rest
of the female population of the world was looking and taking a posture lesson.

Teresa threw her shoulders back and disengaged her ego.
Despite the edge this stranger's beauty gave her, Teresa reminded herself of the importance of a true heart and clear

conscience. Something, possibly knee-jerk jealousy, told her that this gal had neither.

"I'm Teresa Worth. I'm sorry I'm late. Have you been waiting long?"

The woman held out a pale hand and touched the ends of Teresa's fingers. "No. I'm Jordan Morisette." She turned and beamed at the man next to her, as if she was congratulating him on something. "This is my brother, Tal." The blue gaze turned back to Teresa. "You don't mind if he sits in?"

Jordan oozed charm and Patou's Joy, both heady and inappropriate for ten in the morning. "No. Of course not." Teresa fumbled with her keys at the door then finally turned the lock. Making a gesture that felt unaccountably awkward, she forced a smile. "Please come in."

Tal Morisette appeared at her side and held the door. He was slightly younger than his sister, whom Teresa placed at thirty. Tal wore a beige silk suit that was cut to perfection. It had probably cost more than her car, she realized. He clutched a kid leather brief carrier that closed with a gleaming gold zipper. Tal's hair and eyes were sable brown, his skin tanned and his teeth big and strong and white.

He looked so much like his sister that Teresa felt she was staring at a negative and positive image of one gorgeous person. She dropped her briefcase and purse into a heap behind her desk and sat carefully. Slowly she took out a manila folder, opened the first page where a lined notebook page had been stapled in, and wrote "Jordan Morisette."

When she looked up, Tal was still standing by the door looking as if he was waiting for instructions from Jordan. She was relaxing in one of the two straight-back chairs in front of Teresa's desk.

"Won't you sit down?" she asked him.

Without turning, Jordan patted the chair next to her, an emerald cut diamond of about four carats on her long-fingered hand sparkling the way. Her brother shut the door and came and sat. Teresa tried not to react as the two of them scooted their chairs even closer and waited for her to say something. It was getting on her nerves that they were so chummy and that so far Tal had not spoken a single word.

"Now. What is it you need a private investigator for, Miss Morisette?" Teresa asked.

Jordan smiled and nodded to Tal. He unzipped the Gucci brief carrier, took out a picture and handed it across the desk.

She glanced at it quickly. It was a professional black and white of a chubby Hispanic woman. About twenty, she was wearing an off-the-shoulder cotton blouse and ornate earrings, and had a wide space between her top front teeth. The bottom corner was cut off, as if someone had decided to keep the signed inscription.

"Who is this?"

"Cecilia Joachim," Tal answered. His voice was deep like Jordan's, edged with the same upper-class Southern blend of accents that tells of time spent with teachers in expensive private schools and inadequately educated nannies.

"Would you spell that, please?"

Tal did. Teresa kept her face expressionless but her stomach knotted. Tal pronounced Joachim as "Joe-ak-um," not with the intonation her southern California childhood had taught should be "Wa-keem."

"Who is she?" she asked, looking at Jordan.

"The woman Jordan and I need you to locate as soon as possible," Tal answered. He took out another item from his carrier, a folded piece of heavy white stationery.

Teresa unfolded it. Typed on the sheet were three addresses, one a few blocks away in Port Jackson, one in

Pensacola, Florida, about an hour east, the last in Pico Rivera, California.

"Cecilia lived in Port Jackson until a couple of weeks ago, July nineteenth to be exact. At that address on Dauphin," Tal intoned with rehearsed precision.

"Are you sure she's moved out?"

"Yes," Tal answered. "Before that she was in Florida. The California address is, I believe, where some family live."

To Teresa's ears, Tal made "some family" sound disreputable. "Why do you and your sister want to find this woman?"

There was a moment's silence. Tal looked at Jordan. Jordan stared at Teresa as if she amused her. "She has something of mine." Her voice sounded slightly surprised.

"She stole something from you?"

"She has something of mine," Jordan repeated. "I can't have that. I understand your fee is a hundred dollars a day, plus expenses. Tal has some cash for you." She stood slowly and, to Teresa's amazement, held out her hand. It was obvious she judged the interview to be at a close.

Teresa glared at Jordan, figuring that might slow her down. "Miss Morisette, I can't take this case without more information."

"Oh?"

She sounded amused again, and it was beginning to aggravate the hell out of Teresa. *"Oh,"* the detective said flatly.

Jordan favored the sarcasm with a high-wattage smile. "Well, there is nothing more to tell, really. This little girl worked for me as a maid. She disappeared with something of mine. All I want you to do is find out where she's living."

"The police need to be informed if there's been a theft."

Tal dropped a heavy white envelope on Teresa's desk and laughed low in his throat. "We don't need to go bothering those boys with this, Miss Worth. If you'll just locate Miss Joachim, our family can handle the rest. She ran off with one of Jordan's purses what had one of our Aunt Gens's favorite necklaces in it. Nothing real valuable, except sentimental, if you know what I mean."

Teresa leaned back in her squeaky chair and crossed her arms over her chest. Tal Morisette sounded as if he was doing an impersonation of someone older, maybe his father. She let them wait while she mulled. The guy in the tow truck this morning had said her car needed a new solenoid and battery, to the tune of three hundred dollars. The envelope Tal had dropped on the desk was thick. While she didn't like the Morisettes' air of condescending mystery, she was used to clients who were unable to be straight about their own motives for wanting to find someone.

"Is there any reason why Miss Joachim doesn't want to be found?" Teresa pronounced the name as they had. She saw Tal's left eyelid quiver, or thought she did.

"You're the detective," he said.

"I doubt she's in hiding, if that's what you mean," Jordan added, for the first time sounding a touch anxious.

Teresa was tired of dancing around. She picked up the sheet and stared at it again. "Okay." She got Jordan's address and telephone number. "By the way, may I ask who referred you to me?"

Jordan blinked as if the question were too difficult to answer.

"A family friend," Tal broke in. "He said you were discreet and used to working with our kind of people."

Teresa nodded. No discussion was necessary about what Tal meant by his "kind" of people. "I'll call and check with you tomorrow."

"Thank you, Miss Worth." Tal took Jordan's arm and they waltzed away as smoothly as if they'd been choreographed.

"You're welcome," Teresa mumbled as the door shut. Quickly she walked to the window that overlooked the tiny rear parking lot. The couple appeared a few seconds later, surprising her by walking through the car park and strolling down the street.

Teresa glanced back down at the notes. Jordan had given her address as 3 Davis Circle. Of course, she told herself. Antebellum types lived in antebellum inherited mansions. Doobie's mother had lived on Davis Circle. She'd died when they'd first moved to town, and Doobie had sold the house. He'd sold all the property he'd owned in Alabama, she'd found out during the divorce. The better to hide his assets, her lawyer had told her. The better to be the secretive, manipulative jerk he was, she'd concluded.

Jordan and Tal Morisette disappeared from view, sucked into the shadows thrown by the canopy of moss and oak and magnolia branches.

Ten minutes later Teresa deposited ten one-hundred-dollar bills into her business account. They were so crisp she had trouble peeling them apart to count.

Four remained. She tucked those into a white envelope and wrote "Vergel Johnson" along with his address across it, stopped at the post office to insure and post it, then headed back to the office to try to track down Miss Wallace.

Chapter Two

Teresa had got an address and phone number for a Miss Eugenie Wallace by calling Sister Hanks, the woman who lived next door to Verastine, but had received no answer when she called.

Deciding to put Vergel's case aside for a while, Teresa tackled the Morisettes.

The address Jordan Morisette had given for Cecilia Joachim's residence was on Dauphin Street, a lovely wide street filled with hundred-year-old homes. The house she was looking for was set back from the street about two hundred feet. Teresa parked the loaner the Chevy dealer had given her at the curb, and slapped a mordantly buzzing mosquito. Beside her on the car seat the accident report on Verastine lay unread. She knew what it said after talking with Betts Vaut a few minutes ago. Nothing.

Nothing of any comfort to Vergel, or use to her investigation. The only clues were faint traces of dark blue or black paint found on Verastine's clothes. The lab boys had sent them to Birmingham for make and model type, but that would take two days.

It was three o'clock and the humidity was ninety-nine percent and swelling. The typical August day underscored the intelligence of afternoon naps and Creole cottage architecture, although, as she shaded her eyes, Teresa doubted if there was a breeze anywhere to blow below the raised porch of the home sitting beyond the pine trees.

An overgrown path cut at an angle across the yard. Teresa set out, wondering how Cecilia Joachim could afford this part of town on a maid's salary. Port Jackson gentry kept strictly to the minimum wage for the hired help, popping only for bus fare when pressed.

Verastine had worked for some of her "families," as she called them, for over twenty years, and still she was paid the minimum. It had rankled Teresa when she heard this, but it hadn't seemed to upset Verastine. Teresa had paid her what she'd paid her sitter in Los Angeles and Verastine had accepted the money as she did most things, which was without comment.

The path wound through twenty oak trees in desperate need of pruning. The gnarly branches and mossy limbs tangled like linked hands, providing a complete screen from the busy street. The white-painted clapboard house was fully revealed as she came through the last stand of oaks. It had a redbrick foundation, and six round pillars supported an overhanging shingle roof and a raised front porch wrapped gracefully around both sides. A Port Jackson Historical Society marker was nailed onto the wall beside the front door, which stood wide open. Ten-foot floor-to-ceiling windows across the front of the house were too grimy to offer a glimpse of any movement inside.

Paint was peeling off in sheets, and two of the six front shutters had rotted off their hinges and sat on the porch where they had fallen.

Teresa climbed the steps to the left of the door, her ears picking up the strains of Vivaldi from deep within the house. Halfway across the porch she stopped dead. A small cinnamon-colored lop-eared rabbit jumped out the front door and sniffed the air excitedly.

Tears welled up and Teresa felt incapable of swallowing. Last Easter she had bought her seven-year-old daughter, Katie, a lop they named Gussie. Gussie had died two weeks after Katie's father kidnapped her, and the rabbit's death had nearly driven Teresa over the edge.

"Bunny? Where are you, bunny?"

The man's voice was like a splash of tepid water and did little to snap Teresa out of her despair, but she managed to blink away the tears before he saw her.

"Bunny! Come on now, darlin', baths are a treat on a mean old day like this. Then I'll give you some nice—"

He spotted Teresa and stood looking surprised, but not frightened or annoyed. "Hello. Can I help you?"

"Good afternoon," she answered, her voice tight. "I'm Teresa Worth. I'm sorry to bother you, but I'm looking for Cecilia Joachim." She pronounced Joachim in what was to her the correct way, and was pleased when the man knew who she meant.

"Cecilia's gone, my dear. More than two weeks now." He picked up the lop and walked closer. He was short and thin, about fifty years old, dressed in a crumpled white shirt and linen trousers held up with frayed leather suspenders. His voice was creaky but firm, the drawl celebratory of his heritage. "I'm Barron Rinaud. Landlord, bunny baby-sitter and poet. Would you like to have a glass of lemonade? I make it properly, with boiled sugar water and a drop of maraschino juice."

Rinaud seemed delighted Teresa was there to be hospitable to. She relaxed, seeing this as a sterling opportunity to get started on this case and put off disappointing Vergel Johnson another few hours. "Yes. I would like that very much. May I help?"

"No, no. Just sit and I'll be right back." Barron Rinaud waved a big-knuckled hand at two pitiful-looking wicker loungers at the end of the porch and disappeared into the house with the lop.

Teresa took a seat, waiting and listening, trying not to feel the pain gnawing at her. Katie had been gone for eight months, yet the anguish of missing her was first-day fresh. She closed her eyes and rocked, remembering how Verastine had baby-sat for them the day Doobie had taken Katie, and how Verastine had blamed herself for not sensing something was about to happen.

The violins of Vivaldi gave way to a march, cymbals and trombones obscenely energetic in the leaden air. At the sound of ice cubes clinking, Teresa opened her eyes. Rinaud was walking toward her carrying a silver tray that looked as if it weighed more than he did. He sat it on the porch next to the empty rocker and handed Teresa a starched linen napkin and an impossibly tall frosted glass with a gold rim around the top.

"Drink this, my dear. You're looking a bit flushed. Ladies and children and any man with sense should be napping on a day like this."

"I was just thinking that myself, Mr. Rinaud." She took a deep swallow of pink-tinted liquid. It was so cold it made her tonsils ache. "This is incredible. Thank you."

Rinaud raised his bushy white eyebrows at her as he drank and nodded his agreement. After a moment he put down his glass and picked up a chipped china plate. With a flourish he removed the napkin covering it and offered her a coconut macaroon.

She picked one up. "This is still warm. You're baking in this heat?"

"Yes. I'm a slave to routine. I iron on Wednesday, bake on Thursday and give my dinner parties on Friday night. The only time I had to juggle my schedule was when Frederick hit."

Frederick was the 1979 hurricane, a major event to Port Jackson natives. Teresa looked out at the swarm of oaks. "Did you lose many trees?" This was the standard Frederick-related question to ask.

"Braces of them. No chain saws, and no power to run them even if we'd had the monsters. It was kind of fun, though. Not many folks lost, a few stubborn fishermen. I still had my parties, but we had to make do with *frozen* creole from Sissy's freezer."

"Sissy?" Though a common moniker for Southern women, Teresa thought immediately of the woman leaving the wake last night. And of her remarkably handsome grandson who'd noted how small a town Port Jackson was.

"Sissy Talmadge. A dear girl and my cousin. She lives a few blocks away in our grandma's house. Do you know her?"

"No. I haven't had the pleasure."

Rinaud waved his hand toward a line of magnolia trees to the left and leaned toward Teresa. "You'd love her, everybody does. Her husband is rumored to be having an affair, even though he's had two heart attacks. Now Sissy told me she isn't upset about losing her husband as much as she is about the strain it might put on her Monday bridge game at Lucilla Sayer's. 'Cause, you see, Lucilla is the rumored paramour. But they've overcome their differences now."

"And they still play bridge?" Teresa asked, intrigued despite her attempt at remaining aloof.

"Oh, yes. Sissy once said it would be easier to find another man than a decent fourth."

Teresa laughed as Rinaud refilled her glass from the bumpy crystal pitcher. "Did you know Cecilia well?"

An expression that looked like satisfaction puckered Barron's face. "Not really. 'Course, she and I shared a kitchen, and you learn lots about a person when you fix food with them, but Cecilia never did say much. Her English was about like my Spanish, piddling. But we got on fine."

"Did she have a boyfriend?"

"No...." He sounded as if he wasn't sure.

"No dates at all?"

"No, no dates. She worked every day and stayed in at night most of the time, except when she went off to one of her little mystery parties."

"Mystery parties?"

"Oh, that's what I called them." Rinaud licked a macaroon crumb from his lip and went on. "Yes, I think a group of the maids were playing poker or gambling or some such trash. Innocent fun, you know, but they all took to whispering and such like they were going to get in big trouble with the FBI or something. Heck, no one would've cared about a little card party now and again."

Teresa's mind whirred away as she thought of Jordan Morisette's stated reason for wanting to find Cecilia. Had the maid stolen money from Jordan? If she had, it would have to be quite a bit to warrant them spending a thousand dollars to find her. "Did Cecilia have any visitors?"

Rinaud looked offended at this question. "Are you asking if I spied on the girl?"

"No. I just thought, what with all the windows, that you might have noticed if she had visitors. It's that kind of house."

Rinaud sat back and turned the heavy gold signet ring he wore on his left ring finger around several times. "Cecilia's in trouble, isn't she?" he asked, surprising Teresa with his directness.

"I don't know," she answered, though she suddenly thought that Cecilia probably was. "I would like to find her. Do you have any idea where she's gone?"

"No." Rinaud stared at Teresa, his voice dropping to an intimate whisper. "Are you with the police?"

"No. I'm a private detective." After announcing this fact for three years, sometimes it still sounded melodramatic to Teresa. Today was one of those days.

"Do tell!" Rinaud leaned forward. "You know, I think I heard about you. Weren't you once married to India Beaulieu's son, DuBois?"

"Yes."

They stared at each other until Barron was convinced Teresa would say no more. "Well, I hear you are well rid of that boy. He was a real rounder. Robbed a lot of folks of their money in a land scheme several years back. His poor dear mother liked to died of embarrassment, I can tell you."

Teresa took out one of her cards. "If you hear anything from Cecilia, would you please ask her to call me?"

He picked it up and nodded. "I surely will. A private detective, I can't get over it! A little old thing like you. That's wonderful. Who hired you?"

"I can't discuss that," Teresa replied, softening her refusal with a smile. She stood. "Would you mind if I took a look at Cecilia's room? You can come with me, if you like."

Rinaud blinked and slapped at a gnat, mashing it onto his cheek. Teresa waited for him to make his move.

"Have you been in Port Jackson long, Miss Worth?" he asked.

"Five years."

"You like it here?"

"It has its good points."

"It does?" Rinaud giggled and turned his ring around several more times. "You're one of the first outsiders I've ever heard to say that. Cecilia's room is above the garage in the back. The key is under the mat. I don't mind you taking a peek at her things, though I don't think there's any clue as to where the girl's gone off to."

"Have you looked?"

"No. Goodness, no."

He made little effort to hide the fact he was lying and turned his attention back to her empty glass. "Can I pour you some more?"

"No, Thanks." Teresa held out her hand and shook Rinaud's surprisingly strong one. "Thanks for your time, Mr. Rinaud. I'll be off now."

"You sure now, darling? You don't look too good."

"I'm fine, really. Thanks so much, Mr. Rinaud." Teresa couldn't coherently say why, but suddenly she wanted to leave. "Should I let you know when I'm finished?"

Rinaud didn't answer. Teresa watched his eyes drift to the line of magnolias. She noticed for the first time a group of them were dead, the edges of the leaves black, the voluptuous flowers withered and molding on drying branches.

"No need for that, dear, I'll see you go." He smiled and twirled the well-worn band of gold. "It's that kind of house."

She picked up her purse and left her napkin on the corner of the silver tray. "Around here?" She motioned toward the back.

"Just around. You'll see it. Careful on those stairs."

Teresa nodded. It seemed odd that he wasn't offering to show her the way, but she decided she'd worn out her welcome. Hurrying, she stepped off the porch and headed up a wide, weedy driveway. Bleached shells the color of old bones cracked and crunched beneath her shoes, and thunder rumbled in the distance.

She glanced at her watch. It was ten past four. In the summer months in Port Jackson, Teresa had learned she could set her clock by the four-fifteen thunderstorms.

The "garage" sat a good hundred feet behind the house and looked as if it had once been a barn, or a coach house. The structure was over thirty feet high. The owners had knocked out the back wall of what had probably been a hayloft and carved an apartment, complete with small patio and sliding-glass door.

Teresa ran up the stairs but didn't find a key under the mat and looked back toward the main house. There was no sign of Barron Rinaud. Her glance traveled down the twenty shaky steps she had climbed to reach Cecilia's apartment. There was another mat at the bottom of the steps. Could the key be there?

Heat lightning flashed in the distance and a spatter of raindrops, like someone's sweat, hit her in the face as she looked up. She knew the key wasn't downstairs, just as suddenly as she knew the door was open. She tried the knob, and it turned easily.

With a deep breath, she went in.

As TERESA'S EYES ADJUSTED to the gloom, she saw that Cecilia Joachim's apartment was little more than a one-room flat. An open sofa bed covered with a batik spread, two aluminum TV trays and a large, professional-looking drafting table occupied the majority of the square space. On the wall next to the sliding-glass door was a four-drawer oak bureau and a cheap metal bookcase, crammed with stereo equipment.

A door was ajar in the left corner of the flat leading, Teresa assumed, to the bathroom. A baseball bat leaned against the doorjamb. She stepped in and pulled the door closed against the growing threat of the storm. The apartment was dark and stuffy, smelling of cigarette smoke and rotting citrus fruit. Methodically her glance roamed the room until it found a basket of fuzzy oranges atop the stereo turntable, but no ashtrays.

Systematically she began to snoop. Beside the empty drafting table there were piles of paperback novels, a good selection of history, romance and sci-fi. She picked up one. Page 199 was folded in half. *Looks like Cecilia left in a big hurry, if she didn't even take the time to finish a good mystery,* Teresa thought.

There were also several textbooks, science mostly, running mainly to chemistry and agriculture. "F. Reynolds—Auburn University—1947" was written inside *Liquid Fertilizer and the Northern Hemisphere Farm* in faded ballpoint. Teresa put down the book and checked the others, which all bore the same owner's name. Puzzled at what a twenty-year-old housemaid would be doing with forty-year-old chemistry books, Teresa sat at the desk.

The only drawer in the drafting table was open a bit. Tentatively she reached down to slide it toward her and felt the prick of splintered wood. A close look showed the lock had been forced by someone who didn't care that the fact would be apparent.

Inside she found nothing unusual: pencils, two clear plastic rulers that read Rebel Chemicals with an address in Pensacola, Florida, green plastic paper clips and dirt.

She picked up a fingertip full and rubbed it against her thumb. It wasn't dust, it was dirt. Coarse, red soil of the variety that Port Jackson sprawled on.

"In the desk?" Teresa murmured aloud. She copied down the ruler address and took a sample of the dirt, labeled it and stuck it in her purse.

When she slipped the plastic bag inside, she bumped her knuckles against her .38 pistol. She was licensed to carry it and her years in L.A. as a cop had given her the confidence to use it, though so far during her three years as an investigator she hadn't had to once. She hoped it would stay that way, but she found herself wondering if she should load it. Shaking off her paranoia, Teresa snapped her purse closed and left it on the desk while she searched the rest of the place.

There were no photographs, but several empty picture frames of assorted sizes were stacked on the floor behind the sofa bed. Teresa looked through them, carefully replacing the frames as she had found them.

She stood and regarded the double-size mattress, then pulled back the bedspread, revealing a wheat-colored wool blanket and dingy gray-green sheets. One of the pillows had lipstick smudges; the other was clean but there was hair on it—two long blond hairs, curling at the ends, and a couple of short black ones.

As Teresa peered at the remnants of Cecilia's nest, the storm broke outside and the lights flickered, then went off with a crack as a bolt of lightning landed like a missile in one of the pine trees.

Despite the darkness, Teresa kept looking, though her instincts told her there was little to be found. The bureau held no clothes save for a red Fairhope Crawfish Festival shirt with Bite The Head And Suck The Meat emblazoned across the front. She couldn't imagine anyone outside an exhibitionist wearing it. "So you're that kinda gal, Cecilia," she remarked to the dim room. The shirt smelled sweaty and had dried mud, the same iron-choked red as was in the desk, smeared down the front.

Making her way in the gloom, the racket of the thunderstorm above, Teresa hunched in front of the bookcase and pawed through the records. There was more dirt in an unlabeled plastic bag stuck between some albums; someone had made an *M* with a felt marker on the plastic. The records were soft rock, mixed with Dean Martin, Rosemary Clooney and Sinatra.

The selection made Teresa pause and take a deep breath to compute the facts. The picture that formed in her mind about Cecilia Joachim was fuzzy, but she had a hunch that the girl had never intended to stay in Port Jackson for long. She walked to the window and looked out. It was then she noticed it was ajar several inches. The screen was pushed out, but propped against the sill so it didn't fall to the ground.

Teresa leaned forward and gazed down. An old wooden ladder, splintered and paint spattered, leaned against the back wall. "What the—"

An ambush training scene from her police days flashed into her head and she stiffened. Teresa turned and caught a shadow of movement on the door of the bathroom. Her neck tensed and she blinked, her eyes straining for another glimpse as her brain argued she hadn't really seen anything. She glanced back and measured how many steps it would take to reach her purse, and remembered with a sinking feeling that her gun wasn't loaded.

From out of the unseen room a person came toward her, their upper body covered by a length of dark cloth. The person leaped at her with a blood-freezing scream. The force of a huge body sent her tumbling onto the dusty floor. She craned her head around but before she could get the first glimpse of her assailant, Teresa felt blinding pain as the bookcase came toppling down on her. She crashed against the floor and heard the skin on her forehead pop open with a spurt just before dark gobbled up all consciousness.

WHEN TERESA WOKE nearly an hour later, she was lying on the sofa bed. She had been dreaming of Gussie, and having an argument with Katie about letting the rabbit sleep in her bed. Her head hurt with a needle-in-the-eye level pain, all over.

"You're going to be okay," a male voice announced in what sounded like the tone a drill instructor might use with an impossibly stupid recruit. "Lie still."

Teresa turned toward the voice, unable to focus around the incredible pounding in her skull. "What—"

"You've been mugged, lady. Don't talk."

She closed her eyes and felt her stomach churn. Her left shoulder ached and a pulse point of agony beat in the flesh under her collarbone. *The banshee who jumped me did a real number on my body,* she thought. Her fingers found the wound above her left eye and she winced, both from the pain and the sticky hardness of dried blood.

The sounds of running feet, followed by a familiar voice, seeped in.

"I called the police. They'll be right out." Barron Rinaud, breathless from a too-hurried trip up the stairs, leaned into Teresa's limited line of vision. "Is she going to be okay?" he asked.

Teresa started to reply, but stopped as the second man loomed into view behind Rinaud.

Her first impression was that he was a hallucination. He was too big, too much man to be in the same room with Cecilia's sofa bed and Barron Rinaud. He was blond and enormously tall. Six foot three or four. His shoulders were massive, his neck thick.

"This is Wells Talmadge, Miss Worth," Rinaud announced.

Wells didn't speak, but he nodded. Teresa continued to stare, allowing her disabled condition to cover a multitude of etiquette sins. Wells wore blue running shorts and a nylon sleeveless T-shirt. His bare arms bulged with hard muscles, as did his legs.

He was even more incredible-looking in shorts than he had been in a suit, Teresa found her scattered thoughts judging. Wells Talmadge was the kind of man girls like her dreamed of and girls like Jordan Morisette dated. At that dippy conclusion, she scooched up a little on the pillow and forced a swallow. "Hello. Again. I guess you were right about running into each other."

While he stared at her, Teresa realized that if she had to estimate the size of the creature who had done her in, it would be someone *his* size. "What are you doing here, anyway? Looking for your grandmother again?" she asked, knowing she sounded sarcastic but not really caring.

"Wells found you, honey," Rinaud answered, then sat and took her hand in one of his big paws. "Do you two know each other?"

Before Teresa could explain their previous meeting, Wells asked abruptly, "What happened to you, Miss Worth? And what are *you* doing here?"

"Someone jumped me, then pushed the bookcase over on me. I smacked my head against the floor." Gingerly she felt the back of her head. It was swollen and sticky, and she felt a stab of dizziness. She also realized what she probably looked like, and her hand moved to push her bangs aside. The inadequacy of that grooming attempt was obvious even in her groggy state, so she gave it up. "I didn't get a look at him, but he was big. Very tall." Her glance rose to the top of Wells.

He stared back, getting her drift. "Very tall? You mean, as tall as me? Or taller?"

"I didn't get much of a look."

"None at all?"

"Not much," Teresa shot back, wishing it wasn't really true. She glanced to the floor and saw a black windbreaker lying there. It must have been what the assailant had covered his face with. "Is that your jacket?" she asked, pointing to the garment.

He walked to where she directed and picked it up. It had a small insignia on the front that read Rebel Chemicals.

"No, it's not mine," Wells replied.

"Did the attacker say anything?" Barron interrupted, frowning at the jacket Wells held, then turning his tiny eyes back to Teresa.

"Leave her alone, Barron," Wells broke in before Teresa could answer. "The police will find out what she was up to."

"Up to?" she echoed. She stared now at Rinaud, who looked away and nervously chewed his lip. "I had Mr. Rinaud's permission to come up here. If he hasn't told you, I'm a private detective. I'm looking for Cecilia Joachim," she announced hotly.

Wells Talmadge folded his arms across his chest. Teresa noticed how dark his blue eyes were, and became even more irritated with herself. "Not that it's any of your business."

"Is this your first case?"

She wanted to tell him to drop dead, but overcame the urge. "No, I've been a detective for three years. Why?"

"Who hired you to find Cecilia Joachim?" he demanded.

Barron giggled. "She can't say, Wells. Don't you know that? It's part of a detective's code, for heaven's sake. Don't y'all read mysteries?"

"Was it Jordan?" the big man suddenly demanded. He ignored Rinaud and leaned his weight on his hands, which rested on the sofa back. His hard jaw, a deep dimple in the center, was set in a sharp line. "Did Jordan Morisette hire you?"

Teresa tried to hide her shock, but realized in her weakened state she probably didn't do a very good job. Just then she heard the sound of another person coming up the steps. Barron Rinaud jumped up and hurried toward the door, like a welcoming host, but Teresa kept her eyes on Wells. "How do you know Jordan Morisette?"

He made no response, but looked angrier.

"Now, lookie here. If it isn't Miss Teresa. Honey, don't they teach young ladies in Los Angeles that it ain't polite to go breaking into folks' homes?"

Betts Vaut's voice sailed across the room and took charge of Teresa's attention. The Port Jackson police sergeant, all five feet three inches of him, stood smirking and smiling, hiding his considerable savvy behind his country-boy routine. She decided it was time to try to sit up, which was a mistake. The room, with its assorted male spectators, spun. Teresa fell back against the clammy pillow. "I didn't break in, Betts. Ask Mr. Rinaud."

"She didn't, Betts. Poor girl must have caught a burglar in the act."

"That's probably true. I saw a ladder propped against the back of the apartment over by the window. I'd say he got in that way," Teresa replied.

The three men trooped over to the window and looked out. "Out *this* window?" Betts asked.

"Yes."

"Ain't no ladder there now," Betts said.

"Well, then he moved it when he left," she argued, exasperated. She took a deep breath to regain control. "I didn't see his hands, but if you want to get prints you probably should be careful of the sill."

Barron and Wells jumped back and Betts chuckled and wiped the grime from his hands. "Thank you, darling. Now, did you see anything, Barron?"

Two heartbeats of silence passed before he answered. "No, no, I surely didn't. I was baking away in my kitchen. Didn't know nothing was the least bit wrong till Wells came barreling in here and told me to call for some help."

"I didn't see anyone leave," Wells responded, anticipating Betts's next question. He put his big hands on his slim hips. "I came to check on what needed to be cleaned out of this place and found her out cold." He looked past Teresa at the drafting table. "Someone broke into the desk. Was it you?" His eyes were back on Teresa.

"No. I found it that way." Nervously she glanced around and noticed that the plastic bag full of soil and the smelly T-shirt were nowhere to be seen in the mess of books and overturned shelves. The baseball bat she'd noticed earlier was on the floor. She felt her insides churn at the sight of it, lying beside the pool of dried blood that probably had come from her head.

"How did you get in, Teresa?" Wells pressed.

"Hold on here, folks." Betts held up a chubby hand and grinned. "Now, I'm going to get this all down in a report, but I think the first thing we need to do is get Miss Worth over to the hospital."

"I'll call for an ambulance," Rinaud said.

She started to protest, but the ache in her head and neck had spread to her legs. She realized her vision was a little screwy when she saw two copies of Barron Rinaud hovering by the open door. "I'd rather someone just drove me," Teresa said. "No need for an ambulance."

"I'll drive you," Wells Talmadge announced. "I need to apologize, again, Miss Worth, for my manners. Since my family owns this property, we'll gladly take care of any of your bills."

She was too woozy to argue, and the others seemed relieved that Wells was taking charge.

"That would be fine," Betts said. "Barron, you and I can go in your house and I'll call for the lab boys to come out. Come on, help me now with Miss Worth and then you and I can look around the property for that ladder."

Rinaud grabbed her purse and Betts helped her off the sofa bed. Wells Talmadge stood by the door. When Teresa met his eyes he turned away and marched out into the muggy late-afternoon twilight.

By the time the trio made it down the stairs Wells was coming up the driveway in his car. The two men supporting Teresa on either side kept murmuring and chatting about taking small steps and being careful. They handed her off to Wells, and she watched them head toward Barron's back door. Wells Talmadge had the hardest arm she had ever touched, and he made her feel weightless as he wrapped it around her and opened the back door of the car.

Teresa put most of her weight on her other leg and tried to keep from leaning against him too snugly. It was then she noted the make and color of the car. It was an '88 silver Mercedes coupe. Trying not to blink, she glanced at the path and saw that Betts and Rinaud had disappeared into the house. Yesterday's images of the man in the dark glasses outside Verastine's wake washed over her. As Wells gently moved toward the car, Teresa wondered if it was coincidence that he'd been at the wake and now showed up here.

Shaking herself mentally, she questioned whether she could load her gun without Wells seeing her. But then her fears melted away. Wells Talmadge was holding her gently, and the look of concern on his face seemed real. She was in shock, she told herself. This man wasn't dangerous. He was helping her, for God's sake.

Teresa leaned against his broad chest and tried to relax.

"You okay, Miss Worth?" Wells asked in a gruff voice.

"Yes. Thanks." Before she slid into the seat she managed a glance at the bumper. Dull red paint smudged the surface, like rusted bloodstains from long-forgotten road kill. The question of what Wells Talmadge had been doing at Verastine Johnson's wake hummed again inside her skull.

Manners or no manners, when Wells shut the car door, Teresa suddenly had the fear that she was in more danger now than she'd been an hour ago.

Chapter Three

Wells Talmadge drove the Mercedes as if he were a teenager in a stick-shift Ford. He heavy-footed the gas, then withdrew until the car slowed, then hit the pedal again so that the sleek luxury car accelerated like a jumpy cheetah. In the back seat, behind the tinted glass, Teresa watched the familiar mansions of Dauphin Street sail by and tried blindly to load her gun with one hand hidden inside her purse.

In what seemed like less than two minutes, he pulled into the left-turn lane in front of St. Ignatius Hospital, the turn indicator softly clicking like the beat of a mechanical heart. Teresa met his reflected glance in the rearview mirror.

"How are you doing?"

"Fine. Or at least, I will be fine."

"Good. Before I take you in, I'd like to ask you in a more polite way who hired you to find Cecilia."

She wet her lips. "You never said how you knew Jordan Morisette. Is she your girlfriend?" Her fingers slipped around the cold metal of a bullet and she fumbled with the gun's chamber.

"So you're not going to tell me?"

"No."

The smile disappeared. With a jerk, Wells hit the gas and the car flew across the intersection.

Though Teresa had recovered somewhat from the flash of paranoia she'd first felt when she'd worried about Wells showing up at Barron Rinaud's, the day's circumstances made a loaded gun seem wise. But as Wells veered into the emergency-room parking lot, she gave it up.

Her brain told her the man was abrasive, abrupt and intense, but humane enough to help her. She didn't, though, doubt for a moment that personal motives were behind his being a Good Samaritan. With a snap Teresa closed her purse and waited to be helped out of the car.

Wells escorted her into the hospital without comment. At the admitting desk he barked out her name. When asked for a billing address, he turned his navy blues to her coldly. "Give me your purse."

She clutched it tighter. "Why?"

"I need your driver's license and insurance card." His huge hand covered hers and he gave a gentle tug. His hand was hot, strong and callused, and telegraphed maleness.

Teresa glanced at the nurse. "Two zero one two Balboa, Port Jackson, 36609," she said, then opened her purse and yanked out her wallet. In so doing, the purse lining stuck to the leather and she dumped everything onto the floor. Pennies, tampons, lipstick and ten bullets she had taken out of her change purse bounced and clinked and spun in shining, mocking circles around her feet.

Wells and Teresa nearly knocked foreheads as they bent to pick up the mess. His face tightened when he reached for a bullet, but he stood without comment and handed it to her.

"Where's your health card?" he snapped.

"In my wallet."

He took the wallet and opened it. A beautiful child with braids and her mama's eyes smiled out from a picture in the first compartment. He looked at Teresa, and she stared back with a look that kept him from asking any details. He handed the card without a word to the nurse.

Teresa leaned against the high counter. Suddenly she felt a wave of postshock nausea roll through her and gripped the tabletop tighter.

"Blue Cross. Private. Social security number..." she rattled off in answer to the nurse's questions, feeling like a prisoner of war. Wells placed her hospitalization card on the counter and guided her into the wheelchair that materialized next to him.

For the next hour of X rays and sutures, exams consisting of white lights shone into her eyes and rib counting by a young intern, Teresa didn't let her brain work. She had gotten fairly good at this discipline the past eight months. Disengaged, she actually slept in short bursts, awakening to answer no to all inquiries about pain.

She wanted to go back to Cecilia's and check out the bathroom. She should have done that before she left. That loose end gnawed at her. If she had been attacked because of something hidden in the apartment, something her assailant was looking for, she couldn't afford to let much time pass.

At six-thirty Teresa was wheeled out of her examination cubicle and was astounded to find Wells waiting for her. He was sitting in the waiting area, reading a two-year-old copy of *Sports Illustrated*. Upon seeing her, his eyes traveled up and down her body as if he were taking inventory of her injuries.

He frowned. "How are you feeling?"

"Great. You didn't need to wait."

"You're welcome."

Teresa grimaced at her poor manners. "I'm sorry. Thank you for bringing me, and for staying. Would you mind driving me home?"

"Home? When?"

"Well, if it's not too much trouble, now."

Wells glared at the orderly waiting quietly behind Teresa. "You're letting her go?"

"Doctor says she can, if she rests. You make her rest, okay?"

"She should stay. For God's sake, look at her!"

He sounded upset, like a dad would, and Teresa found herself oddly touched. She had seen the blue-green blotch on her forehead, and her scalp prickled where the Novocain was wearing off around three stitches. But no woman liked hearing how bad she looked, especially when the opinion was being offered by someone who could pose for the cover of *Gentlemen's Quarterly*.

Teresa fluffed her bangs and smiled. "I'm fine, Mr. Talmadge. Can we go now?"

"She'll look better in a few days. Don't y'all worry," mumbled the orderly. Teresa and Wells looked doubtfully at the red-cheeked young man, but allowed him to wheel the chair out to the parking lot.

Ten minutes later the Mercedes was hopping down Dauphin Street with Teresa now ensconced in the front seat beside an obviously aggravated Wells Talmadge. "I live at—"

"Two zero one two Balboa. I know."

He remembered. For some reason that unsettled Teresa. She looked out the window and took silent inventory of her physical condition. She was sore and woozy, but didn't want to down the stiff little envelope of pain medicine just yet, figuring she would need it more tonight, and even more so in the morning. The emergency-room doctor had ruled out concussion, but had warned her to check her pupils for dilation and to have someone keep an eye on her for forty-eight hours.

The thought made her throw a glance at Wells, then look quickly away. She'd call and ask her friend Zelda to call her in the morning to check if she was still among the living. Teresa rotated her shoulder in an attempt to unbunch the muscles, but they were knotted tight and seemed set on staying that way. She sighed, wondering again who had tackled her. And why.

As soon as she did that, the why became evident. Cecilia Joachim was in a lot of trouble. Two people who wanted her found were paying Teresa to track her down while at the same time some other someone was willing to risk felony assault to keep her from that task.

"You still doing okay?" Wells asked suddenly.

Teresa turned and studied his profile. The skull was impressive and well shaped, his skin tanned and clear. He had a day's growth of beard, which she noticed for the first time. A small, wedge-shaped scar puckered his top lip, and his nose had a strong curve to it. It was an accessible face, ill matched to the prickly personality she'd so far seen.

"I feel like hell. But I'll be fine." Teresa stared back out the window. It was only then she realized Wells had missed the turn to her house about five blocks ago.

"Where are we going?" Her voice sounded alarmed even to her own ears.

Wells cut his eyes to her. "You said you were fine. And since you're a professional detective, I thought you'd be up to a little more snooping tonight."

"Thank you for remembering, but I work solo. So just turn this car around and take me home and I'll go snooping tomorrow. *By myself.*" He stayed silent, but the car sped up as he ran a yellow light.

"Just let me out here," Teresa demanded.

"I'll take you home as soon as we're through. I'm sorry, Miss Worth, but I need to get to the bottom of something before it gets any bigger, and you're going to help me do it." Wells made a left and nearly hit a parked car. The Mercedes fishtailed, bopped around, then settled down.

"Did your grandmother teach you to drive?" Teresa asked, gripping the door and trying to read the street sign.

They were on Davis Circle. The house where her ex-husband's mother had once lived zoomed by, then he stopped in front of a beautiful columned house with the widest front porch she'd ever seen. A brass signpost held the number three.

"Where are we?" Teresa demanded.

"At my grandmother's," Wells replied.

Holy cow, she thought to herself. Wells Talmadge's grandmother lived at the same address as the blue-blooded Miss Jordan Morisette.

WELLS ESCORTED TERESA up the front stairs in a frustrated rage. Mostly he was angry with himself. Damn my impetuous hide, he was thinking. What had seemed a sensible plan a few minutes ago—to confront Jordan with the delectable Miss Worth and demand that his harebrained cousin terminate her services immediately—was now quite clearly not so sensible.

Jordan was sure to balk and revert to her dumb-as-dishwater belle routine, which he knew was sure to make him angrier. And the sharp-eyed woman next to him was sure to know that there was more to the disappearance of Cecilia Joachim than a simple spat with a housemaid. He'd overheard Jordan talking with someone on the phone about hiring a detective and had guessed it was about Cecilia. Why in the hell had his cousin gone against his wishes? Why couldn't she ever think of the family first? Damn!

In a barely controlled fury, Wells held the front door and led Teresa into the formal sitting room off the wide center hall.

"Please have a seat, Miss Worth, and I'll try to get you out of here as soon as possible."

"Why don't you start by telling me exactly why I'm here?"

"I'll do that soon. Can I get you some tea or a soft drink?"

"No, thanks." She crossed her arms and stared at him, her lip slightly puffy from her earlier fall. "I'll wait to drink at home."

The sight of her injured and disheveled appearance caught Wells by surprise and made him feel even more the heel. Maybe if he explained something of his position, he thought. Wells closed the doors and sat on the sofa, casting around for something conciliatory to open with, but, noting the flash in Teresa Worth's hazel eyes, he gave up. He'd be direct. Damn, it was the only way he knew how to be, despite his grandfather's best efforts to teach him the art of negotiating. "I'm sorry. It was thoughtless of me to drag you over here after what you've been through. But I need your help, and now seemed as good a time as any to get it."

"My help?" Teresa sat across from him, but still looked ready for a fight. "You mean you need the services of a private detective?"

"Yes, actually, I do."

"Who's Jordan Morisette to you?"

"My cousin."

This news was not unexpected. "I see. And you live here?"

"No. I live in Pensacola. I'm visiting here, though, for a few weeks." Wells leaned forward, suddenly aware that he was dressed casually in shorts and that Teresa Worth was staring at his thighs. "I'm president of my family's company. We're in the midst of a very difficult time right now, which I won't bother to completely explain, but the biggest part of the problem is a company called Tiger Development. All I've been able to find out is that they're a holding company for some mysterious group with a lot of funds who are showing an unacceptable interest in my firm.''

''Unacceptable?''

Thinking he should check with his grandfather before going on, Wells decided to risk taking Teresa into his confidence. ''We're fairly sure they're organizing a takeover attempt on the company. I need to find out who the principals in the firm are so I can stop them.''

Teresa let her gaze drop to Wells's arms. They were tense; the smooth muscles bulged with pent-up emotion. While she didn't like the way he'd shanghaied her into this discussion, she admired his spirit. ''I take it this is very sensitive. You can't just show up at their offices and ask to see them?''

''They have no offices I've been able to find, or I would. And yes, it is very sensitive. All I want you to do is find out a name, or names. I'll handle the rest. Is that something you'd be interested in?''

''Possibly. But how does someone take over a privately held company?''

Wells clenched his impressive jaw. ''They turn the stockholders against one another.''

''I see. That can be messy when it's a family-owned business.''

Bingo, Wells thought, his respect for Teresa's analytical ability going up a notch. ''*Especially* when it's a family-owned business.'' He sat back and stared at Teresa. ''So, do you think you can help me?''

''Yes. As long as...'' She stopped, unsure of how to phrase her next sentence.

''As long as what?''

''As long as it doesn't interfere with my investigation into the disappearance of Cecilia Joachim. I accepted that job first. Since you seem to be irritated by that, I'll have to ask for your assurance that there's no conflict here.''

''So you are working for Jordan?''

"That's confidential. But if I were, why would that be a problem? Or is Cecilia Joachim the problem?"

"Meaning?"

"Meaning, do you think Cecilia Joachim is involved with Tiger Development?"

Wells snorted. "Not at all possible." Inside he was livid, and nearly ready to scream with the accuracy of Teresa Worth's instincts.

"Were you and Miss Joachim involved?"

"No. I never met the girl."

"So why don't you want her found?"

"Miss Worth, my cousin Jordan has a knack for turning a molehill into a mountain. I simply do not want any publicity or gossip going on, particularly now. Doesn't that make sense to you?"

Teresa didn't answer. While his argument seemed easy enough to accept, she read something else going on. It bothered her that he had the sudden urge to hire her to help his company. Teresa pulled back and decided to make no judgments until she was alone in her own home and away from Wells Talmadge and his compelling personality. "I'll let you know about this, Mr. Talmadge. I'll need some time to think it over."

"I have no problem with that. But I do beg your indulgence and ask that we go see my cousin. I'm going to ask her to stop this foolishness one more time. If she won't, well, then, I'll drop my objections. Would that enable you to take on this other job for me if I did that?"

Teresa took a deep breath. She sensed he was concealing more about Cecilia Joachim from her, but she knew enough to pretend to take people at their word, then find out the truth herself. "Okay. I'll be glad to take on some more work. As long as I have your assurance about the other issue."

Wells's face twitched as he mulled over her terms. He stared at the woman in front of him. She was small and delicate boned, but nothing about her suggested weakness. On the contrary, she exuded will. Her thick auburn hair, her clear-eyed, direct gaze, the set of her chin, even with its bruise, all telegraphed strength. All in all, Teresa Worth projected two things—intelligence and control. Wells liked what he saw. He just prayed he could control it.

He held out his hand. One thing he'd learned from his grandfather was to keep your family close and your enemies closer. "Then we've got a deal. Do you need a retainer? I can drop it by with all the details about Tiger Development tomorrow."

"That'll be great." She took out a card. "I should be in the office by ten."

"Banker's hours, eh?"

"No. A lot of nighttime hours, though."

"Right. Now, one last thing. Please keep your work for me confidential. I don't want anyone else in my family to know I've hired you."

"Fine," Teresa said. But she thought it a very odd request.

"Well, if you'll give me a minute, I'll change, then we'll go have a drink with Jordan and give her a chance to come to her senses. Sure I can't get you something?"

"No, I'll wait. Thanks." Teresa used all her effort not to stare at his gorgeous legs as he stood and walked to the door.

"I'll be right back."

Teresa sat, not really unhappy for the chance to see the inside of 3 Davis Circle. After all, Teresa told herself, she was getting more work out of this.

The three-story home was quiet around her, though she caught sight of a white-uniformed woman pass by the doorway. The room she sat in was comfortable, furnished with satin-upholstered furniture that spoke of another era.

Her glance roamed the walls, which were covered with family portraits.

The residents of 3 Davis Circle were prosperous, Teresa judged. You didn't have to be a detective to see that. She turned away from the walls and stared at the Baccarat vase on the piano next to her. It was full of pink roses, which she could smell from where she sat. Suddenly Teresa wondered if she was dressed properly to be meeting the family in whose house she waited. A glance confirmed her yellow cotton suit was presentable, though wrinkled. She marveled that it had no blood stains.

Just as she was congratulating herself on this small luck, into the room swept a woman who made Teresa feel like a ragpicker. *Swept* was the right verb to use for this person, for the woman had sheer drama about her. Tall, nearly six feet, she was good-looking in a striking rather than pretty manner, with a round face and slim figure. She had the same fabulous posture Jordan Morisette carried herself with.

The woman got to the center of the room, her white eyelet collar and black linen skirt crisp with hand-ironed labor, before she noticed Teresa. When she did she stopped, put a graceful hand to her throat and stared. But only for a moment.

"Hello, my dear. I'm so glad to see you. May I get you something to drink?"

She was looking at Teresa with a wide smile. With a start Teresa realized two things. One, the woman was older than her first impression. Two, she was heavily medicated. Teresa had seen before that look ill people have in their eyes, a tense, anxious questioning, as if they know things are wrong somehow, but they're not sure just how to fix them. Due to drugs or disease, or a combination of both, this woman had that look.

Teresa decided not to rock the boat. "It's nice to see you, too."

"You here with Jordan, honey?"

"Yes, ma'am."

"Good. Good. Jordan needs to spend more time with her girlfriends. She'll be down in a few minutes. She's helping Tal pick out a shirt." The woman draped herself on a settee and reached for a green crystal cigarette box. "Those two are so close. It's wonderful for a sister and brother to be so close, don't you think?"

Teresa moved next to the woman on the sofa, uneasy suddenly. She watched the woman select a cigarette, smooth it and stick it in her well-drawn mouth. She made no move to light it.

"I wasn't close to my brother, you know," the woman continued. "'Course, he's eighteen years older than me, so that explains it. I was lonesome as an only child, always hanging on to one of the maids, trying to catch a glimpse of what was going on with Mama and Daddy and Bay."

Teresa wasn't sure how to answer, so she nodded sympathetically.

"'Course, it's hard enough being a girl in a family like this. I shouldn't be too surprised about Jordan being so willy-nilly with all the beaux. Even in the 1990s it's hard for a girl to be anything but a decoration in this family. She and I both graduated from university, you know. That's some achievement, don't you think?"

"Yes, ma'am."

The woman nodded and sucked on her cigarette. "Tal never did graduate. He couldn't stand being up there once Jordan was finished, so Bay let him come on home. Tal's got a bright mind and should have a bright future. If Bay would just give him the chances he gives *other* people around here, Tal will be a big success."

"Tal's never been married, has he?" Teresa asked.

The woman shook her head. "No. No, he hasn't. Still very young, though. Jordan's the one I'm worried about.

She'll be thirty-one next week, you know." Her voice had dropped discreetly. "She has so many beaux, but that can't last forever! Honestly, if Wells would just—"

Teresa stiffened at the mention of his name, and nearly bolted upright as his voice boomed from the doorway behind her.

"Aunt Gens!" He strode into the room, threw Teresa a glance as sharp as a dart, then continued to his aunt's side. "You going on with all that bragging nonsense on Tal and Jordan? You're going to bore our guest, darling." His firm voice softened and lilted as he joked with his aunt. He leaned down tenderly and kissed her proffered cheek, squeezing her arm lightly, then removed the cigarette and stuck it in his pocket. "I'm glad to see you're feeling well enough to come by for dinner. Two days in a row out and about. That's wonderful."

"Well, Sissy brought me some of her whiskey a bit ago and we're both just fine now." She put her fingers on Wells's face and smiled.

"Dr. Cousin said no whiskey. You know that."

"Dr. Cousin don't count." Wells's aunt startled Teresa by winking at her. "We girls got our tricks to stay happy, don't we, darling?"

Teresa smiled and looked back to Wells. He had changed into linen trousers and a crisp white shirt. The effect on his aunt, and Teresa, was dazzling. He looked to Teresa as if he'd stepped out of the pages of *The Great Gatsby*. Casual. Confident. The fair heir. She wondered suddenly about the woman's remarks about Bay favoring certain members of the family, and wondered at the competitive intrigues between Wells and the furtive Tal.

This line of thought made Teresa tense up all over again.

"Auntie, this is Teresa Worth. Miss Worth, this is my Aunt Gens. Auntie, Miss Worth and I have to run talk with Jordan. Will you excuse us?"

"Of course, darling. Good day, Miss Worth."

Teresa stood and let Wells guide her out of the room. Where he had been friendly a few minutes ago, he was suddenly back to the distracted brooding she'd first observed at Verastine's wake. Silently the two continued down the center hallway, past four other rooms, out to the veranda. Moving from the icy, air-conditioned interior to the thick evening air made her feel dizzy.

Jordan and Tal Morisette were sitting on a swaying white porch swing, deep in conversation. Tal glanced up and saw Teresa. He looked annoyed, then confused. He turned back to Jordan.

"Jordan, I believe you know Miss Worth," Wells said, an edge to his deep voice.

Jordan glanced up at Teresa, patted Tal's leg as if she were soothing a startled pet, and stood. "Yes, I surely do. How are you, Miss Worth? I didn't know you knew my cousin."

"We just met yesterday," Teresa replied.

"She was mugged out at Cecilia's," Wells added. "Working for you, I'd wager."

Jordan's blue eyes widened at so much surprising information. "Are you all right, Miss Worth? Tal, run get Miss Worth an aspirin or something. She's got a terrible bump on her head."

"No, no, I'm fine," Teresa said.

"No thanks to you, Jordan," Wells added roughly. "I thought we agreed that your hiring a detective was nonsense."

"I thought you weren't supposed to tell who hired you," Tal said angrily, his dark eyes huge in his pale face.

"I didn't—"

"She didn't tell me," Wells interrupted. "I figured it out. And I think now would be a good time to unhire her, don't you?"

Tal got a strained look on his face and Jordan looked as if she were going to cry. Teresa was very irritated that Wells seemed to be going back on his word to allow her to work unmolested on the Cecilia Joachim matter, but she should have expected that. Wells Talmadge obviously wielded enormous power within his family.

She sat on the chair Wells was holding for her and decided to let this little domestic drama play out.

Jordan talked very fast. "Wells, honey, what are you so upset about? Don't use that tone with me." She linked her arm in his and led him away from Teresa. "I did hire Miss Worth to find Cecilia. That girl took my best evening bag and I want it back!"

"You should have called the police, then. That's what they're there for."

"Don't patronize us, Wells," Tal retorted. "Besides, if we want to hire a detective, we don't need your permission." Tal looked over at Teresa and waved his finger at her. "You just ignore my cousin's bad manners, Miss Worth. And keep looking for Cecilia."

Before Teresa could answer, Wells turned to Jordan. "I told you to lie low for a while. You know the difficulty we're having with the business and how people in this town talk! If I go to Bay about this—"

"About what?" an authoritative male voice boomed from behind Jordan. Everyone turned. A heavyset elderly man in a gray summer suit stood in the doorway. His thick white hair was brushed back in a gleaming wave. He rested heavily on a black walking stick. Beside him stood a tall woman with brilliant, probably artificial, green eyes. Lanky and restless, this beauty had the firm jaw and stature Teresa immediately identified with Wells Talmadge. Her manner was one of indifference. Something told Teresa she paid little attention to conversation unless it was about her.

"Grandpa!" Jordan peeped. She skirted Wells and embraced the large man. "Come on in and sit. Tal, run get some drinks for us. Charlie's not working tonight, his mama's dying. Be sure and bring ice."

At the odd clump of orders and information, Tal scurried out. Wells and Teresa moved out of the way and let the tall woman lead the man to the swing. After she'd helped him sit, the woman turned to where Wells and Teresa were standing, kissed him and let her neon gaze travel over Teresa's rumpled appearance. "I'm Durinda Talmadge," she announced suddenly. "Wells's mother."

"Teresa Worth," she offered with no further explanation. Her head was beginning to throb from the pungent scent of gardenia floating heavily above the hissing summer grass. She was having a heck of a time keeping the fast-breaking relationships and names straight, but this much was clear. Wells was Jordan and Tal's cousin, and Durinda was Wells's very young mother. She'd bet the elderly man just helped in was the grandfather and older brother Aunt Gens had spoken of. The man looked sick but still in control of this show. Teresa had no earthly idea how Cecilia Joachim fit into this mix, and had the sinking feeling that this case was going to be more of a challenge than the average missing person warranted.

"Do you know what happened to me today?" Durinda demanded of Wells, who seated her in a blue-striped lawn chair and leaned against the porch railing next to her.

"What, Mother?" he asked absently, intent on getting Teresa's attention.

Teresa ignored him, choosing instead to cross to where Jordan was making cooing noises at the big man no one so far had introduced her to.

Durinda launched into an irate story about the lack of courteous salesclerks at Gayfer's department store and how she'd left nine hundred dollars' worth of dresses in a heap at the dressing-room door because she'd been told to hang them back up herself.

"You got no business buying so many clothes, anyway, Durinda," Jordan said. "Everyone knows you're broke."

"Isn't that a bit like the pot calling the kettle black, darling?" Durinda shot back.

As that battle heated up, Teresa tuned it out and sat in the chair opposite the swing. The old man's eyes flicked over her and he nodded.

"I'm Bay Davis Talmadge." He patted Jordan's leg. "Jordan's grandpa. You here with Tal?"

"No, sir. Wells brought me." Teresa had the odd sensation of her skin burning from the intenseness of Wells's eyes, but she kept her glance averted from him.

"What in damnation happened to you, girl?" Bay shot back.

Teresa touched her forehead. It was clear her bangs didn't cover her stitches and bruises as well as she'd thought. "Minor collision."

"You look like hell," Bay replied, then bellowed, "Durinda, stop arguing with Jordan and go find Tal. Tell him to get out here with some drinks before our guest and myself expire."

"You go, Jordan. You're the only one who can get Tal to move," Durinda replied.

Teresa saw malice and rage wash across Jordan's features at her aunt's remark.

"Grandpa asked you." Jordan pouted.

"How ungracious of you," Durinda shot back.

Bay's face flushed red and he crashed the cane onto the floor. "Damnation! All I asked—"

"Here we are!" Tal announced as the door opened. He wheeled in a creaky wooden cart loaded with a pitcher of lemonade and several bottles, along with glasses, ice and napkins.

Wells wished he'd never tried the direct approach with Jordan and wished he could make a quick exit. There was no chance of that now, though, until Bay was finished holding court. "What can I get you, Miss Worth?"

"Some of that lemonade would be great," she replied.

He splashed it into a tall glass and added a nip of gin and two cherries. He then poured vodka neat into a highball glass, turned and handed it to Durinda and bowed as he gave Teresa her glass.

Jordan, trying to appease her grandfather, sauntered over and poured whiskey for Bay. Teresa felt her mouth water, and realized she was starving. Fat green olives sat in a small cut-glass bowl. She didn't like martinis much, but she was willing to order one next just to eat something off a stick. Unfortunately, she didn't get the chance.

Wells walked toward her. "Grandfather, did Miss Worth tell you what she does for work? It's very interesting."

Bay grinned and sucked the ice in his glass. "No one tells me nothing anymore. What does she do?"

"She's a private detective, Grandpa," Tal cut in. "She's helping to find Jordan's housemaid."

Teresa heard Durinda suck in her breath in surprise and watched as Bay and Wells exchanged a look she could not read.

"Is that so? I think I heard of you, honey. You married to India Beaulieu's boy?"

Carefully Teresa returned the glass she was holding to the table beside her and pressed the linen napkin into a ball. "Not anymore, sir. We divorced."

"Good thing for you, I'd say. Doobie Beaulieu wasn't worth the powder to blow him to hell, I always said. Durinda went with him for a time, didn't you, girl?"

Wells looked shocked at his grandfather's less-than-tactful remark, but Durinda seemed pleased the conversation was thrown back to her.

"I did go out with him once or twice, Daddy. I heard he married a girl who was much younger than him, but you're a surprise, Miss Worth."

Teresa wanted to say, "So are you," but bit her tongue and said what she always forced herself to say when Doobie's name came up. "Have you heard from DuBois lately?"

"Not for years! Why? That scoundrel behind on his alimony?"

"No. But he kidnapped our daughter and there's a warrant out for his arrest. So if you hear from him, I'd appreciate your letting me know."

That news startled them all and it was Jordan's turn to gasp. "Well, at least you're in the right profession."

"That little bastard," Bay muttered into his glass.

Wells looked as though he wanted to turn and run, but instead held out his arm to Teresa. "I hadn't heard that. I'm sorry. It must be very difficult."

"Yes, it is."

Unable to take his family's bickering any longer, Wells said, "Good night, everyone. I'm going to take Miss Worth home now."

"Let the girl finish her drink first, Wells," Bay barked. "Have Jesse set a plate. Your grandma likes company. Especially when she's upset." He pointed his cane to Durinda. "You should've never told Sissy about that maid getting killed the other night, honey. She ain't slept at all since then. You know how she suffers when a woman's killed and leaves little ones. It reminds her of when Jordan and Tal's mama was taken."

"She'd have heard from someone else soon enough," Durinda said hotly, though she looked away quickly.

They must be talking about Verastine, Teresa thought.

"Can you stay with us, Miss Worth?" Bay demanded.

"Oh, no, I couldn't—" Teresa began.

"She's got to take medicine tonight, Grandpa," Wells broke in with a glare at his mother. He guided Teresa out of her chair and toward the door. "Come on."

The only reason she didn't dig in her heels and stay was that she knew she was going to be sick soon if she didn't eat more than cherries. But she would have loved to ask Durinda Talmadge why she'd told Sissy Talmadge about Verastine, and *when*.

Glad to have Wells's arm for support, Teresa turned to the assorted family members. "Nice to see all of you."

"Nice to meet you," they chorused with a notable lack of enthusiasm. Jordan looked at Tal, Tal looked at the floor. Bay waved. Durinda stared off the porch toward the trees.

So much for Southern hospitality, Teresa found herself thinking. *I wonder what they're hiding.* She and Wells silently made their way back down the huge hallway. As they passed the sitting room, Teresa spotted another woman sitting with Aunt Gens.

Both held highball glasses and silently stared at one another. Gens had another cigarette, still unlit, dangling from her mouth.

"Who's that with your aunt?" Teresa asked Wells.

He seemed surprised at the question. "My grandmother, Sissy Talmadge. Do you want to meet her?" He opened the front door and waited for Teresa to step out onto the porch.

"Next time," Teresa replied.

As the door shut behind her Teresa took a deep breath. Sissy and Eugenia were the same women she had seen at Verastine's wake. Often there was a moment at the beginning of an investigation when she knew she was in possession of a pertinent piece of a mystery but would have to be patient—and a little lucky—before that piece would fall into place. This was such a moment. "So you can handle me working for Jordan as well as for you?"

"Yes. I promise not to raise the issue again."

"Well, then, thanks for hijacking me," Teresa said with a smile. "I'll be glad to take your job on, and I enjoyed meeting your family. They're all very interesting."

"Very trying, you mean. I'm sorry my family's manners leave so much to be desired." He flashed her a smile. "You see I come by my rudeness honestly."

Teresa smiled back. "Everyone's got a family. There's no choosing them, so you just have to accept them, my mom used to say."

"She didn't know this bunch," Wells replied. "Come on, let's get you home."

Chapter Four

Wells held open the front screen door of the small house at 2012 Balboa and waited for Teresa to go inside. She looked even slighter than she had earlier and was definitely more pale. A pang of guilt tore at him over forcing her to go to see Jordan. He chewed the inside of his cheek. "You sure you wouldn't rather go back to the hospital?"

"No, I'm fine."

"Someone should stay here with you."

Teresa looked at him, alarm in her hazel eyes. "I'm fine. If I need anything, I'll call my friend. Really. You don't have to worry about me."

Wells sighed. He was disgusted with how the evening had turned out. He seemed to be exercising all the bad Talmadge traits with this woman and none of the good. If he wanted to manage this thing properly, he was going to have to be more controlled. She was a woman who studied the world around her and gave careful, measured responses to it. Even when she'd dropped her purse and that cache of bullets had jumped all over the floor like silver bugs, she hadn't lost her cool. And when his mother had trapped her into telling the horror story of her child's abduction she'd also been cool. But he'd seen the torment.

"Sure I can't call someone or go get some food? How about some Chinese? I'll run to Peking Seafood. They've got great chow mein."

"No, really. I'm going to go to bed. Thanks for everything, Wells," she said as he grasped the door handle. "I really appreciate it."

"How about if I come in and make you some dinner? I scramble a wicked egg."

"I'd rather you didn't." Teresa glanced away and stepped across her threshold. He released the door with a delayed swish and it closed. She looked at his face through the screen, aware that she had once again been abrupt. She didn't want to sound that way, but opted for rudeness if it meant giving her some time alone to think. The drive from the house at 3 Davis Circle had been silent and tense. The pounding in her head and tightness of her stomach had blocked any ability to analyze, which she badly needed to do.

Teresa smiled in what she hoped was a sincere manner. "It's just that I really need to rest."

"Let me just say one last thing about your working for Jordan—"

"I thought I made it clear that was none of your business," she cut in, surprising them both with the level of anger in her tone.

The intent expression on Wells's face faded into one of vulnerability. He cleared his throat. "Look, I told you I accept that. All I wanted to say was to be careful. After what happened today, I mean."

Teresa relaxed a bit and leaned against the door. "Do you think Cecilia's in some kind of danger?"

"No, I didn't mean that. I'm sure whoever attacked you was a burglar. Totally unrelated." Wells began to sweat. God, he hadn't really thought that through. Was the person who'd attacked Teresa after Cecilia? Was someone else looking for the maid's brother? He'd better stop and see Barron and find out if anyone else had made any inquiries. "I just want you to be careful, is all."

"I always am. Now, I'll see you tomorrow morning, right?"

"Right. At ten?"

"Fine."

"Good. But hey, before you go in, let me just explain that my grandfather is not well. Lots of things are happening right now with his company and he doesn't need any more stress."

"Stress? Why would the disappearance of his grand-daughter's maid give him any stress?"

Wells folded his arms across his chest, slapping unconsciously at a mosquito. "Bay keeps an eye on all elements of our family's private and public life. Like I said before, if any rumors start—"

"What rumors would start about a maid?" Teresa asked. Had the grandfather also had a fling with her? she suddenly wondered. What if Sissy had heard gossip and gone looking for Cecilia and run down Verastine instead?

"We don't need to stand here and do this any longer, Miss Worth. I can see you're exhausted. I apologize again. Go in and get some rest."

Wells's calm words brought her out of the wild speculation and she gratefully nodded. "Fine, I will. But by the way, what's the name of the company your family owns?"

"Rebel Chemicals." Wells took a step back and looked nervously toward the car, then back at Teresa, as if he were worried he'd said something indiscreet. "Why?"

Before she could give any credible answer, her phone began to trill.

"Better get that."

The phone rang a third time and Teresa's arm twitched, so anxious was she to pick it up. "I will. Good night, then."

"Good night. And thanks again," Wells replied.

Teresa didn't watch him walk away. She hurried into the darkened house and pounced on the phone, the tormenting expectations she lived with daily chasing away all concerns about Wells Talmadge. "Yes, hello?"

Silence greeted her on the other end of the receiver.

"Hello. Who is it, please?"

"Teresa? Hang on, darlin', I'll be right there." The woman caller's voice then turned away from the phone. "I'll be right there!" she shouted at some unseen third party before she returned. "Sorry, honey. Somebody's just at the door. Let me get right back to you in a minute."

"Hang on, Zelda. You can't call me back because I'm going to bed. But could you come by in the morning and take me to my car on your way to work?"

"I'll carry you anywhere you say, darling. Where's your car?"

Teresa smiled at Zelda's manner of speaking. Her friend, a Port Jackson native, always blended English grammar with hometown expressions. Zelda was one of the few people Teresa had ever met who sincerely refused to accept anything but friendship from everyone she came into contact with.

"On Dauphin," Teresa answered. "Near the Greek church."

"What's it doing there? And why you going to bed during the daylight hours, if I might ask?"

"It's a long, boring story. Now go answer your door and I'll see you about eight, right?"

"You sick?"

"I'm fine. Go answer your door."

"Yes, ma'am. Sleep tight, darling."

A click sounded, then the dial tone buzzed loudly. Teresa put the phone down as hot tears burned at the corners of her eyes. She refused to let the waves of disappointment blow into a full-fledged crying jag, even though tonight the possibility that her daughter might never be on the other end of a ringing phone presented itself to her as a fact she could no longer avoid.

Outside she heard the sounds of the Mercedes pulling away from the curb. Teresa fell onto the couch and closed her eyes. She ached over every square inch of her body, her head throbbed and her knee was stiffening up. Teresa remembered the pain medicine in her purse and glanced at the beige bag resting on the table beside her, but was suddenly incapable of standing and getting water to go with it. So she lay there.

She pushed away the tearing memories of her blond little girl and prayed for a word from her. She wasn't fearful DuBois would harm her in any way. He had loved Katie in his own way, and had been very proud of the child. Once he'd told Teresa that Katie was the only good thing he'd ever been a part of.

But despite her lack of fear for her daughter's physical safety, Teresa didn't know how much longer she could remain sane, how many more days she could go through without some relief from worry or yearning, some lessening of the pain of missing Katie.

Teresa blinked away the tears and rubbed her forehead. She willed herself to think about what had happened today in order to chase away the demons of the past. *Let yesterday and tomorrow take care of themselves,* Verastine Johnson had told her once. *'Cause today's gonna beat up all over you if you don't give it your full attention.*

Teresa exhaled deeply and replayed the Talmadge clan encounters. The fact that a ruler with Rebel Chemicals' name on it was in Cecilia Joachim's apartment probably had little significance, but maybe the jacket did. And despite what the charming Mr. Talmadge said, it was clear he had some other reason than gossip for not wanting her to look into the disappearance of Cecilia Joachim.

What wasn't clear was why Jordan and Tal really wanted the girl found. She didn't believe the story about a missing necklace, and wondered if Jordan and Tal were the family members Wells was worried about being on the side of the shadowy Tiger Development.

Tomorrow Teresa would have to call on Jordan, and also make some calls to Pensacola. She had two friends who were on the force there who could check out Cecilia and her family, and also find out if Cecilia ever worked at Rebel. First thing in the morning she would also go and look in the bathroom in Cecilia's apartment. And a trip to the police station for a chat with Betts Vaut wouldn't hurt, either. Something told her the officer wasn't sharing all he knew about Verastine.

Then there was also the strange Mr. Barron Rinaud.

With a grimace Teresa burrowed deeper into the sofa cushions. Tomorrow. She'd worry, like a famous Southern belle, about Wells and Betts and Jordan and Tal tomorrow.

Tomorrow she would also go over and try to see Miss Wallace and find out what had brought Verastine Johnson out at nine in the evening. While not an unusual occurrence, it was odd that Verastine would rush out like that, or that one of her employers would ask her to.

Teresa felt an ache in her chest for Vergel, so bewildered and frustrated by loss. Teresa knew those emotions well. When that thought quickly triggered a return to the raw nerve she'd just managed to numb, Teresa squeezed her eyes tight together and exhaled deeply. In less than a minute she was sound asleep.

ACROSS THE STREET from Teresa's house, in the deepening shadows thrown by the three-hundred-year-old oaks fronting a vacant lot, a red-haired man watched Teresa's windows for some sign of life.

After five minutes of no lights or movement or sounds, he figured Teresa had gone straight to bed to sleep off her injuries. He glanced down at his watch. Seven-thirty. He'd wait an hour, he decided. If she made no move to leave, he'd risk it. It should be safe then, if he took his time.

The man leaned against the rough, dusty-smelling bark, shifted his left arm so that he couldn't be seen from the street and waited. He hoped no one came by who would recognize him. He hoped Teresa's door would be unlocked. He'd been told to get a gun, and this was the easiest and least traceable way to do it.

The man smiled grimly. With any luck he could commit a small crime that would tie Teresa Worth up in court for weeks and give him the time he needed to get away.

TERESA WOKE with an awareness that it was raining. She opened her eyes and shivered, not from cold, for it was nearly eighty degrees at 3:30 a.m., but from the sound of the storm lashing the shingles and the thunder rumbling as it tumbled and skittered over the brown waves of the gulf.

She inhaled and sat up stiffly, then felt nausea roll through her. In Port Jackson, summer rain tasted of the paper mills, an unforgiving blend of sawdust mingled with grass, hundred-year-old moss and dying azaleas. The scum coated her throat and nasal passages and made her wish she was home in Los Angeles. There the smog burned your eyes and lungs by day but it was a rare night that didn't bring sweet fresh breezes off the Pacific.

Teresa tried to stand and nearly crumpled into a heap, so stiff was her right leg. It must have taken the full force of the fall this afternoon, she realized. She rubbed it a moment then tried again, hobbling in the direction of the bathroom. In the dark she yanked back the shower curtain and turned the faucets on full bore, then peeled off the rumpled yellow suit and her underwear and stood under the shower. The water beat against her back, stinging her skin, but her muscles were so numb she still felt as if she was asleep.

She soaped her face and neck and wished she could wash her hair, but the throbbing from her stitches reminded her she couldn't. Two minutes later she stepped from the shower and wrapped herself in her terry-cloth robe, no longer cold and stiff but already uncomfortably hot and more than a little aware of how sore her bones were.

Silently she made her way to the kitchen, her path lit by the moonlight flooding the house. Teresa walked into the living room, searching for her purse on the coffee table. When she didn't see it she continued on into the kitchen, found the coffee filters and the Chock Full O'Nuts and set the pot to perking.

Her pocketbook was on the table beside the back door. Teresa had no recollection of having put it there, but sat down and pawed through it for the pain medication. She dumped one of the bullet-shaped yellow pills from the small white envelope and got up for water, when fear, sudden and overwhelming, gripped her.

Though physically battered, she was suddenly clear-headed and wide awake. She distinctly remembered tossing her purse onto the coffee table and answering the phone. The explanation for how it got into the kitchen could only be that someone else had moved it there. Frantically she pressed the kitchen light switch, cringing as the fluorescent illumination flooded the room. Quickly she searched the area with her eyes. Nothing else seemed amiss, but the idea that someone was in the house with her brought a scream to the base of her throat.

Teresa reached back inside the purse for her gun, debating whether to call the police before searching the bedrooms, then froze. She emptied her bag on the table, the sharp commotion of falling items jarring her nerves until she thought she'd scream from tension. Instead she gulped for air and collapsed slowly onto the kitchen chair. The gun and the bullets, all ten of them, were gone.

It was then that she noticed the back door. It wasn't closed completely, but was wedged half-open in the humidity-swollen doorjamb, the knob shiny with rain that had blown in from the storm. Carefully she put the pain pill back in the envelope and wiped the sticky residue it left onto her robe. She picked up the phone and dialed 911 and waited, wondering who had stolen her gun. The reasons someone would do that were numerous, and all bad.

Sixteen minutes later, her coffee undrunk and tepid in her cup, she let the police sergeant in the back door. He was tall and black, with graying hair and a competent manner. After taking the details he looked at her bruised face and asked, "You weren't attacked?"

"When do you mean? Tonight? No."

"But you were attacked? Lately, I mean." The man, his dark eyes sharp, looked up from his notepad.

"Yes. I'm a private investigator. Betts Vaut knows all about the incident that caused me to look like this."

The patrolman met Teresa's glance and she saw something register in his eyes. "Oh, yeah. I've heard about you." He nodded, then continued. "And you didn't see anyone strange outside when this Mr. Talmadge brought you home at seven-thirty?"

"No one."

"And you never heard anything?"

"Nothing."

"You don't remember unlocking the door, maybe to let the cat out? Or some air in?"

"I don't have a cat." Teresa sipped the cold coffee. "And I never leave the door unlocked at night."

"Good idea. Even if it was just some kids who took this gun, you don't want to go making it easier for them to get in."

Teresa doubted it was "just some kids" who took her pistol, but she remained quiet. It didn't pay to argue with police, or offer opinions. Either course of action usually led to one thing—suspicion.

"Okay," the cop continued, "let me look around."

Teresa remained in the kitchen. Two minutes later the officer returned and told her everything was clear. "You lock the doors now, Miss Worth. I'll be calling you tomorrow. Nothing else is missing, right?"

"Right."

"You counted your money? It's all there?"

"Every penny."

"And you don't want me to call anybody to stay with you? You'll be okay?"

"Fine. Thanks."

"Lock the door behind me, now."

She nodded, her nerves tensing at the slightly condescending attitude the man had suddenly adopted. "I will. Thank you for coming so quickly, sergeant."

"No problem, ma'am. Lock that door."

"Good night." Teresa locked the door and sat down, realizing she was frightened. A thief had broken in but left eighty dollars in cash in her wallet. It was as if he'd come specifically for the gun. Her stomach roiled at the thought of what that could mean. First attacked and now robbed? Was there some connection? Teresa wondered.

The thought made her reach for the coffeepot. There'd be no more sleep tonight.

TERESA WAS LOCKING the door, her friend Zelda Zurales chatting a mile a minute about what a "fine, upstanding, though somewhat audacious group" the Talmadge family was, when the ringing of her phone sent Teresa racing back inside.

She caught it before the answering machine clicked on. "Hello?"

"Teresa? This is Betts Vaut. How are you this morning?"

"Did you hear about the burglary?" Teresa was in no mood for one of Betts's circuitous talks, and decided to push him so that Zelda wouldn't be late for work.

"Yes. I just went over Sergeant Watson's reports and your name just leaped off the page at me. I think we might have some information on it, as a matter of fact. Can you come in and see me this morning?"

"You found it already?"

"I can't say that for sure. Now, can you stop in now?"

"I have a couple of things to do. How about nine?"

The officer hesitated. "Okay. But no later, okay?"

Teresa hung up and frowned. While not alarming in itself, an invitation from a police officer to visit him at his place of work was never an idle request. She relocked the front door and got into Zelda's car.

"You okay, darling?"

"I'm fine, Zelda. We'd better hurry up. I don't want you to be late."

"Don't worry about that. Doctor knows to expect me when he sees me." The sixty-two-year-old redhead patted Teresa's knee. "He wouldn't dare yell at me for being late. When he made me unretire last year to straighten out the mess that little Dupree girl made of his billing files he told me to work my own hours. I've just spoiled him being there first thing. Be good for him to wonder when and if I'm going to be in today."

"You're a smart woman, Zelda."

Zelda beamed at Teresa, then narrowed her eyes. "Now why don't you tell me how you came to meet up with the Talmadge family."

Zelda had become Teresa's closest friend since she moved to Port Jackson. They'd met at the park behind Teresa's house when Katie's ball had flown through the air and knocked Zelda's glasses off her face as she had sat reading the *Port Jackson Journal*. Zelda had said she welcomed the interruption, since it gave her an excuse to stop reading "the mullet wrap," and the women had become fast friends ever since. Zelda was a Port Jackson native who had a dizzyingly busy social life, and her considerable appetite for gossip had been piqued as soon as Teresa had mentioned Wells Talmadge.

"There's not much to that story," Teresa replied. "As I already told you, I was investigating a case and he showed up after I got bopped over the head. He and another guy called the police. End of story."

Zelda pulled up to the light on Japonica and smirked. "I doubt that that's the end of it. If I remember correctly, Wells Talmadge is a rather intriguing young man. He wasn't raised here, you know."

Teresa kept her face expressionless. "No? Where's he from?"

"Born and reared by that wild thing of a mother in Boston. She ran away from school and married Yankees, twice if I remember right, but was forgiven by her father when she promised to move home. That was about fifteen, twenty years ago. According to what I hear, Bay Talmadge is passing the family mantle to that boy."

"Why is his last name Talmadge? If his mother was married twice..."

Zelda cut her eye and looked over her glasses at Teresa. "'Cause Durinda never did marry the boy's daddy, is why. If you ask me, that little escapade all those years ago is what led to Sissy Talmadge's drinking problem. That and a few other things.''

"A few other things like what?''

"Like her sister-in-law what isn't all there, for one thing.''

Teresa smiled. "You mean Gens? I met her. A very beautiful, if aloof, woman.''

"Nice way to put it, Teresa. Eugenie's bats now, but used to be beautiful and brilliant. She should have never gone back to live with Bay and Sissy when her husband was killed. She should've had her own, separate life, but of course that's going against the grain here in Port Jackson.''

"You say her name is Eugenie, and that she was married?''

"Yes. To a young, bright boy who was a friend of Bay's. It was rumored she was going to marry some poor boy she met at college, but Bay paid him off and had her marry Gerald Wallace.''

A bell, followed by a buzz, bang and whistle went off inside Teresa's head. Aunt Gens's full name was Eugenie Wallace. The same Eugenie Wallace who had—or had not—called for Verastine at Sister Hanks's house the night Verastine was killed. Teresa waited for her friend to finish the story, but Zelda fell silent. "Well, what happened?''

"I don't really recall. She came home from Auburn and did as her brother said, then Gerald was killed. In a car accident, I think. Her life was over.''

Teresa remained facing the front window. Zelda was a gold mine of information on Wells Talmadge and his family, but she didn't want to compromise her client's security by asking pointed questions about Eugenie Wallace, the Aunt Gens with the stolen necklace. Just knowing that Zelda's knowledge was formidable cheered her considerably. She would let a little time pass then ask a few choice questions. "There's my car, Zelda. Just stop next to it and I'll get out. Don't park.''

Zelda did as Teresa asked and patted the younger woman's arm. "I'll call you tonight. You come over for gumbo, okay?"

"I'll see. Thanks for the ride, Zelda." Teresa waved and moved onto the sidewalk as she watched Zelda's Oldsmobile go down the street. She shaded her eyes and glanced through the trees toward Barron Rinaud's home. She decided she would have better luck staying away from the big house and going up to Cecilia's apartment without announcing herself. Private detectives often skirted the full implications of trespassing, though her reasons for not wanting to spend more time with the charming Mr. Rinaud were mainly due to time constraints.

Teresa crunched her way up the wide, shell-paved driveway, past the stately dying magnolia trees, and up the rickety stairs of the garage apartment. She paused and searched under the mat for the key. It wasn't there but when she tried the door she found it, as it was yesterday, unlocked. With the words of the cop who had visited her this morning echoing crazily in her head, she went in.

Cecilia's apartment looked exactly as she and Wells and the others had left it. The covers on the sofa bed were rumpled from where she had lain. The desk drawer was open, as was the bathroom door. Steadily Teresa walked toward it, banishing the hysterical fears that tried to catch fire in her imagination. The bathroom was empty. Long and narrow, it held a toilet, pedestal sink and stall shower. A dingy window with a yellowing plastic curtain provided tepid light.

Methodically Teresa searched. The medicine cabinet had aspirin, toothpaste and mouthwash. Gingerly Teresa moved the shower curtain aside and peered in. A pair of yellow galoshes sat on the chipped shower floor, caked with the hard, red mud of Alabama. Teresa picked each up and looked inside. When she dumped the second one over, a plastic bag tied with the same red tie as the one she'd found in the bookcase yesterday, bounced out.

D.M. was marked on the surface. The bag was full of dirt. Red anonymous-looking dirt. Carefully Teresa tucked it away in her purse, washed her hands and shook them dry on the way down the stairs. She was onto something, of that she was sure. She didn't see Barron Rinaud on her way out, but when she reached her car she had the distinct feeling that someone was watching her.

Without further ado Teresa started the car and headed for the police station, wondering if the lab boys would do her a favor and find out if the silent chunk of earth might have something to say about Cecilia Joachim's disappearance.

Chapter Five

Betts was standing beside the front counter, scowling at the day sergeant.

Teresa waited a moment, then caught his eye. "Good morning," she said.

"Hey, Teresa. How you feeling this morning?" Betts came around and looked at her forehead, still frowning. The fluorescent lighting did nothing for his complexion, so she was sure hers looked ghastly.

"I'll live," she replied. "Your men find my gun yet?"

"Not yet," Betts said. "I was hopeful we had a lead with some boys we picked up trying to hold up a convenience store with a .38, but it didn't check out. Come on back and sit with me for a moment. I want to talk to you about something else."

Her heart began to pound. "Katie? Did you—"

"No. Nothing there, darling. I'm sorry. You still running those ads and things?"

"Yes."

"I need you to get me a copy of her dental records when you get a chance, for the FBI." He shifted uncomfortably, knowing how the possibility a child would have to be identified by her teeth would sit on a mother's heart. "Those boys are sticklers for technicalities. You know Katie's going to be fine."

"I do," she replied with more confidence than she felt at that moment. "I'm still on a waiting list for a spot on the milk cartons, but I'm doing all I can."

"Everyone knows you are, honey. Those ads you're running all over the country must be costing you a fortune."

They were, but until she spent every cent she had, Teresa wasn't going to stop putting Katie's picture in front of the public. "Besides, it's only money, Betts, and I'm afraid to stop." Teresa reached into her bag and took out a stack of photocopied flyers. "I'd appreciate it if you'd hand these out to the men again. Keep their memories refreshed."

With the strained look of a man who wished he could do more, Betts took the papers and left them on the front counter. "I'll do that. Now, let's talk about Verastine Johnson."

Teresa kept the surprise she felt from showing on her face and followed Betts into the bullpen area of the precinct, over to a corner where his desk was third in a line of seven. She took the chair Betts pulled out and crossed her legs at the ankle. "So, what's up?"

Betts shuffled through a stack of phone messages, then sat behind his oak desk and opened the gray folder in the center of it and read something from a lined sheet. "I talked to Miss Eugenie Wallace yesterday. She said she did not call Verastine Johnson Tuesday night at Sister Hanks Harper's home, or anywhere else." Betts looked up. "What do you make of that?"

Teresa considered the question. The police were not in the habit of soliciting opinions or help from the public, despite what one saw on TV. Which meant that Betts was fishing, trying to find out what she knew without asking. "That surprises me."

"Surprises the hell out of me, too. No reason for Sister Hanks to lie. I don't like this one damn bit, Teresa. A fine, upstanding, hardworking woman like Verastine Johnson don't have enemies that would be calling her out in the middle of a summer night pretending to be someone they ain't just to knock her over with a car! Not in this town.''

Betts might as well have said, ''Not in my town,'' Teresa found herself thinking. ''Has Sister Hanks ever talked to Miss Wallace on the phone before?''

''Why?''

''So she'd know her voice.''

Betts snapped the folder closed. ''You suggesting this elderly woman with a very well-connected family is lying to the Port Jackson police department?''

''I'm not suggesting anything, Betts.''

Betts blinked. ''I didn't ask Sister Hanks if she was in a regular habit of talking to Miss Wallace. When I told her this morning that Miss Wallace said she hadn't called for Verastine, Sister liked to had a cat. I didn't press the issue 'cause Sister's got high blood pressure, but I don't like this one damn bit.''

''No one does, Betts.''

''Didn't Sister used to work for your ex-husband's family?''

Teresa shifted on her chair. Damn small towns, she thought. Everyone knows too much of everyone's past. ''Yes. Sister Hanks worked for Doobie's mama until she died three years ago. Why?''

''You know her to be an honest woman?''

''I never heard anything to the contrary.''

''What do you mean?'' Betts replied. ''You mean you never heard or you won't say?''

''I never heard.''

They stared at each other, their game of cat and mouse frustrating them both. Finally Teresa asked, ''Do you think Sister had any reason to set Verastine up?''

''For what? A hired killer?''

Said out loud, the notion was absurd to her ears, though Teresa reminded herself that stranger things had happened. "Sounds ridiculous, I know. So let's drop this and I'll ask you straight out if this means you'll change the investigation to one of murder from vehicular manslaughter?"

"Why would I do that?" Betts asked gruffly. "I got no proof of that."

"But if Sister says one thing and Miss Wallace another—"

"You been off the force too long, Teresa," Betts interrupted. "Sister Hanks Harper is a seventy-eight-year-old woman who gets confused. Everybody knows that. It's a mystery, all right, who called Verastine out, but it's just a little old tiny mystery. Not a big, Hollywood-movie-of-the-week deal."

"Vergel Glenn thinks it's a big deal," Teresa couldn't help but retort.

"Vergel's being foolish to not relax a while and let the police handle this. It's a waste of good money." Betts crossed his arms and sat back in his chair. "As a matter of fact, I'm kind of surprised you agreed to work for him. Business a little slow these days?"

"No, actually I've taken on three cases in two days and have more than I can handle comfortably." She leaned on his desk, anger sparking in her eyes. "And if you're asking why Vergel feels the need to hire me, maybe you should ask yourself that. Vergel's not old and confused, Betts. He's young and smart and hurting. And he's going to be pushing for answers. Pushing me and pushing you."

"Well, me and you got separate responsibilities," Betts replied. "And the responsibility for finding whoever killed Verastine Johnson is mine. Just you don't forget that." His voice rose.

"Has someone asked you to warn me off this investigation?" she asked quietly, running through a mental list in her mind. None of the usual names of councilmen or the mayor seemed plausible, but the tenseness on Betts's face made her worry. But Eugenie Wallace was well connected. Maybe someone was putting a little political pressure on this death. Someone with enough pull to get a bug into Betts Vaut's ear.

"Don't go blowing this little talk out of proportion, Teresa. I just got enough on my hands right now, is all, and I don't want you stirring things up that don't need stirring."

Teresa stood and picked up her purse. "Let me know if you find my gun, Betts. I'll see you around."

"Wait a minute."

She turned back.

"Wells Talmadge called here about thirty minutes ago. Said to go ahead and start an active burglary investigation on that incident on Dauphin Street yesterday."

"I had permission to be in there."

"Hey, simmer down, now. Legally, of course, you didn't have permission from the owner, but Mr. Talmadge isn't asking us to give *you* any grief about it. He's more interested in finding whoever jumped you."

"Oh. So what, you want another statement?"

"Yes. I do. Why don't you wait outside?"

Teresa took a deep breath. *So it's going to be like that,* she thought. Betts was going to try to harass her by wasting her day with reports. "Fine. I'll be just outside."

She turned and stalked out. It wasn't the right day to ask Betts a favor about analyzing the soil she'd taken from Cecilia Joachim's apartment this morning. It might never be the right day for that again. Teresa picked up the pile of flyers bearing her daughter's likeness and description, jammed them in her purse and continued walking out to the parking lot.

Let them come to her if they wanted a statement. She had work to do, and it was going to take more than some manufactured red tape from the Port Jackson police to keep her from it.

THE LAST PERSON she wanted to see was the man waiting beside her office door. Teresa came through the elevator doors and Wells Talmadge stood and smiled.

"Good morning. How are you feeling?"

"Lousy," she replied, then stuck her key in the door and shoved it open. "Come in, please. I'll be right with you."

He followed her inside and sat in the chair to her left, looking cool and calm and well rested. His dark blue eyes glinted and his hair was softly curled around his collar, the way that made a woman want to reach out and rest her hand there. Teresa caught her reflection in the dusty chrome of her electric coffeepot and stifled a sigh. She looked limp and beat-up and tired.

There was no justice. "Want coffee?"

"No, thanks," he replied. He pulled a briefcase up onto his knees and clicked it open as Teresa walked over to her desk and sat across from him. He could see she was out of sorts and felt a pull of the same remorse as last night, but pushed it aside. He had to do what he had to do and just hope that he didn't hurt anyone else along the way. He took out a folder and handed it to her.

"These are copies of the investigation I've been conducting for the past few weeks into this Tiger Development company. As you can see from the Dun and Bradstreet and stock exchange correspondence, no one has heard of them. Rebel Chemicals received two letters from a French attorney who states he is representing the firm, but we've been unable to get him on the phone, so I don't know if that letterhead is legit or not. It's not much to go on, I realize, but it's all I've got."

"Why do you think they're trying to gain control over Rebel?"

"Because of this." Wells removed another envelope from his jacket pocket and handed it across to her. Inside was a letter addressed to Josephine Talmadge, 3 Davis Circle, Port Jackson. It was dated two months before and offered to buy two hundred thousand shares of the Rebel Chemical Corporation preferred stock owned by Josephine Talmadge for $26.75 a share. It listed a fax number in Paris—the same number as on the lawyer's letterhead—as a number to contact, and was signed P. Verlaine.

"Is this a fair price?"

"Yes. Actually, more than fair."

"And who is Josephine Talmadge?"

"My grandmother, Sissy."

Pretty arrogant on the part of the letter writer, Teresa thought to herself. Attempt a takeover by approaching the wife of the corporation president to throw in with them. "Did everyone who owns stock get one of these letters?"

"I don't know."

"What?"

Wells shifted on the chair, aggravated that he no longer felt in charge of the conversation. "Well, no one admits to getting one but my grandmother and Jordan. Bay didn't get one and neither did I. But the others may have."

"And how much stock do you and Bay own?"

Wells shifted again. The lawyers would have a heart attack if they knew he was divulging this kind of top secret information about their privately held company to any outside source, but he wanted Teresa Worth to help him and before she'd do that, he knew he had to give her the facts. "I control seventeen percent. My grandfather, thirty-two percent. The rest of the family owns fifty-one percent."

Teresa was writing down what he said, her head bent over a notepad. "And the rest of the family is who?"

"You mean all the stockholders?"

Their eyes met. "Yes. I'll need all their names, Wells."

"Why?"

She put her pencil down. "Look, the only reason you're worried about this is because you and Bay don't want to sell and you're worried some of the others do. Isn't that right?"

"Yes."

"Well, then, I need to know the other players if I'm going to see the whole picture."

"The whole picture? I'm not asking you to get involved in the politics of my company." He felt his temper rising and tried to calm down by lowering his voice. "Look, I just need you to find out who's behind this Tiger Development. I'll do the rest."

Teresa folded her hands. "What are you afraid of, Wells?"

"I don't get your drift."

"Okay. I'll spell it out. I think you must be concerned one or more of your family lied about getting this letter and either is planning to sell or has somehow else aligned themselves with Tiger Development."

He swallowed. Damn, how did she figure that out? he wondered. "So?"

"So, if you can't go to them and find out who Tiger Development is, I may be able to. Or am I only allowed to find out who your adversaries are if they don't have a blood relation to you?"

Wells's face grew hot. "Look, I know my family didn't make a very good impression on you yesterday, but they're still family. I can't believe they'd be working against us on this and I just don't want to accuse any of them of anything before I know all the facts."

"That sounds like a solid plan. But I can tell you first-hand that families turn against each other in the most hateful and destructive ways every day of the week. So you're going to have to decide your priorities. Risk your company, or risk hurting someone's feelings. It's your choice."

"Okay, I'll give you the information. But I don't want any of them to find out what you're doing. You'll have to do your work without raising their suspicions."

"I'll do my best."

Wells looked at his hand and took a deep breath. "Aunt Gens, Tal and Jordan own a joint share amounting to thirty percent that shifts to three equal parts next year when Tal is thirty. My grandmother's shares are ten percent of the company, my mother controls five, and assorted other relations and two trusts own the other six percent."

"That's a lot of people to convince to gain control. Is it really a threat?"

Wells ran the palms of his hands down his perfectly creased gray suit pants and looked worried. "Yes. Even with part of the company in outside hands we'd risk big changes. The industry we're in is as hard-pressed as other American companies to tool up and spend a lot on research in order to compete in the next century. With new members on the board who are more concerned with profits, our plans could be ruined."

"What happens to Bay's shares when he dies?"

Wells snapped his head back and looked at Teresa in horror.

She leaned forward and added in a soft voice, "I'm sorry to ask such a thing, but it might make a difference."

"They're to be held in trust and administered by the family member holding the largest percentage of shares."

"Which is you?" Teresa asked.

"Now it is."

Teresa got up and poured herself some coffee, letting the silence work to calm the tension in the room. She sat and stared at the notes. "Well, I've got a lot of work to do here. Do you have anything else you want to add?"

He was glad to hear her say that. If she was buried in work trying to find Tiger Development, it would give him a little more time to hunt on his own for Cecilia Joachim and attempt to defuse the hidden time bomb that threatened to blow Rebel Chemicals sky-high. "I think that's about it," Wells said, then took a check from his briefcase and laid it on Teresa's desk. "This should cover a month. Is that sufficient?"

She looked at the check and swallowed, forcing herself to look unimpressed. "It's fine. I'll call and update you a couple of days a week. Have you told no one in your family that you've hired me? Not even Bay?"

"No, and I don't intend to. I think it's better all around if no one but you and I know how seriously I'm taking this thing. As I told you before, my grandfather isn't well. I see no reason to give him any more stress."

"Fine. I'll be discreet."

"I'm sure of that," Wells replied. "Take care."

"I will. But I need to ask you one more thing."

Wells stood, his body relaxed but his mouth in a tight line. "Is your father in the picture anywhere?"

He blinked. "No. My grandfather paid him off long ago. He died ten years ago in New York. He's not an issue."

Teresa felt her neck color. She detected pain in Wells's voice. It would have been easy for him to hate his grandfather for what he'd done, but Wells had obviously come to terms with what his family was. *What a cool customer you are, Wells Talmadge,* she thought. "Okay. Thanks."

"No problem."

Teresa watched him leave, then sat back and reread her file. After a moment she closed her eyes and tried to clear her head. What the song said about families was true. You only hurt the ones you love. Slowly she picked up the phone, wondering who it was that was going to hurt the most before the Talmadge civil war was over.

AT ONE-THIRTY Teresa drove over to Zelda's office in search of a favor and a lunchmate.

"Hey, baby girl! What a nice surprise to see you two times in one day," Zelda exclaimed, peeking around the frosted glass panel of her office on Jackson Street. "You had lunch?"

"No. Why don't you let me buy you some chicken salad at Mama's?" Teresa answered.

"You don't have to make that offer twice." Zelda smoothed her black silk pants over her expansive hips. "Let's go right now. I got no more appointments until four o'clock. I'll just call the service."

Teresa wandered around the empty waiting room, wiggling her fingers to work out the cricks she had developed making twenty phone calls. Rebel Chemicals' office in Pensacola had been less than helpful about anything; the corporate public relations person, Miss Sandy Gutierrez, had taken the word *guarded* to new heights in answering questions Teresa had asked about the family members and the next board meeting.

Calls to the Paris telephone company in an attempt to get a lead on the fax machine phone number were equally numbing. She'd finally been referred to AT&T in the United States when she couldn't make it understood that she wanted an address for the owner of the fax machine phone number. She also got nowhere with the French bar association, though the woman who'd answered the phone had promised to call her back once she checked.

Calls to the Pensacola police station about Cecilia had earned her promises of callbacks, and a furtive call to the Port Jackson crime beat reporter hadn't revealed whether the police had gotten back the report about the paint on Verastine's clothes. So, all in all, she'd worked hard on three cases and gotten nowhere.

"Well, let's go. Mama's is packed now, but if we hurry she'll still have pie."

Fifteen minutes later they'd walked the two blocks past Teresa's office and were settling into a cracked red leather booth at Mama's Favorite Cajun Country Fried Chicken Restaurant. Mama herself, eighty-year-old beauty Rosie Goughis, handed them napkins.

"Miss Zelda, ain't you looking pretty today? You going to have some of my ribs or you going to let Miss Teresa boss you into some chicken salad?"

Zelda winked at Teresa. "Ribs, definitely. And extra potatoes, Mama."

Teresa ordered, feeling her gray mood lift a little. "You want to broil that fish for me, Mama?" she teased.

Mama shook her head, her black eyes opening dramatically. "You knows better than to ask such a thing, honey. My mens fries things here. You ladies going to have tea?"

"You have any made up without sugar?" Zelda asked.

"Lord have mercy, Miss Zelda. Miss Teresa's done ruined your manners," Mama replied. Tea, as Zelda well knew, was served iced and insulin-shock sweet at Mama's—three teaspoons of sugar to every ten ounces, Mama had once proudly announced.

Teresa grinned, then got down to asking the question that had been her ulterior motive for coming to Mama's today. "Mama, before you take that order, let me ask you about someone who used to work here. A little gal by the name of Cecilia Joachim. You remember her?"

Mama nodded her head. "Of course I do. Little bitty old thing. Couldn't cook, but was good with the tables. She's a housemaid now over to the Talmadges, I heard."

"Did you have any problems with her when she worked here?"

"Problems? No, she was a good girl." Mama bent down a little and put her wrinkled hand on Teresa's shoulder.

"She did a bit of gambling, though. Went to a cockfight out in Semmes one night with those boys that wash up. Can you believe that?"

"Not my taste, that's for sure," Teresa replied. "Which one of the dishwashers did she go with?"

"I think it was Jimbo Harper, Sister Hanks's grandson, you know. I'll check for you and call, okay?"

The mention of Sister Hanks sent a small zing through Teresa. Port Jackson was small, but there seemed to be too many connections between Verastine and the house at 3 Davis Circle to ignore. "That'll be great, Mama." Teresa had asked Mama for information before and the woman had always complied. She seemed to get a kick out of helping Teresa, and had bragged more than once that she knew the county's only female private eye.

"What was that all about?" Zelda asked as soon as Mama drifted off.

"Just something I'm working on," Teresa replied.

"And I shouldn't ask, I know." Zelda undid her huge paper napkin and shook it out in anticipation of her rib lunch. "But you know I always do. You have ruined my manners. I've become much more nosy since I've become acquainted with a private detective."

"Is that right? I thought you told me once you've always been nosy."

Zelda sniffed. "I never said that." Her eyes roamed to Teresa's forehead. "What happened to you yesterday? Linda Muhl told me she saw you in the emergency room. Are those stitches?"

Teresa patted her bangs and silently damned the humidity that was making her hair curl up like ribbon. "I told you, I got bonked by a bookcase but I'm fine. Look, I want you to do me a favor."

"What's that?" Zelda's eyes were sparkling.

"Can you find out how Bay and Sissy Talmadge are getting along?"

"What?" Zelda's face lit up ever brighter. "Have you heard something? I knew someone who said Bay and a fresh little piece of work from Biloxi were seen together down at the Grand Hotel. Is that what you mean? God, poor Sissy. First that daughter of hers, now this husband!"

Teresa put her hand on Zelda's arm to quiet her agitation. "Now don't go jumping the gun. I'm just wondering about some things and thought you'd know if anything was going on there. Try to find out, okay?"

"Okay."

Before Teresa could explain any more her attention was drawn across the small, crowded restaurant. Standing at the narrow space in front of the cash register were two women. The shorter wore lilac cotton and a white hat and gloves, the taller a floral print swiss dress with a black patent leather belt. Both seemed to have stepped out of a twenty-year-old magazine.

"Speak of the devil!" Zelda hissed in a loud whisper. "My gosh, there's Sissy Talmadge now with her sister-in-law, Gens. I haven't seen those two out together for years!"

"Did you say you knew the sister-in-law personally?"

"Years ago—"

"Is she okay?" Teresa asked.

"Well, I told you, she was brilliant in school. But if you mean is she crazy, well, maybe a little bit. But in that nice, eccentric Southern way." Zelda peered at Teresa, who was still watching the Talmadge ladies. "Now who's being nosy?"

"I am. But it's my profession, not my avocation."

Mama ambled up, carrying a tray of bread still steaming from the oven and two plates of food.

When she hurried off Zelda picked up her fork. "I wonder what brought those two out for lunch. Neither of them look too happy, do they?"

"No. They don't." Suddenly Teresa had a burning desire to find out just what had brought Gens and Sissy out, especially since she'd seen them both at Verastine's wake, and since Gens had supposedly called Verastine just before her death. She'd promised Wells she would be discreet, but that didn't mean she couldn't follow up her hunches. "Save my lunch, Zelda. I'll see you later."

"Where you going?"

"I'm not sure." Teresa laid a ten-dollar bill on the table. "My treat. See you soon." She crossed the restaurant and hurried out, hoping her surveillance skills would yield more than her phone calls had this morning.

Chapter Six

Teresa followed Gens and Sissy as they made their way down Government Street toward Davis Circle. She assumed they were headed home. Sissy kept a gloved hand on her sister-in-law's elbow, and seemed to be guiding her.

They were moving faster than the other people on the street, and were easy to keep in sight amidst the slow-moving traffic. Men in suits, their creases wilting, walked with ladies in limp but elegant dresses, all practicing the common-sense habit of citizens of Port Jackson never to hurry or rush in midday.

Teresa glanced down at her own dress, glad she'd worn the green-striped silk. Coming from California, she had been shocked at how formally and fussily the folks in Port Jackson dressed. Where in L.A. she had favored jeans and T-shirts and denim skirts, here she had found suits and heels and church-formal dresses on women shopping at the supermarket any day of the week.

Once she'd become a detective, she'd had to spend a small fortune on clothes, just to blend in. She had perfected the slow, strolling way of walking, had deciphered most of the colloquial expressions and felt at home in Port Jackson now. Slowly Teresa adjusted her shoulder bag to the other arm, amazed at the speed Gens and Sissy were walking. Despite the heat and ever-present humidity, the two gentle ladies kept up a most un-Southernlike clip, evidently unafraid of using up their day's allocation of energy.

Teresa glanced at the sun and wished she had thought to wear her sunglasses. Squinting, she pushed the hair off her face and increased her pace, her interest quickening when the Talmadge ladies jaywalked across St. Catherine Street and stopped in front of a small brick building. As Teresa watched, Sissy consulted the front wall listing of the building's residents, said something to Gens, then both walked inside.

Teresa crossed the street. She glanced at the same directory, which had three captions: Parker and Malt, Attorneys-at-Law; Jackson Leasing; and R. Eckert, Interior Design. She didn't have a clue as to which office the women would visit, and hesitated for a moment about going inside. She decided quickly to simply blunder through the three offices as if she were lost. A hunch had bidden her to follow the Talmadge ladies, and she wasn't about to come this far and not find out a little something more.

Teresa reached for the brass knob, aware suddenly of hurrying footsteps approaching behind her. Before she could pull the door open, a deep male voice stopped her cold.

"Miss Worth. What a surprise."

Teresa felt chill bumps skitter up her arms, and turned to face Wells Talmadge. "For me, too."

"What are you doing here?" he asked, his big hands gripping his waist. He had on a navy summer suit and blue-striped shirt, a red silk tie and gold tie bar. He looked cool, handsome and as snappy as a junkyard dog.

"Following up on some things," she countered. "What are you doing here?"

"I've got a family meeting to attend."

"Anything I should know about?"

"No."

"Fine."

He glanced around. "Well, don't let me keep you."

"You're not. I'm coming to see my decorator," Teresa answered. "I need some advice on wallpaper."

"I'll give you some advice," Wells shot back, pointing his right index finger in the air near her face. "Don't get carried away. I told you I didn't want my family to hear about Tiger—"

"Don't point at me," she interrupted. "I get the message." Teresa sighed and crossed her arms over her chest. This was the toughest case she'd ever taken on. An assignment to investigate, but not get too close. She looked into Wells Talmadge's eyes, wanting to quit but unable to picture herself giving back all that money she'd already earmarked to help her find Katie.

Besides, despite his words and the tone in which he spoke them, he wasn't menacing. Powerful, male, yes. But not a brute. She had a quick, hot memory of how he'd looked in his athletic shorts last night and smiled. Her action seemed to unnerve him, but not before Teresa judged that what Wells Talmadge was, was *scared*. Not fear scared, but loving scared. Worried about his family.

"I'll try to remember all your rules." She turned away, but when she grabbed the doorknob, he did, too. His hand was solid and warm and she pulled her hand back.

"How *are* you feeling, anyway?" he asked, his voice gruff and tender all at the same time.

Teresa met his blue stare, which seemed to be measuring her health from forehead to feet. "I'm okay. Don't worry, I won't sue."

"I wasn't worried about that. I just don't want you to get hurt."

"How would I get hurt?" The tension Teresa saw in his face mirrored what she felt in her gut.

"Things aren't as simple as they seem, Teresa...." Wells let his voice die. He clenched his jaw and decided to ignore the impulse he'd just had to appeal to Teresa Worth's good sense. Something told him that nothing short of the entire truth would get her disentangled from him now. And he had no intention of telling her that. "Just be careful, Miss Worth."

Wells pulled the door open. The whoosh of cold processed air washed over her flushed cheeks. She turned away from Wells and said a quick thank-you, then stepped into the lobby.

The phrase "out of the frying pan, into the fire" buzzed inside Teresa's head as she recognized the four people sitting in the space that proved to be the reception area for the law office. Teresa nodded, read the brass sign stating the company's name and smiled again. An iron railing braced a stairway curved above an empty desk to the second floor, where the two other offices were located.

Teresa glanced at the doors, then returned her gaze to the assembled group of people on the long black leather couch, trying to ignore Wells Talmadge.

Aunt Gens stared off in a daze. Sissy Talmadge met her smile with a confused blink. Next to Sissy, Wells Talmadge's mother, Durinda, lolled in a low-neck white dress, white silk stockings and scuffed red shoes. Her artificial green gaze was focused on her image reflected in a mirror of a tiny gold compact.

But the surprise to her was the fourth person. Beside Durinda, in a baggy white linen suit and snappy straw boater, sat Barron Rinaud. Had he arrived with Durinda, Teresa wondered, and were the two as close as they looked? Her suspicions about Wells's mother rose another degree.

"Why, Miss Worth! How are you feeling today?" the skinny little man asked, leaping to his feet.

"Fine, Mr. Rinaud. And you?" Teresa asked.

"Hello, Wells," Gens broke in, her head swiveling to greet her nephew. She did not show any flicker of recognition when she saw Teresa. "We can't see the attorney yet, he's not back from lunch. And I'm still not sure about the new—"

"Let's not discuss that now, Auntie," Wells said smoothly, cutting off his aunt's words.

Teresa met Wells's glance and saw that he wanted her gone. She moved away from him and extended her hand to Barron, shook it and turned to Sissy. "Mrs. Talmadge, I'm Teresa Worth. I didn't get a chance to introduce myself yesterday when I met the rest of your family."

A delicate hand, blue veined and trembly, touched her fingers. "Isn't that nice? You a friend of Jordan's, darlin'?"

"A business associate," Teresa replied.

"Oh?" Her voice registered shock that Jordan would have anything that odd. "Well, that's very nice. Let me introduce you to my sister-in-law—"

"I remember you," Gens suddenly announced, stopping her sister-in-law's introduction short. "You were at Verastine's wake." She nudged Sissy. "She was at Verastine's wake, Sissy. Don't you remember?"

Teresa felt her heart thud against her chest at this amazing gathering, thinking as she often had that most detective work was more luck than skill. She caught the eye of Wells's mother, and was unsettled by the bright greenness staring at her. Teresa realized that Durinda was very much interested in Eugenie's conversation.

"Hello, Miss Talmadge." Teresa suddenly realized she didn't know Durinda's married name, but guessed no one called her by it since she wasn't corrected.

"You're working for Jordan, I understand, trying to find the missing maid?" the woman replied, snapping her compact shut. "And you also ran into my grandmother and aunt at that wake? Port Jackson certainly is a small town."

"Everyone does seem to know everyone else," Teresa replied.

"And everyone's business," Wells murmured.

Durinda arched a drawn-on eyebrow at her son. "Hello, darlin'. No kiss for your mother?"

Wells stiffly walked to his mother's side and gave her a perfunctory kiss on the cheek. Durinda kept her eyes on Teresa. "You two been seeing a lot of each other?"

"We met by chance," Teresa replied.

"You said it's a small town, Mother," Wells offered.

"And so it is. Very interesting."

Teresa couldn't agree more, but wondered at the reason for Wells's mother's attitude. "Did you know Verastine, too?" Teresa asked.

"No. No, I didn't. But my mother did."

"Verastine Johnson was a lovely woman. Did you know her, dear?" Sissy asked Teresa, her soft voice filling with tears.

"Yes. She did some baby-sitting and cleaning for me."

"Oh," Sissy replied sadly. "Horrible, terrible waste. I've known her for years. Cooked the best fried chicken I ever ate. Can't stand that something like that would have happened."

"Did she work for you long, Mrs. Talmadge?" Teresa asked.

"Well, she never really worked for us. We have Margaret, you know. But I met Verastine years ago over at Eugenie's place. She used to help out sometimes before Durinda came back to town." Sissy turned to Gens. "Remember those luncheons we had in the garden, Gens? Weren't they fun?"

"Let's not talk about that maid anymore, Mother. You're getting too upset about it," Durinda cut in, annoyed the conversation had drifted away from her control. The redhead turned dark-lashed eyes to Wells. "Come sit down by me, honey. I want to ask you some questions about Rebel and this damn nuisance with the State Department before we go inside."

Teresa's ears pricked up, but before she could ask any further questions a barrel-bellied man in too-short navy wool trousers and a snug seersucker jacket opened the front door and strode into the lobby. "Hello, hello. I'm so very, very sorry to keep you all waiting. But Judge Thibodeaux wanted to talk, and y'all know how that boy can go on!"

Wells marched past Teresa, took his aunt Eugenie's arm and helped his grandmother to her feet. Teresa smiled at Barron, who took Durinda's arm and seemed to her to be enjoying the whole scene immensely.

"Goodbye," Teresa said. "See you all later." As the voices trailed into the attorney's office, she marched up the stairs.

When the door shut she tiptoed back down, then out the front door. "Very interesting," she said, her whisper excited. "Very, very interesting."

TERESA WENT BACK to her office and sat for several minutes. Finally she pulled out Vergel Johnson's file and reread the accident report, adding notes covering her conversation with Betts. She also wrote down the fact that Eugenie Wallace was Jordan and Tal Morisette's great-aunt with the missing necklace. What that meant to the hit-and-run case was total speculation at this point. Teresa, however, could not shake the terrible feeling that Wells Talmadge's family and Verastine Johnson's death were linked.

She rang up Vergel and asked him how often his mother had been to Eugenie Wallace's home. The young man replied that he hadn't known his mother to go there in years, which was one of the reasons he'd been so surprised Verastine had rushed out the way she had.

Vergel also told her that Betts Vaut had been by.

"Did he warn you to stop throwing your money away on a detective?" she asked.

"No, ma'am. But he did say the police were looking for a Cadillac with a dent in it."

"A Cadillac, huh? They must have got the report back matching the paint." A memory fluttered in Teresa's head but she couldn't catch hold of it.

"Yes, they did. Sergeant Vaut asked me if I knew of a car like that. I told him I'd seen some in Port Jackson, but not around our neighborhood."

"Well, keep your eyes open, Vergel. The police will appreciate it if you see anything."

"I will, Miss Worth. But you're going to still be looking, too, right?"

"Absolutely." She rang off with a promise to call him within a day or two.

A second after she hung up she called Jimbo, Sister Hanks's grandson. He'd known Cecilia Joachim, but heard she'd run off. He verified that Cecilia liked to gamble, but could give her no other names of people she might be gambling with.

At four-thirty Teresa shifted gears and went to work on Wells's case. She ran down a copy of the annual report for Rebel Chemicals at the Port Jackson library. It didn't take long to find a connection other than filial between Barron Rinaud and the other members of the Talmadge clan. Listed on the third to the last page, above a picture that was nothing but pure American Gothic, was the following caption: "l. to r. Chairman Bay Davis Talmadge; seated, President and Chief Operating Officer, Wells Talmadge; Vice President of Finance, Elton Cullard; Vice President of Marketing, Eldon Kendall; Member at Large, Durinda Talmadge; Member at Large, Barron Durkey Rinaud; Member at Large, Mrs. Bay (Sissy) Talmadge; Member at Large, Dr. Winton Smithson."

Teresa stared at the faces, then shuffled through the pages again. She called the *Wall Street Journal* and made some inquiries about Rebel Chemicals. The man on the desk that handled trades and buy-outs didn't know the company, but transferred her to a woman reporter who did.

"Rebel's a private company rumored to be courting a public offering of stock," the reporter commented. "Though there are some reports of a family fight over management, Rebel's very solid. Should make the family a pot of money if they go public before one of the big guys like Dow or Ciba picks them off."

"There's been no scandal connected to the company?"

"Nah. Family-owned companies have a lot of infighting, but nothing serious with the Talmadges. There was talk that the new president, Wells Talmadge, wanted the company to divest itself of its government work, but I haven't heard much about it."

"What do they do the for government?"

"I'm not sure. But I'd guess chemical weapons."

"Germ warfare?" Teresa felt her stomach wrench at the thought.

"No, nothing like that. Research into chemical protective agents for the field forces. I think one of their products is used on the germ gear the army wore during the Gulf War."

"Have you ever heard of a company called Tiger Development?" Teresa asked. "A small holding company with some big buy-out money available?"

"No. Sure haven't. Where are they headquartered?"

"I don't know," Teresa answered truthfully. "But if that name comes up, would you give me a call?"

"Sure thing," the reporter answered. "If you'll call me if you hear Rebel Chemicals is about to be sold."

"Fair enough," Teresa replied. She asked a few more questions, then thanked the reporter and turned back to the annual report. It listed chemical production uses of its products for agriculture and waste management, as well as work with the Defense Department.

The glossy, thick stock was hard to turn, but she wanted to recheck the financials. As she flipped the pages a somber young man with a mustache, wearing a white lab coat, caught her eye. Teresa stared at the picture a moment and whistled at the name beneath. "Raoul Joachim, senior chemist."

Her first reaction was shock. Her second was anger. Anger and a feeling that Wells Talmadge, with his charm and sexy blue eyes, had bald-faced lied to her. "So Cecilia Joachim has nothing to do with Tiger Development, huh?" she muttered aloud. "How about her brother?"

Furious, Teresa reached for the file, pulled out Cecilia Joachim's picture and held it beside the smaller black and white. There was little doubt in her mind. The missing maid, Cecilia Joachim, had a brother who worked at Rebel Chemicals. She pulled her notepad beside the phone, rechecked the number for Rebel's Los Angeles office and dialed. The personnel manager came on the line, her voice friendly but officious.

"Yes," Teresa started. "I'm calling from the *Port Jackson Portrait*," she lied, citing the town's monthly travel magazine. "We're profiling the Talmadge family, and we'd like to interview a few key people for our article. Can you put me in touch with a Mr. Raoul Joachim?"

There was a long pause as the long distance wires hummed. "I'm sorry, Mr. Joachim is no longer with Rebel Chemicals."

"Oh?" Teresa wrinkled her brow. This was an unexpected turn of events. She was hoping through Raoul to get a lead on the missing sister, and possibly a handle on Tiger Development. After all, it made sense that someone on the inside of Rebel might know something about the competition. "Could you tell me where he's working now? I'd still like to talk to him. Mr. Talmadge recommended him as a source."

"Which Mr. Talmadge?"

"Wells." Teresa allowed a note of seduction into her voice, hoping it would cow the woman.

"When did Wells Talmadge do that?" the woman replied, very much uncowed.

"Three months ago. When we initially spoke."

"I see," the personnel manager replied. "Well, then you haven't heard."

"Haven't heard what?" Teresa replied, impatiently tapping her pencil against the empty page of her notepad. "Was Dr. Joachim fired?"

"No."

"Can you give me a home phone number?"

The personnel manager drew a deep breath. "Dr. Joachim has disappeared."

"Disappeared? I don't understand."

"I really can't go into this. Let me direct you to our public relations office. Sandy Gutierrez can help you with this."

I doubt that, Teresa thought. "Have the police gotten involved?"

"Uh, no. I mean . . . Miss, what did you say your name was again?"

Without answering, Teresa hung up and sat back in her chair. A day full of leads had just become uncomfortably fuller. She would have to call Pensacola again and have them run Raoul Joachim through the computer and see what came out. Frissons of worry skittered across her mind. First Cecilia, now her brother, doing a vanishing act? It didn't sound good, for them or for her. Especially since Wells Talmadge hadn't mentioned a word about it.

Teresa wondered just how two members of the Joachim family had come to be involved with the Talmadges, and reached for the phone. A sharp rap outside her closed office door made her look up. "Yes?"

The door opened and Jordan Morisette floated in. "Hello, Miss Worth. I need to speak to you."

Teresa put the receiver down and slipped her file closed, her gaze traveling behind Jordan to the empty space in the hallway, expecting to find the shadowlike Tal. "Certainly. Come in and sit down."

Jordan didn't move, but a second later Tal appeared, closed the door and approached Teresa's desk. He was holding a thick white envelope identical to the first one he had presented.

"This is for you," he said, then placed the envelope in the middle of Teresa's desk. He looked at Jordan. The willowy belle smiled her approval, then they both stared at Teresa.

She ignored the envelope and locked glances with Jordan. "What's up?"

"We've decided not to pursue Cecilia's disappearance any further. We think she's gone to stay with her brother in California."

"Her brother?"

"Yes. She has a brother who she's very close to." Jordan smiled again at Tal. "I've decided to let sleeping dogs lie, so to speak. Despite what she did to me, I wish Cecilia all the best."

"We both do," Tal added hurriedly, like a grade-school boy blurting out his sole line in a school play.

"The envelope is final payment for your trouble," Jordan added, her baby blues clear.

Teresa leaned back and let the silence thicken. The color began to drain from Tal's tanned face at the same moment a red stain began to spread on Jordan's pale one.

"You can check to see if it's enough, Miss Worth," Jordan said, her slender hands fidgeting with her straw handbag. "It's five hundred dollars. I made it generous, to cover your hospital bill. You can let me know if it's not enough."

"It's five hundred," Tal echoed. "Besides, we found my aunt's necklace. The little old scrolled silver locket was in one of her coat pockets. Wasn't even lost in the first place. So there's no problem."

Teresa smiled. "Did your cousin Wells pressure you to drop your search for Cecilia?"

Jordan laughed, the sound high-pitched and full of forced gaiety. "Wells? Honey, I don't do anything Wells Talmadge asks me to. I don't work for him."

"But you want me to drop the case. After only two days."

"Right." Jordan took a step toward the door.

"And for two days' work you're paying me fifteen hundred dollars?"

Tal took a step toward the door, then looked quickly at Teresa. "Right. For your doctor bills."

"What about Jordan's purse? Did you find that, too?"

Jordan shrugged. "No. But I'll get over it. It's not really important."

"It's costing you fifteen hundred dollars," Teresa shot back.

"It's a good deal for you, Miss Worth," Tal said with more energy than she'd heard before. "I wouldn't complain, if I were you."

"Are you the one who knocked me out yesterday, Tal?"

"Miss Worth!" Jordan gasped.

"What?" Tal asked, his face now devoid of any color. He took another step toward the door and stared at Jordan. "What does she think I did?"

"Did you attack me, Jordan?" Teresa made her voice harsh.

"Certainly not. How could you even ask me such a thing?" Jordan's knuckles were white from clutching the wide wooden handle on her purse.

Teresa reached for the envelope and picked it up. She held it out, toward Jordan. "Then why are you feeling responsible for my doctor bills?"

"Because you were injured on my behalf. Looking around in Cecilia's place, I mean."

"I don't want your money, especially since I haven't even earned what you advanced me," Teresa said, then tossed the envelope onto the corner of her desk and picked up the manila envelope. "Which brother has Cecilia gone to stay with?"

"Michael. I think his name is Michael. He lives in La-Jolla, near the border."

"LaJolla." Teresa felt a chuckle in her voice. It sounded to her own ears as if she was doing a Jack Webb impersonation, but neither of them seemed to notice.

"Right. Near the border," Tal squeaked.

Teresa stared at the young man. "Tell me what you know about Raoul Joachim."

Tal flinched and looked at Jordan. Teresa followed and found Jordan staring at her, her pretty mouth tight. She didn't bother looking back at Tal. It was obvious the young man was petrified; his fear was a palpable force in the room.

"Who?" Jordan chirped sharply.

"Cecilia's *other* brother, Raoul Joachim." She pronounced it the way Jordan used to. "I understand he was a chemist at Rebel Chemicals' plant in Pensacola. Until he disappeared, just like his little sister. Do you know anything about that?"

"I never met him," Jordan said levelly. "Or heard of him."

Teresa had a hunch she was lying and shifted her gaze to Tal. Jordan's brother looked as if he was going to be physically ill. "How about you, Tal?" she added softly.

Tal bolted toward the door, threw it open and ran down the hall. Jordan glared at Teresa. "This is ridiculous. We don't have to answer any questions. You no longer work for me,'' she said, then glided out behind her brother, leaving the envelope and the scent of her rich, heavy perfume behind.

Teresa leaned back in the chair and let out a deep breath. They were lying. And scared. "My, my," she said aloud, then turned back to the phone.

Chapter Seven

Teresa parked her car in the long, winding driveway of the three-story house on Hope Avenue. She hadn't called before her visit, deciding not to give Eugenie Wallace any time to rethink what she'd said to the police.

She knocked on the door, catching the lovely smell of creole sauce. For the tenth time in as many minutes Teresa wished she'd eaten something at Mama's.

"Yes, ma'am?" a female voice asked through the screen.

Teresa smiled at the white-uniformed woman behind the door. "Hello. Is Miss Wallace at home, please?"

"Yes, ma'am. Come on in out of that hot sun and I'll get her for you."

Teresa walked into the cool parlor. The maid rushed off to find "Miz Wallace," allowing Teresa a few seconds to look around. Silver-framed pictures and crystal memorabilia graced the tops of several tables in the room, and a painting of three Confederate soldiers gleamed in a place of honor above the fireplace. Teresa thought she discerned a resemblance between one of the men and Wells Talmadge. She sat back under their intent stare and ordered her thoughts, running through what she was going to ask.

She'd discovered Eugenie was a member of one of the so-called "fifty families" who ruled everything from the awarding of city refuse contracts to which debutante was named Mardi Gras queen.

According to Zelda, the Talmadges were business and civic leaders, with social connections leading to several generations of Mardi Gras queens. Zelda said that Sissy Talmadge had been a queen, and that Durinda could have been except that she ran off and got pregnant with Wells.

These were the people who had depressed Teresa at the social affairs she'd attended with Doobie, for though most of Port Jackson's elite were nothing if not gracious, they were not really interested in becoming friends with an outsider. Teresa glanced nervously toward the doorway, wondering how it was going to sit with these folks that she'd dropped by to question one of them about a murder case.

Not well, Teresa was willing to bet. Not well at all. Port Jackson citizens took less kindly to personal questions than any people she had ever met. Privacy was like property with most, with Keep Off signs posted prominently.

"Well, hello, Miss Worth. How nice to see you." Durinda Talmadge floated into the room a second later, the smile on her face not quite hiding a calculating tone in her voice. Dressed in a red silk kimono and gold sandals that were scuffed along the sides, Durinda gave the impression of wealth without taste. "This is a surprise to run into you so soon again."

"It's nice to see you, too, Miss Talmadge. But I really came to see your aunt, Miss Wallace."

The maid followed behind Durinda, carrying a pitcher of tea, glasses and cookies on an enormous brass tray. She set it on the table near Teresa while the two women chatted.

"Thank you, Mazie," Durinda said without moving her eyes from Teresa's face. "Run tell cook to put dinner on now, will you?"

"Yes, ma'am," Mazie answered. She met Teresa's glance and gave her a searching look, then headed toward the back of the antebellum home, the tread of her rubber-soled shoes silent on the oak-planked floor.

"I'm afraid that's impossible," Durinda said in answer to Teresa's earlier request. "Aunt Gens is not in the best of health these days and she's napping now. I don't expect her to see anyone for the rest of the week."

"I'm sorry to hear that," Teresa replied.

"But why don't we chat, instead," Durinda suggested, pointing to the chair across from her. "I'll pour you some tea and you can tell me all about being a private eye."

Teresa wanted to tell Durinda to stick her tea in her ear, but instead she smiled and sat. While she still wanted to question Miss Wallace, Durinda Talmadge might be able to shed some light on the inner workings of the Talmadge clan. It was worth a shot, she told herself, accepting a glass of tea.

Durinda poured herself a glass and sighed. "That meeting at the lawyer's nearly did us all in. Barron had to run out and get us colas, it was so hot in that lawyer's office. As much as Rebel Chemicals pays him, you'd think he could serve refreshments himself."

"Rebel Chemicals," Teresa repeated. "That's your family's business, isn't it?"

Durinda smiled an old-cat smile. "Yes. Started by my grandfather and his brother-in-law when they were just boys younger than my Wells. Daddy's always saying the women in our family aren't worth the powder to blow them to hell, but the men are all solid as a rock."

There was little rancor in Durinda's voice, though Teresa noted that a small muscle near her right eye quivered. Hardly evidence enough to think the woman was angry or hurt enough to be intent on plotting her father's overthrow. Which only made sense, Teresa thought, when one considered the fact that Durinda's only child was being groomed to take over the company.

"You must be proud of Wells," Teresa said.

"Oh, I am. I just wish that boy would settle down and get married. He needs someone to look after him. One of these little debutantes who doesn't have anything else to do in life but lunch and shop at Parisians is what he needs. Don't you think?"

"I don't know him well enough to guess at what he needs, Miss Talmadge."

"Is that so? But can't you guess, honey? After all, you are a detective." Durinda laughed and Teresa felt her neck begin to redden.

"I was surprised to see Barron Rinaud at your meeting today," Teresa said suddenly, watching to see how Durinda reacted to that name. She didn't seem alarmed over the turn of the conversation. Maybe she'd been expecting another line of questions, Teresa found herself thinking. Another stickier line having to do with Verastine, in which case questions about Rebel might be a relief.

"Barron? Wherever did you happen upon him? At a bridge party? That's his favorite thing in the world, next to gossip and playing fetch for Aunt Gens."

"No, I met him at his home. I was working."

"Working?" Durinda's eyebrows rose and a look crossed her face that showed just what she thought of Teresa's kind of work. "Well, aren't you the industrious one. Are you investigating my whole family, or is Barron in some kind of difficulty?"

"No. No, not at all. I met him when I went to see Cecilia Joachim's apartment the other night. And at first, I didn't realize he was a Talmadge family member."

"He is. Poor old Barron, for all the good it's done him." Durinda waved her hand dismissively. "I don't blame Wells for being upset that Jordan hired you to find that little thief of a maid. Waste of time, if you ask me. She's long gone."

"Do you know where?" Teresa asked smoothly.

Durinda pursed her lips. "Well, of course I don't know where she ran off to. Nobody does, if that's why you came by to see Aunt Gens."

"No, that wasn't why I need to speak to Miss Wallace. I want to ask her about Verastine Johnson."

"Verastine?" Durinda repeated dully. "What on earth would you be needing to ask her about a dead woman?"

"Did you happen to call her the night she was killed and ask her to come over?"

"I most certainly did not. I think I told you once today that I didn't even know the woman. And I also told Betts Vaut that, on two occasions now. Why, may I ask, are you asking me the same thing again?"

"I'm looking into her death."

"In what capacity?"

Teresa glanced toward the door, feeling in her bones that someone was listening in on this conversation. A conversation that had suddenly become much more strained than she'd meant it to. "I've been retained by Verastine's family."

"I don't believe this!" Durinda put down her glass with a bang and stood, her hands on her waist. "Those poor people have all this grief to deal with but you're telling me that they've *hired* you to do what the police are quite capable of doing?"

"Yes, they have. You see, they're not convinced everything that could be done will be done."

"They're as bad as Jordan." Two red patches appeared on Durinda's face, and Teresa saw for the first time the pockmarks that were expertly covered with thick makeup. "So that's why you're now asking me about this so-called telephone conversation."

"Yes."

"I didn't call Verastine to come over, nor would I have. If I needed something, or Aunt Gens did, we would have had someone else carry her over in the car. It was late. I treat my help better than that, Teresa."

"Can you think of anybody who would call and pretend they were your aunt?"

"I certainly cannot."

Teresa knew better than to say, "Are you sure?" Instead she nodded and picked up her purse. "I appreciate your time, Miss Talmadge. I'll be going now. Please give my best to your aunt Eugenie."

Teresa walked into the foyer but not before she caught a glimmer of a white uniform ducking into the room across from the parlor. Durinda was on her heels, for even if she had been offended by Teresa's questions, her ingrained good manners would not allow a guest to see herself out.

Teresa turned. "Thanks for your time."

Durinda ignored the pleasantries. "I'm betting Verastine's children have very little money, Teresa. I'd think you'd advise them not to spend what they do have foolishly."

"I don't think they're being foolish. I think they're after some answers. It will help them all if they think they can find the person who killed their mother."

"Well, yes, I can see that. But tracking down a hit-and-run driver is work for the police."

"Yes. As is tracking down a murderer, Durinda."

"Murder! Who's calling Verastine getting hit by a car and left for dead that?"

Teresa registered a tone of very real fear in Durinda's voice. She had a mad impulse to run outside and check the garage, but instead smiled steadily. "What would you call it?"

"An accident. A tragic, terrible accident. They happen in life. Believe me, I know that!"

"I'm sure you do," Teresa couldn't help saying. "Anyway, no one is calling it murder. Yet. And no one *ever* will if I can clear up any suspicions that someone called Verastine out into the dark night with ulterior motives.''

"Who would ever want to kill that woman?'' Durinda pressed. "People like that don't have enemies.''

"I wouldn't have thought so, either,'' Teresa replied. "But until I know for sure, we can't just assume it was a hit and run.''

"I think the police are doing a little more than assuming, Miss Worth.''

"I don't.'' Teresa met the other woman's stare. "I was a cop for five years and I know the police are only human. They make mistakes. Every day.''

Durinda pulled open the door. "That may be true in some places. But not here in Port Jackson.''

"I hope, for Verastine's children's sake, that you're right,'' Teresa replied, then left without another word.

The door banged closed behind her before she was three steps out into the thick, hot afternoon. Immediately she wished she'd handled that meeting with more tact. People like Durinda always got to her. The combination of self-centered arrogance and teasing rubbed her the wrong way.

Doobie had that same manner about him, she realized with a shock. He used to make her feel ill-mannered, when he had been the one to act like a cad. She knew it was counterproductive to let people like that get to her, but they did. She hadn't learned much, she told herself. Questioning Wells's mother had been like wrestling with Jell-O laced with razor blades. The only thing she was sure of after their talk was that Durinda didn't want her around looking into Verastine's death, or for any other reason.

Two steps away from the curb Teresa suddenly realized another car, a familiar car, was parked behind hers. She stopped short as the door of the Mercedes opened and Wells Talmadge emerged, his blue eyes covered with black, mirrored sunglasses.

"Great." She sighed aloud. The man must be following her. She marched over to him, ready to read him the riot act, but before she could open her mouth he started yelling.

"I don't believe this. What are you doing here?" he said, then slammed the door.

"I'm working. Or trying to, at least. Are you following me?"

"No. But maybe I should be. I thought you were going to be discreet! Make a few calls, check around. But instead I keep finding you lurking in the shadows of my family."

"Look, Wells Talmadge, I don't appreciate whatever it is you're trying to pull. For your information, I'm here on another case that has nothing to do with Tiger Development. So get off your high horse and stop jumping to conclusions."

"Another case?" he answered, but looked less agitated. "What other case?"

"That's none of your business," Teresa said, yanking her car door open and getting in.

He was beside her in a minute, his hands grasping the hot metal frame of her door before she could slam it.

"I understand Jordan has terminated her contract with you so I assume this isn't about Cecilia."

Teresa flushed. He sounded delighted that she'd been fired. The seat burned the backs of her thighs and made her back sweat. She fumbled in her purse but finally pulled out her keys, which she pushed into the ignition. She could see Wells's hands on the door frame beside her, could feel the heat from his body near her. She looked him in the face, meeting twin reflections of herself.

"Do you or do you not want me to work for you?"

"Well, yes. But I told you—"

"Then back off!" she interrupted. "I can't even consider working for you if you're going to keep running hot and cold on me. Talmadges may be powerful and rich,

Wells, but they aren't above the law. So you remove your hands from my property and stop harassing me or I'll quit your case altogether."

"Look, calm down. I'm sorry I jumped the gun."

"And while we're having this talk," she replied, "why don't you really tell me what's going on with Cecilia Joachim? Why did you *really* want Jordan to stop looking for her?"

"I told you. Publicity. I didn't want people talking about Jordan chasing around after the hired help."

"Well, then, what do you have to hide about her brother?"

"Whose brother?" His tan seemed to fade a degree or two. "What are you talking about?"

"Raoul Joachim. He is Cecilia's brother, isn't he? And he did work for Rebel Chemicals until he disappeared, too, didn't he?" Teresa gripped the steering wheel tighter and gambled that her hunch was right. "Funny you never mentioned that. Care to give your opinion on why one of your chemists disappeared in the midst of a corporate takeover attempt, Mr. Talmadge?"

Wells's opinion of Teresa's detective capabilities rose several notches, as did his blood pressure. What he hadn't wanted to ever happen already had. *Damn Jordan!* he thought to himself, staring into Teresa's challenging eyes. By hiring Teresa Worth she'd inadvertently involved her in the most dangerous and volatile aspects of Rebel's fight for survival.

Damn his family and their closetful of skeletons! "Look, I don't know what you're getting at with a crack like that, Teresa. But there are some things I can't discuss with you. And as for Cecilia Joachim, all I wanted to do was clean up one of Jordan's stupid little messes."

"How is Cecilia's disappearance Jordan's mess?" she asked, but then bit her tongue. Maybe Cecilia wasn't the mess Wells was referring to. Maybe it was the brother. "Was Jordan seeing Raoul Joachim?"

Wells went paler still. "She dated him once, but that was long over."

So Jordan had lied about knowing him. Teresa filed that fact away and stared into Wells's dark blue eyes. "Why don't you tell me the truth? What's going on with you and Jordan and the Joachims?"

Wells grimaced but knelt, eye level with Teresa. He removed his sunglasses. "Look, Teresa, I'm not comfortable acting like a bully with you, but I can't tell you any more. Just find out about Tiger Development. Don't worry about Cecilia, or her brother."

"Or what? You'll fire me?"

Wells bit the inside of his cheek and looked for a moment as if he'd like to yell. "I probably should do that now. But I don't want to. For several reasons."

Teresa swallowed, angry and more than a little intrigued by Wells Talmadge and his head full of secrets.

"Just be square with me, Wells. Maybe if you tell me the whole story I can help."

"All I can say is this. Jordan and Tal and I have a very difficult relationship. Tal is by rights the heir. But when my mother and I reappeared on the scene several years ago, Bay and I clicked. We're cut from the same cloth, I think. We're both aggressive, and put our family ahead of anything. Tal faded to the background and has lived a kind of wasted life in Jordan's shadow. Sometimes the two of them get involved in things they shouldn't. I don't want to go into this any further, but I often bail them out of a mess before it gets too big to handle."

"I imagine that endears you to them," Teresa replied, liking him more for his honesty than his actions.

"Sometimes I think Tal hates me. But that doesn't matter to me. Bay wants me to watch out for the two of them, so I do."

Teresa studied the wide-shouldered man leaning against her car and felt the pull of attraction. It wasn't only his charm and good looks, Teresa thought. He was so sincere. Even when he was hiding things, which he was doing now.

"I can understand your wanting to protect your family from bad publicity, Wells. But I don't believe that's why you wanted Jordan to stop looking for Cecilia Joachim."

He chewed his lip and glared at Teresa. "Oh? Care to share your opinion on my motives?"

She turned her eyes away. "No."

Wells sighed, realizing he was at a crossroads with Teresa but unsure of what to do next. It was very tempting to tell this fresh-faced woman the whole story. But finally he decided that it just wasn't safe to trust Teresa with the kind of explosive information he'd have to reveal to put the whole thing in perspective. Wells searched her face and noticed the small line of stitches under her bangs. No, he couldn't tell her the truth, he decided. She'd already borne the brunt of the danger involved.

He was going to have to fall back on his inbred Talmadge tactics and try to scare her off. Wells narrowed his eyes and leaned closer to Teresa. "Look, you've been taken off the case of Cecilia Joachim. Raoul Joachim has nothing to do with my problems with Tiger Development. Now I think I've said enough on that matter, don't you?"

"No."

"No?"

"No." Her eyes flashed. "I'm not going to work for you anymore, Wells. I'll send your check back. When you want to stop treating me like a moron, call me. Until then, we have nothing more to say to each other."

He grabbed her arm through the open window as his temper flared. "Stay away from the Joachims or it might be you who gets some unfavorable publicity in the paper. Or even a review of your investigator's license by the state board. It just so happens the Talmadges have a family member on that panel. Things could get very, very nasty, Teresa."

"Things already have, Wells." Teresa turned, a look of betrayal flashing in her eyes. She wrenched her arm away and put the car into Drive. Wells jumped back, but not before she heard him use several ungentlemanly oaths. "Same to you," she said aloud.

So much for being attracted to the man. When the chips were down he was nothing but a spoiled rich guy who was used to getting his way through his family's connections. And if connections didn't work, then he'd just shown that he didn't mind using good old-fashioned intimidation.

"Same to you," she said again, louder. Intimidation was something that had never worked on her when she was a cop in the field, arresting men a foot taller and a hundred pounds heavier. It hadn't worked when she divorced Du-Bois and he threw four three-hundred-dollar-an-hour lawyers at her, either. It surely wasn't going to work now.

Didn't Wells Talmadge know that the harder he tried to get her to drop her search for Cecilia, the more he showed that there was something he and his family were trying to hide?

Chapter Eight

Wells hurried through the back door into the Talmadge mansion. He nodded a greeting to Jesse, the cook, turned down her offer of a piece of freshly frosted angel food cake and bounded up the back stairway. Taking a deep breath in an attempt to calm his churning temper, Wells paused outside Jordan's closed sitting-room door. It did little good to yell at his cousin, he reminded himself. She was stubborn and willful and spoiled, and like the other great beauty in the family, his mother, was never moved to action merely by someone else's anger. Talmadge women responded when they saw fit, and only if their way was paved with charm or adulation.

Since his disastrous meeting with Teresa Worth had shown him how little of the latter he could manage, he'd just have to concentrate on the former.

He raised his hand to knock but before his knuckles could meet the smooth wood, the sounds of an intense argument behind the door made him pause. The angrily spoken words, "This is your doing, Jordan!" reverberated through the barrier. "If you'd never taken up with Raoul Joachim and started having those little parties we wouldn't be in this dangerous position."

"Don't throw that up to me," Jordan retorted in her un-mistakable deep drawl. "We needed the money until Tal comes into his inheritance. And for God's sake, if anyone's put us in danger, it's you!''

"All I wanted you to do was distract—"

"Tell that to the judge some day!" Jordan interrupted, rudeness and outrage mixed in her voice.

"Shh," a third voice ordered. "If Bay finds out about any of this..."

The answer to this command was an instant of silence, followed by the low rumble of angry whispers. Wells leaned closer to the door, trying to guess at the meaning of the conversation, as well as with whom Jordan was having it. Was it his aunts or his mother? It sounded most like his grandmother, Sissy, but he couldn't imagine her yelling, nor could he imagine Jordan ever admitting to her less-than-ladylike behavior on her weekends in Pensacola. Straining to concentrate, Wells made out possibly three voices tumbling together, then nothing. He heard a door shut, then another.

Sharply Wells rapped to gain entrance. "Jordan?" he called out. "I need to talk with you."

Several seconds passed before the door opened. Tal stood before him, his expression blank. "Jordan's dressing. She's got a dinner engagement."

Wells looked beyond Tal into the room. The small, chintz-covered settee and wicker chaise were empty. Three glasses stood on the tea table, and cigarette smoke hung in the air. The door leading into Jordan's bedroom was closed. A second door, leading into a hallway skirting the other suites on the floor, was open.

"Would you get her for me, please? I've got to talk to her about something before she disappears for the evening."

Tal's eyes narrowed, but he turned away and walked to the closed vestibule. Wells followed him in and sat on the sofa, noting that all of the glasses had smudges of lipstick on them.

"Jordan," Tal yelled, "Wells wants to talk with you."

"Be out in a sec," came her reply. A moment later the blonde emerged. She was wearing a blue-and-green paisley robe and soft slippers. The curves of her body showed clearly that she wore nothing else under her prebath ensemble. "Hello, cousin," Jordan offered. "What can I do for you?"

"Did you make it clear to Teresa Worth that you didn't want her looking for Cecilia anymore?"

"I told you I did, yes." Jordan paused and looked at Tal and raised her right eyebrow. "Honey, could you run get me another glass of tea while my bath's running? Extra lemon, if you please."

Tal looked as if he didn't want to leave Jordan alone with Wells, but reluctantly turned to go.

"Oh, and take those glasses with you, would you, sugar?"

Tal leaned in front of Wells without meeting his eyes. "What time are you supposed to be at the Carletons?" he asked his sister.

"Seven-thirty. You going to be a love and drive me?"

"Yes," Tal said, then picked up the dirty glassware and headed for the door. "You better hurry. It's nearly six-thirty now."

Jordan sat on the chaise and folded her hands over one knee. She made no attempt to rearrange her robe, which at that moment slipped aside to show nearly all her naked legs and thighs. "Now, what's got you in such a temper, honey? I told you I was going to fire that mousy little old detective and I did."

"Don't underestimate Miss Worth, Jordan." He wanted to add that, with that body and her thick, shining hair, Teresa was anything but mousy. Wisely, he chose not to. The quickest way to alienate Jordan was to openly appreciate another woman. "Everyone can't be as beautiful as you.

But you're sure she understood her services had been terminated . . . ?"

"I am, I am. So I'd think you'd be a little sweeter to me now." Jordan leaned back into the chaise, the slippery robe offering Wells a glimpse of cleavage.

"Well, thank you for doing that. But do you know why she showed up today at our attorney's office?"

"No."

"Did you know why she was over at Aunt Gens's?"

"When?"

"Just now, for God's sake. I thought she was there looking for information on Cecilia, but it turned out she was looking into another matter. Something about the woman who was hit by the car the other night."

Jordan batted her eyes but looked worried. "She went to Aunt Gens's? I have no idea at all why she'd go there, Wells. Maybe she's working for her, too. About time Gens hired someone to watch that your mama didn't steal all her silver and sell it to buy makeup."

Wells gave Jordan a scathing glare, remembering too late he was supposed to be charming information out of her. He allowed a lazy smile to soften his expression and looked slowly down her sleek and pale body, hoping she would read interest where he felt only distaste. "You're going out tonight, so I guess I'll be off. But I wanted to tell you that I appreciate your following my advice about trying to find Cecilia. That girl and her family have caused us nothing but trouble, so it's better for all of us that she's gone now."

"You're probably right, Wells. But if I ever do hear tell of where she's run off to, I'll scratch her eyes out. She stole Aunt Eugenie's necklace, and my favorite evening bag. After all I did for her." Jordan covered her mouth, as if she'd suddenly said too much.

"What is it you did for her?" Wells asked quietly.

"Got her a job, is all I meant."

Wells leaned closer. "You sure? You and Tal aren't running one of your little scams on the working class again, are you? Ripping off the maids' paychecks on some little floating crap game?"

Jordan stuck out her chin indignantly. "Of course not."

"Good. That's real good to hear, Jordan. And since you've been so good, I'll be sure to see you get a new bag and Aunt Eugenie gets a new necklace."

"Why, thank you, Wells. I love presents." Jordan wiggled in her seat and smiled. "Anything at all I can do for you, cousin, you know I will." She leaned forward, her gown splitting open to her waist, and ran her fingers over her bottom lip. "Anything at all."

"I appreciate that, too, Jordan." Wells gave her knee a quick squeeze and rose. "By the way, you're telling me the truth about Raoul, aren't you? You haven't heard from him for months?"

Jordan's chin tipped up defensively and a guarded look came into her eyes. "No. Of course not. I'm done with that old boy. Why do you ask?"

"Because it would not be a good idea at all for you to be seeing him on the sly, Jordan. I told you I've got the police in Pensacola looking for him because of some trouble at the plant." He didn't have to elaborately lie with Jordan. She wasn't interested in the plant at all. "It would look real bad to Bay, and to me, to find someone in the family knows where he is and isn't saying."

"You threatening me, cousin? Because I've already told you the truth and I resent you implying I haven't."

Exasperated suddenly, Wells leaned over his cousin and grasped both arms of the chaise, his face inches from hers. It was time to give up on charm and give fear another shot. "Yes, I am threatening you, Jordan. I've hired lawyers for you before and kept your name and this family's reputation from getting smeared. But I promise you I will not help if you are lying about this. Raoul Joachim is no friend to anyone in this family."

She gave him an ice-cold glare. "I understand you, Wells. You don't have to raise your voice. I told you I haven't seen him, and I haven't."

"Okay. But his landlady said a young woman wearing dark glasses and a scarf who looked very, very much like you was seen leaving Raoul's apartment the night he disappeared."

"And you believe that?"

"I believe you're selfish and spoiled, Jordan Morisette. I believe you were shacking up with him in the little room you had Barron give Cecilia. I just hope you're smart enough to see how dangerous this could turn out for all of us. And I'm hoping you're not stupid enough to have hired a private detective to find Cecilia when it was really Raoul you're looking for."

She blinked. "I'd never have thought of that."

"Well, don't think of it!"

They both looked toward the doorway as Tal entered, his hand wrapped tensely around a frosty glass. "Here's your tea, Jordan," Tal said. "Everything okay?"

Wells jabbed a finger in the air toward Tal. "Make sure he's on board about this," he snapped, then turned on his heel and walked out, the back of his neck twitching under what he was sure were looks that could kill.

As he reached the stairway he glanced over his shoulder, catching sight of a shadow against the wall. He heard Jordan's bedroom door close. "Now what the hell . . . ?" he muttered, staring at the haze of cigarette smoke hovering in the person's wake. But he had neither the time nor inclination to retrace his steps and find out which of the other female members were in on Jordan and Tal's latest scheme.

He went down to the kitchen and grabbed a piece of Jesse's cake for the drive to the plant in Pensacola. He would meet with the security people there and find out if they had determined anything about Raoul Joachim's whereabouts or come up with any proof that he'd tried to alter the computer program by which the pesticides were produced.

This was the secret he was furiously trying to keep a lid on, for if any one of several sources got wind of his fears that someone was sabotaging Rebel Chemicals, the economic impact could be enormous. When several people on his staff had brought their fears about Raoul to him, he had immediately wondered if Raoul had been approached by the Tiger Development people. And when he'd approached the young chemist, Raoul had been surly and uncooperative. Then he'd disappeared.

And Wells was left trying to piece together what, if anything, Raoul had done to hurt his company. It wouldn't take much of a scandal before creditors, clients and the press would be tagging Rebel as another victim of the recession.

"You be home for dinner, Mr. Talmadge?" Jesse asked, lifting a platter down from the shelf. "We's having shrimp and rice—your favorite."

"No, no, I won't be, Jesse. But you save me some, okay?"

"Yes, sir."

"Thanks," he replied, then left the way he had come in, never noticing the person standing motionless on the stairway, anxiety and concentration pulling at the blue eyes, and fear tightening the mouth.

When Wells slammed the door, the listener stepped into the kitchen. "Would you go see where Mr. Bay wants his supper, Jesse? I need to use that phone for a minute."

Jesse nodded and wiped her hands on her apron. "Yes, ma'am."

"Thank you, Jesse," came the woman's reply as she dialed, her attention focusing on just how to frame the order that must be given if her long-dreamed-of goal was going to be reached. She lit a cigarette and said softly to the man who answered, "We need to meet with him tonight. Call and set it up now."

"You sure? Now? I—I don't like this. It's much more than we ever discussed, you know. I say let him be. If he goes to the police he can't prove anything. Besides, he took our money. Who would believe he'd changed his mind?"

She thought of one man who would, and he'd just left the house. "We can't chance it. We'll have to meet him. Set it up and let me know when to be ready."

"Okay."

"Be sure you bring the gun," the woman said. "We might have to scare him."

The man sighed. "This isn't smart."

"It is if you let me handle it," she replied, then softly hung up the phone.

THE DARK-HAIRED MAN DROVE into the open garage and watched as the dark-haired girl standing inside hit the switch beside the door to close them off from view. He waited a moment before getting out of the car, trying to read the expression on her face. She looked calm, but sad. He opened the door as she came around to him. "Well? Did they call?" he asked.

"No. Nobody's called. And I can't stand this hiding out anymore, Raoul. I want to go back to California today."

"Cecilia, I told you we can't go until they call."

His pretty, plump sister folded her arms, and tears welled up in her eyes. "I told you never to get involved with this stupid plan. You had a good job, Raoul! A future!"

Raoul Joachim got out of the car and slammed the door shut. "Don't start lecturing me, little sister. I don't need it!"

He stalked into the house through the side door, Cecilia on his heels. She watched silently as he grabbed a beer and sat at the small dinette.

"How long are we going to wait? What if he never calls?"

"He'll call." Despite his words, Raoul frowned. The "he" Cecilia spoke of was a wealthy man who had contacted him two months ago to steal the formulas for Rebel Chemicals' line of pesticides for the sum of three hundred thousand dollars. A mysterious man Raoul had met only once, who had approached him at a party Jordan Morisette gave. The man had known Raoul worked at Rebel Chemicals, and had asked if he was interested in any "freelance" work.

The free-lance work, Raoul had learned later that evening, had been to alter the mix of ingredients for one of Rebel Chemicals' agricultural products in order to cause some "positive market trends" for the mystery man's friends.

Raoul had refused that night, and several times after. But then the man had called his house and offered him enough money to cover the cost of education for each of his four brothers.

The man had promised that Raoul's tampering would do no long-term damage to Rebel Chemicals. He'd even implied that Wells Talmadge was in on the plan. But when Wells had approached Raoul a few weeks ago and asked him, man to man, if he knew anything about some alteration in the programs, Raoul knew he'd been tricked. He'd thought of admitting everything to Wells, but it looked so bad. Raoul had run tests for months on the formula, coming up with minute changes that turned the alkaline-based fertilizer into a killer for the crops it was meant to improve.

So he ran. He thought if he gave the man the money back before anything happened to Rebel, that he could *then* go to Wells Talmadge and explain it all.

Cecilia was doubtful, but the way Raoul saw it, it was his only chance. He turned to his sister. "We'll wait as long as it takes, Cecilia. Now why don't you fix us something to eat? I'm hungry."

Her eyes filled with tears but she hurriedly brushed them aside. "You've been played for a fool, Raoul. I still say Jordan Morisette set you up. You know she's no good. I told you about what she and that brother of hers are doing. It's stealing! Only with a fancy name."

"I don't want to hear this again, Cecilia." Raoul stood and hugged his young sister, then helped her with the food. They worked side by side for several minutes, chopping onions, tomatoes, grating cheese.

The small duplex in the heart of Pensacola's rental district began to smell like his mother's house in California. Raoul closed his eyes and imagined himself and Cecilia going back there, living in those tiny, cramped rooms with his four younger brothers. It sounded like hell, but if it got them out of the trouble he'd gotten them in, it also sounded a little like heaven.

Except he'd have to give up Jordan Morisette, and giving up that woman was harder than he imagined it was to give up a drug.

"I hope that at least you aren't going to see Jordan anymore before we go away," Cecilia warned softly, as if reading her brother's mind.

Raoul sat back down at the table and finished the beer. He didn't meet his sister's eyes. "No, I'm not seeing Jordan anymore."

"You lying to me? She might turn you in to the cops, you know. It would be just like her, making you the fall guy for all this."

"Jordan wouldn't do that." He thought of the silky blonde, of the nights they'd spent in Cecilia's fold-out couch making love.

"I hate her," Cecilia said spitefully.

"She's probably mad as hell at you for doing what you did. I told you to stay put. You shouldn't have run off the same day I left my job, Cecilia. The police are going to think you were involved with me."

"I don't care about that," she said, wiping fresh tears away. "I was too worried about you, Raoul."

"Is that why you stole Jordan's purse?" Raoul shot back. "'Cause you were worried? Or were you mad you lost all your pay at that party Jordan had?"

"I deserved to take more than that purse," Cecilia threw back. "It didn't even have any money in it. Just some old dumb necklace."

"I heard from one of the girls who works in Port Jackson that Jordan hired a private detective to find you. I think that was the girl I saw at your apartment."

"The one you knocked over?" Cecilia asked. Her eyes were wide. "That was a woman, you said. A woman is a detective?"

"This is America, Cecilia. I keep telling you, you got to set your sights higher in America. It's not like it was in our country."

"Right. In our country the police would have already shot your sorry butt." She turned back to chop garlic, and added it to the sizzling ground beef mixture she had frying on the stove.

"Maybe you should call Wells Talmadge now. Maybe if you confess, we can work something out with that man. He was always very nice to you."

"I got to give the money back first. Then I'll be in a good position to negotiate."

"I don't know," Cecilia retorted. "I think you might be dreaming about this whole thing, Raoul."

Raoul squared his shoulders and set his jaw. "We'll see." He laced his fingers together then stretched his arms and cracked his knuckles. "I'm going out later. You stay in and keep the door locked, okay?"

"Where you going?"

"Just out to have a few drinks with some friends." Raoul was supposed to drive over to Port Jackson and meet Jordan at ten in his sister's empty apartment. It was dangerous, but the thought of her blue eyes and soft mouth made him willing to risk it one last time.

"I don't like it, Raoul." Cecilia threw a package of tortillas on the counter. "I don't like having to stay in by myself. Take me with you. If you're going to Port Jackson, I've got friends I can see."

"Who said I was going to Port Jackson?"

"I'm not stupid, Raoul," Cecilia replied.

Their eyes locked and Raoul frowned. His temper was frayed, but his compassion for Cecilia kept him from arguing any more strenuously. "Look, I'm just trying to do the right thing here. Don't bite my head off. I'm going to get us out of this." His eyes went to the top of the refrigerator where the package of money he was going to return lay. "But we can't take chances. We can't be seen, or the Talmadges are going to hear about it."

"That's what I'm afraid of," Cecilia replied. She turned back to the stove, muttering in Spanish. Before he could speak to her again the phone jangled shrilly.

Raoul blinked and Cecilia ran to the phone. He pointed to the answering machine. "Hit the memo button before you answer. If it's him, we want to get him on tape."

She nodded, hit the button as well as the broadcast speaker so they could both hear the conversation, then Raoul picked up the receiver. "Hello?"

"Mr. Joachim?"

"Yes. Where have you been? You should have called two days ago."

"Hold on now with the scolding or I'm going to hang up this phone." The man's accent was as thick as Mississippi mud.

Cecilia pulled on Raoul's sleeve and motioned for him to calm down. He took a breath and nodded. "I'm sorry, it's just that I was worried. Please go on. Have you told your people about my change of heart? I have all their money—not a penny is missing. I just want the Rebel Chemicals information I copied for you back."

"Yes. I spoke with my people a few minutes ago, as a matter of fact. Can you make a meeting?"

"With your boss?" Raoul replied quickly. "When? Where?"

"You're in Pensacola, right? Can you drive the fifty miles over to Port Jackson by nine tonight? It should be dark by then. We can meet and decide what to do."

Raoul stiffened, sensing danger with every word. He motioned for Cecilia to write down the directions. "Of course, of course. Where should we meet?"

"You know the empty warehouse on Columbus Avenue where we met before? Wait there. Alone. I'll be by to take you to my people and we'll exchange the money and the documents you took then."

"That's wonderful," Raoul said, his young voice high-pitched with excitement. "So, they've agreed? There's no problem?" A click signaling the end of the conversation sounded out over the speaker, then the dull buzzing of dial tone.

Raoul tightened his left hand into a fist and stared at the phone. "I don't like this."

"Why? If they're going to take the money back, it's okay." Cecilia hugged Raoul and danced around with relief. "Hey, you can even stop and tell Jordan goodbye. You can give her that purse back. We'll all make up and have a party before we go to California."

"You're not coming to Port Jackson with me," Raoul shot back. "You stay here. I've got to go alone."

"You let me come or I'll call the police," Cecilia said, folding her short arms across her chest. "It could be dangerous. I'll wait in the car and go for help if I need to. Please, Raoul, don't make me stay here by myself."

"Okay. We'll eat and go early. I'll hide inside, check everything out. But you're waiting outside! We've got to be careful here, Cecilia. It's not over yet."

Cecilia gulped and turned back to the stove. Raoul watched, and realized what he said was very true. It made the skin crawl on the back of his neck. He suddenly thought of the young woman he'd knocked a bookcase over inside Cecilia's apartment. She'd been snooping around. She had even found one of the test samples he'd carelessly left behind.

Could that have had anything to do with his contact's sudden agreement to back out of their deal?

Raoul shook his head to clear the thought away, sickened at the possibility that it was already too late for him to undo what he'd done. "Let's eat and then get going, little sister. We've got a lot to do before we celebrate."

Chapter Nine

"You want me to send *this* to the lab for you?" Zelda peered closely at the plastic bag full of red dirt Teresa had handed her. "Why? I can tell you what it is. It's dirt. Good old red Alabama clay dirt, I'd say."

"I know it's dirt, Zelda," Teresa replied, "but I'm betting there's something interesting about it. Which is why I would be very grateful to you if you would send it to Dr. Smithson's lab folks and get a breakdown on it for me. Tell them one of Dr. Smithson's clients ingested some of it, and you want a chemical analysis. I'll pay you for it now if you like."

Zelda wrinkled her eyes behind her thick glasses. "Don't you usually take this kind of thing to Betts Vaut's boys?"

"Yes."

"But not this time?"

"Right."

Zelda crossed her arms, gingerly holding the bag away from her white blouse. "And I suppose you're not going to tell me why, right?"

"Right." Teresa leaned toward her friend and gave her a kiss on the cheek. "Thanks for bringing my lunch home. Now I've got to run. I'll talk to you tomorrow."

Zelda looked at her watch. "Okay, I know you've got to run. But tell me quick how you made out following the Talmadge ladies today?"

Teresa kept walking down Zelda's front steps, trying to hide the smile on her face. "Fine. Fine. I'll call you tomorrow, Zelda!"

She waved from the car, put it in gear and drove the short block to her house. Teresa chuckled as she thought of Zelda and her curiosity. It wasn't fair, she knew, to tease her friend so by not telling her more about her work on the Talmadge case, but that was part of the job she had.

Detectives had to be able to keep secrets. Even when it would be easier to discuss her cases with Zelda, she bit her tongue, knowing that it took only one slip to get a reputation for being untrustworthy. And, through no fault of Zelda's character, giving her friend any information was likely to lead to a slipup. After all, Port Jackson was a small town. And if there was one thing small towns were good at, it was passing secret information along in a hurry.

Wearily Teresa unlocked her back kitchen door and slammed it behind her with her foot. She set the foil-wrapped container Zelda had saved for her from lunch, a bag of groceries, her purse, briefcase and an alarmingly high stack of mail on the table. She glanced at her watch. It was 7:55 p.m., and still as light, hot and humid as midday.

She grabbed a soda from the fridge and went into the living room, switched on the overhead fan and sat by the phone. She stared at it for several minutes, willing it to ring.

When she and Katie had lived in this house after her divorce and she'd had to work late, she had always called Katie at exactly eight o'clock. They'd played a good-night game that now echoed mockingly in her head. . . .

"Hello, Katie-bug," she'd said many a night, "it's tick-tock eight o'clock, time to go to bed."

"Hello, Mama-bug," her daughter had replied, "it's tick-tock eight o'clock, but can I stay up for five more minutes?"

After Teresa had told her no and that she loved her, they'd said good-night and Katie had gone to bed. Many a night it was Verastine Johnson who had tucked her in. Teresa had never warned Verastine not to let Katie see her daddy if he should drop in. Until the night he'd taken her, there had been no reason to.

Verastine, blaming herself, had been as inconsolable as Teresa. That was one more score she had to settle with her ex-husband someday, she realized. The pain he'd caused Verastine. She'd have quite a few things to say to Doobie if she ever saw him again. "*When* I see him again," she said aloud, forcing another mouthful of soda down her tight and aching throat.

She blinked away tears and wished for the phone to ring, for her daughter to be on the other end. When Katie was three Teresa had taught her their home phone number. The child loved to repeat it and knew how to dial it. In her heart she knew that some day Katie would call that phone number looking for her. Teresa held on to that hope. Some days it was all that kept her going. And for eight months it had kept her in Port Jackson.

But at fifteen past eight Teresa decided tonight wasn't the night her daughter would call. She got up and went into the kitchen, moved the groceries aside and peeled the foil off her leftover lunch.

Teresa stuck the paper dish in the microwave for three minutes and washed out the coffeepot, forcing her mind off thoughts of Katie. She wondered what Wells Talmadge was doing, and imagined him sitting in the cool, lovely dining room in the mansion at Davis Circle, laughing with Jordan and Tal Morisette over firing her.

Teresa chewed the inside of her cheek and said, "Same to you," aloud to her empty kitchen. She then pushed her mind into an analysis of the day's events.

She'd made a few more calls after she'd left Durinda's, and found out from the police that no missing person's report had been filed on Raoul but that there were rumors he'd stolen some documents from Rebel Chemicals before he'd disappeared.

She'd also—amazingly—heard back from a French official of the bar association, who'd verified a P. Verlaine was a member, and gave her two addresses where she could contact him. One was in New Orleans. A call to that office had yielded a post office box number in Fairhope, a small, rural city an hour across the bay from Port Jackson.

Even though she'd resigned from Wells's case and been fired from Jordan's, she was curious about the Joachim sister and brother as well as the mysterious Tiger Development. She might just bop over to Fairhope tomorrow morning and see if she could dig up an address to go with that post office box.

She'd also received a surprise callback from the *Wall Street Journal* reporter, who said that the Talmadge family was having a meeting with their lawyers over a rumored sale of several hundred thousand shares of stock, and, off the record, someone else was reporting a rumor that one member of the Talmadge board was bragging that he was going to wind up controlling a bigger share of Rebel than Wells Talmadge before too long.

Though no one could confirm which family member was trying to sell out, the reporter implied it was Tal Morisette. Teresa had also learned through a source on the Pensacola police department that Jordan Morisette had been questioned about a bar fight involving Raoul Joachim shortly before his disappearance and that all charges had been dropped.

So the day that began with her gun being stolen and later saw her fired had also sent her investigation about Cecilia Joachim in a new direction. "Don't forget bullied by both Betts Vaut and Wells Talmadge," she said aloud to herself, lifting the plate of steaming food out of the microwave as soon as it buzzed.

How all those events fitted together eluded her, but she knew from experience that detective work was like cooking stew. One had to assemble and then chop up all the ingredients, stir the pot and be patient enough to let things simmer.

Teresa thought of Wells Talmadge and wondered for the tenth time today what made him tick and what he was hiding. She planned to pay him a visit tomorrow and stir his pot a bit more when she returned his check. She might even give him the information about Tiger Development, if he was halfway civil.

And if he paid her for it. She chuckled at her mercenary thoughts, knowing deep down her reasons for going to see him didn't all revolve around work. Even if he was a major control freak with a bad temper, she'd seen his kindness and compassion and had liked that side of him immensely. Plus he was what they described in the South as "drop-dead gorgeous." Teresa looked hungrily at the mound of butter beans on her plate, but before the food could get to her mouth the front doorbell rang.

"I'll be right there," she hollered, took one forkful of food, burned her mouth and ran to the door. She opened it to find Eugenie Wallace's maid, Mazie, standing there.

"Hello, Miss Teresa," the teenager said nervously. "I'm sorry to come busting in on you like this, but I need to tell you something. About Verastine. It's real important." The girl's black eyes were huge with worry. "Is it all right if I come in for a minute?"

"Of course. Please come in," Teresa said, pushing open the screen. She glanced out at the darkening night, wondering if anyone at the Wallace house knew of their maid's visit. "Just sit over there and I'll go get us a soda."

Mazie sat on the edge of the couch where Teresa pointed, and looked down at her shoes. When Teresa returned with the sodas and set one in front of the girl, she smiled in what she hoped was a trust-inspiring way. "Now, what can I help you with?"

Mazie cut her eyes to Teresa, took a long sip from the soda then turned her glance back to the floor. "I heard you with Miss Durinda today. I heard her tell you she didn't call Verastine out the other night."

"Yes, she did tell me that," Teresa said. "Do you know anything about that, Mazie?"

"Yes, ma'am." The girl tapped her foot and continued to stare downward.

"If you tell me about it, I won't say anything to anyone else," Teresa offered.

"Oh, Miss Durinda is telling you the truth about that," the girl replied. She looked at Teresa and her eyes were tearing up. "She was in the front parlor with Miss Eugenie, who was fussing about Miss Sissy's husband and his girlfriend. I know that for sure 'cause I brought the ladies some tea about ten minutes before nine."

Teresa kept her surprise from showing, though her stomach tightened at the news Bay Talmadge had a mistress that his wild-eyed sister knew and was upset about. "I see. Well then, do you know who did call Sister Hanks looking for Verastine?"

"Yes, ma'am." The tears rolled, clear and fat, down Mazie's pretty face. "It was me that did it, Miss Worth. It was me that got poor Verastine killed." She began to cry hard then, and buried her face in her hands.

Teresa rose quickly and sat next to the girl, her arm hugging the shaking shoulder. "Don't cry, honey. What are you saying? You didn't get Verastine killed. It's all right now."

Mazie continued to cry, however. Several minutes passed before Teresa could get her calmed down enough to talk. But, finally, she did.

"I didn't want Sister knowing why I was calling Verastine 'cause it was a secret and everyone knows Sister Hanks can't keep no secrets no matter how hard she tries. Verastine told me to call her if I ever heard about something happening again that she wanted to come to...a party-like. But Verastine didn't want me to call at her house 'cause she didn't want her family to know she was going. So she told me if I ever heard about a party to call and tell Sister the story about the tablecloth." Mazie's eyes filled again but she bit down on her lip. "And now poor Verastine got hit by that car and it's all my fault."

"It's not." Teresa squeezed the girl's hand and looked at her closely. "It's not your fault at all. You just did what Verastine asked you to do. But I don't understand what you mean about a party. What kind of party?"

"A club, kind of like. Where people can make a whole lot of money if they bring their friends. My aunt in Mississippi had one and she made over four hundred dollars. Verastine said she heard tell of a white lady in Biloxi who made five thousand dollars. 'Course, her friends had more money than our friends do. But it's still possible."

"These are gambling parties?"

"No. No gambling, nothing that ain't legal like that. 'Course, the police don't like them, which is why you have to be real careful about saying where they's going to be."

Teresa was completely mystified. "Tell me how these parties work, Mazie."

"Say if you was to have one, you'd call and tell five friends to come and bring one hundred dollars each. If they'd bring five friends each, they'd make twice their money back and you'd get twice again that much." The teenager saw the doubt in Teresa's eyes and picked up the pad and pencil lying on the table by the soda. Quickly she sketched some boxes and filled in the boxes with excitedly drawn one-hundred-dollar bills. "See—" she pointed to the paper "—it works like this."

Teresa took the paper from her young visitor and stared at the stack of boxes. "My God. A pyramid scam." She looked at Mazie. "How long have you heard about these parties going on in Port Jackson?"

Mazie looked upset at Teresa's use of the word *scam*. "Couple of months now. Maybe a little more. But it's no rip-off, Miss Worth. I know people who've made plenty of money. Even Miss Morisette—" Suddenly the girl covered her mouth and looked ashamed.

"What about Miss Morisette? You mean Jordan Morisette, Miss Durinda's niece?"

"It's just I heard someone say she's made some money that way, too. Which means it's got to be legal, if Mr. Bay's kin is involved."

Teresa mentally shook her head with anger that reputation allowed people to take advantage of others with a minimum of effort. "Some people do make some money. But most people lose *all* their money." Briefly she outlined the staggering numbers of people necessary to keep these games afloat, but stopped after a minute because of the blank look in Mazie's eyes. The girl was nobody's fool, but she'd stopped listening to the facts. Like anyone enamored of making something for nothing, she believed these pyramid parties were the chance of a lifetime.

And so, evidently, had Verastine. "Anyway, so you called Verastine out. And you didn't tell the police about it because you know they don't like those parties, right?"

"Yes, ma'am." Mazie looked miserable again. "But I will go to the police if you say I should, Miss Worth. If it might help find the person who hit Verastine with the car."

"That's good to hear, Mazie. But before you do that, tell me where the party was you were sending Verastine to. Maybe I can handle things so we don't have to have you go to the police."

This news relieved the young girl. "It was on Dauphin Street. A big old house near Columbus, back behind a lot of trees. You can't hardly see it from the street. I was going to go myself but I couldn't leave until Miss Gens and Miss Sissy came out of that parlor. Then they took off in that big old Cadillac of Miss Sissy's, and I thought the party would be over. They don't last long, those parties."

"The white house with the pillars, across from the cemetery?"

"Yes, ma'am. A white man lives there. But the girl that was having it knows Margaret, Miss Sissy's maid, and said it was okay for anyone to come."

An image leaped into Teresa's brain of a sagging front porch and Vivaldi music. "Mr. Rinaud lives there," Teresa said softly.

"That's right," Mazie said, shaking her head. "He's a real good cook and from what I hear, a real nice white man. Cousin or something of Miss Durinda and them."

"I see. Who else went to the party, do you know?"

"That's a funny thing, Miss Teresa. They never had it. Margaret and Opal Jackson that works for Mrs. Dupree, they told me they went but nobody was home, and nobody never came home, either. So they left." Tears began to well up and drip down Mazie's face in a fresh spasm of regret. "Verastine didn't even need to be going out, 'cause the party never did come off. I should've never called her that night."

Teresa patted the girl's leg and listened to her cry, knowing she could do little to alleviate the guilt but more determined than ever to find out who had acted as an instrument of fate and ended Verastine Johnson's life. The fact that Barron Rinaud—cousin to the Talmadges—was involved, and maybe Cecilia Joachim, her mind suggested, gave her a sick feeling in her stomach that would not go away.

"Did you know Cecilia Joachim? She worked over at the Talmadges' on Davis Circle."

Mazie blinked her tears away and shook her head. "No, ma'am, I never met her. But Margaret said she was a nice girl. She saw her at Miss Sissy's house one time. But she said she wasn't really a maid, 'cause she didn't know how to clean or iron or nothing like that."

"Did you hear why she left her job?"

"Don't know for sure, but somebody said something about Miss Jordan losing her purse or some such thing." She made a face when she said Jordan's name.

"You don't like Jordan much?"

"She's okay. For a spoiled rich girl."

Teresa could see that Mazie was too loyal to say something about a Talmadge relative. "Do you know if anyone knows where Cecilia went?"

"No, ma'am." Mazie's eyes strayed to the clock on the table and she stood quickly. "I need to be going, Miss Teresa. My mama's fixing to go to work and I got to mind my brothers."

"Let me take you home, Mazie."

"No, that's okay, Miss Teresa. It's way out by the airport. I'll get the bus."

Teresa smiled at Mazie's indication of great distance. Port Jackson was three miles by seven, built around three boulevards and the interstate. To someone from Los Angeles it wasn't big enough to change gears in. "No, I'll just get my purse." She grabbed her bag from the counter, gave her heated-up food a regretful look and hustled the girl out into the thick night air, her mind buzzing over the fact that two separate cases seemed once again to have more than a co-incidental amount of common threads.

Chapter Ten

Barron Rinaud arranged his baggy features into an appearance of welcome. His voice, however, held surprise and, if Teresa wasn't completely mistaken, some fear.

"Well, now, Miss Worth. What's a beautiful young woman like yourself doing out all alone at nine-thirty on a Friday night?"

"I'm sorry I didn't call first, Mr. Rinaud, but I have a few things to ask if you have a minute."

"Of course I do." Rinaud fumbled with the hook on the wide screen but finally pushed it open. "How you feeling, darlin'? Come on in here out of the bugs and night air."

"Thank you, Mr. Rinaud." Teresa hurried through the open door, anxious to allow the man no time to reconsider his offer.

She found herself in a cavernous front hall, dimly lit and fragrant with old wood and vanilla candle smells. Rinaud let the screen drop and gestured to the parlor leading off the center hallway where a fringed pink lamp threw a circle of inviting mauve light.

"Come on in and sit down here, my dear. I'll run get us something to drink."

"Don't go to any bother, Mr. Rinaud," Teresa replied. "I don't want to take a lot of your time. I just wanted to ask you a few questions."

He blinked his pale eyes and smiled. "More questions about little Cecilia? Certainly. But let me run get us some iced tea. It won't take a minute."

Teresa remained standing and listened to the echo of his footsteps trailing toward the rear of the house, where she assumed the kitchen was located. She glanced around the room, marveling at the amount of bric-a-brac and mementos heaped on every surface in the room. On a small, drum-shaped table next to her stood a dozen porcelain angels posed in innocent and fanciful positions of flight, while on the bookcase beside it hundreds of metal Confederate soldiers stood shoulder to shoulder, lances thrust out and battle flags raised.

It must be a nightmare to clean in here, Teresa found herself thinking, then noted thick inches of dust and realized the inside of Rinaud's house was in the same disrepair as the outside. It was odd that she'd never seen a maid or cleaning woman on the premises. "Poor relation..." a voice inside her head whispered, and she wondered suddenly about the pressures of being a member of a rich family with little of that wealth to call one's own.

"Now here we are, honey. Sit down! Sit down! Take a load off. Did you hear the news reports that a hurricane is kicking up in the Atlantic? You never been in Port Jackson during a hurricane, have you?"

"No, I haven't. There was Juan a couple of years ago, but that went into Mississippi and just brought us a lot of rain."

"Nothing new about rain in Port Jackson, though, is there?" They shared a laugh and Barron studied Teresa's face. "Now, let me ask you again how you're feeling. That was a nasty bump the other day."

Teresa accepted the frosted glass Rinaud handed her across the table, elegantly decorated with mint and a silver spoon. "Fine. My head's a little sore but I'm none the worse for wear." She sat on the horsehair couch and took a drink.

"You modern women never cease to amaze me," Rinaud said, moving the leather-bound cookbook he'd been reading before she arrived off the chair across from her and sitting down. "Look so pretty and delicate but work all day and night. 'Course, Southern women are famous for that— steel magnolias and all that mess—but it seems to be true 'bout all you'all." He smiled and tipped his glass. "Cheers!"

Teresa let him drink, measuring in her mind how much he'd ask him. She didn't want to get Mazie into any kind of bind, and hoped again that no one from the Wallace household had seen her come to the door. "That's delicious. Thank you very much."

"You're very welcome. Now, what can I help you with?"

"Just a couple of things. Did you ever meet Raoul Joachim, Cecilia's brother?"

Barron blinked several times and took a sip of his tea. "Well, yes, I did. A good-looking boy. Came to visit once or twice. Sunbathed out by the magnolia trees with Cecilia, seems like. Stayed the weekend a couple of times, if I remember."

"Did anyone come with him?"

"No. But a good-looking young boy like that wouldn't need to bring no girl with him. One would find him, soon enough."

"Did Jordan Morisette find him?"

Barron began to laugh and shook his head. "Oh, I doubt that. Jordan's tastes run a bit more genteel than one of her grandpa's hired hands."

So Barron Rinaud knew Raoul worked for Rebel, too. Teresa decided to let that drop for a moment and pursue the major topic of interest. "I was wondering if you'd tell me what you know about pyramid parties here in Port Jackson."

"Pyramid what?"

"Parties. Have you heard of them?"

"Some kind of card parties, are they? Like mah-jongg?"

"No. These are parties that make people a little cash : they bring their friends. They form a pool—first in is pai first, last in take their chances."

"Is that so?" Rinaud took another big gulp of his tea an removed the starched napkin covering the plate of cookie he'd also brought in. "How about a praline, honey? These pecans are a little on the puny side but they're real fresh an sweet."

"No, thank you," Teresa replied over the growling com plaint of her stomach. "So you haven't heard of these pa ties?"

"I might just have, but I can't say from who. Seem Juanita or Cutty Levelle might've mentioned somethin about it last week, or was that Tupperware? Maybe it wa No, can't say as I have heard of pyramid parties. Did Cec lia go to them?"

"I don't know. But I heard a rumor that one was su posed to be held here last Monday night."

"Here, you say?" Barron's eyebrows rose, though th surprise in his voice did not sound sincere. "Humph. Wel you know how rumors fly around Port Jackson, honey. Th maids hear something, or think they do, and pass it on u til a big story is told that don't have no more truth to it tha an Alabama governor's campaign promise. Besides, la Monday I was in New Orleans at a dinner party. So someone was having a pyramid party here, they must'v broken in."

Teresa let his words float over her, checking them fo shades of emotion. Rinaud's speech had become more an more slurred and accented as the visit wore on, and she wa wondering if he had spiked his own glass of tea with a litt gin, a common Port Jackson treat. New Orleans had be pronounced as a single word, "Norlins," and she was su denly worried that if she didn't hurry, he'd pass out before her questions were all asked.

"The maids do have a great news delivery system," Teresa said. "Did you know Verastine Johnson, Mr. Rinaud?"

"Verastine . . . ? Yes, I did know sweet old Verastine. She was a fine woman. A sin what happened to her. A sin it was." He drained his glass and sat back, a faraway look in his eyes. "Twenty years ago or so she used to come iron for my cousin, Ouida Morisette. I'd lived with them since I was eight and Ouida ten, which was when my mama ran off with that white trash oilman from Baton Rouge. Anyway, when Ouida's kids, Jordan and Tal, were little and I was studying for my entrance exams for Auburn, those children would yap around and hang all over Verastine and me. I'd chase them off but Verastine always was kind to them and they'd pester her to come play in their room instead of doing the ironing, and Verastine always would. She brought them sausage from a fast-food joint as a treat. Ouida never allowed that stuff in the house. She was a diabetic, and blamed it on Southern food. She died eighteen years ago, bless her heart. I think her kids were as upset at losing Verastine as they were their mama."

"So that's when Jordan and Tal went to live with the Talmadges? What happened to their daddy?" Teresa asked, no longer surprised that every question she asked seemed to yield an answer that brought her back to the family on Davis Circle.

"He left Port Jackson in a big hurry. I think Bay gave him some money. Eugenie, who had just recently come back into the family fold after some very peculiar behavior upstate, was a regular spinster by then, so I think Bay decided Tal and Jordan would be a good project to keep her occupied."

Barron sighed and Teresa murmured, "It sounds like a very sad time."

"Oh, that it was. Eugenie never did let me visit with the children much, she was too busy mothering them in her own peculiar way. I miss old Ouida. And I think Jordan could've used some of her mama's firmness. That boy Tal got even more withdrawn, but I expect he'll be okay. Eugenie did right by them. Or tried to, anyway."

"Did you live with the Talmadges, too?"

"No. Bay didn't much want 'someone of my influence' around. But I was given this place to live in, rent free as Bay so generously tells everyone who'll listen, so everything turned out fine. But we all missed Verastine and her sausage." Rinaud sat forward suddenly and shook his finger at Teresa. "Family's everything, you know. The last safety net in life. They might drive you insane, might treat you bad and scare the tarnation out of you with their pranks, but they's all that a body's got when things go badly."

Teresa nodded. "Bay Talmadge took in his daughter Durinda and her son, Wells, a few years ago, too. He certainly proves your point."

"You don't know the half about that, darling. Durinda's one of them girls never can seem to concentrate on anything but herself, no matter who else might be in danger of getting hurt. Reminds me of Eve, she does. Tempt whoever with whatever just to keep things around her exciting. If she wants a bite of that apple, she's going to put her teeth into it no matter what God or her daddy says. Her boy's a good one, but even he ain't going to keep her from trouble. After all, family can only do so much to protect a person, if you know what I mean."

Teresa had found that questioning people to be more specific often alerted them that they had said too much, but she needed to understand what was going on with the Talmadges and felt Wells's mother might hold the key. "Why does Durinda Talmadge need protection?"

"From herself, mostly. And the law, from time to time." He winked. "James Robert what works at First National said that woman bounced over two thousand dollars' worth of checks last month. The district attorney is a young man who don't react too kindly to that kind of nonsense going on in Port Jackson, no matter who your daddy is."

"Do you think she's being prosecuted?"

"No. Grounded by Bay Davis is more like it. Same thing happened last year when she tried to sell some stock, or some trash like that her daddy didn't like. I reckon he done got Wells to carry his tired old bones to the bank to straighten out Durinda's little shopping spree. But if I know Bay, Durinda's going to have to look elsewhere for some money. He and Wells are trying to keep the waters smooth around their family name, especially now that their company might be bought right out from under them."

Teresa nodded and took another sip from her glass, showing no surprise at this story involving stock. She hoped that ruse would convince Barron she knew more than she did. "I heard a firm was anxious to buy them and that some members of the family had been approached about selling their stock. Is that what the big meeting was for at the lawyer's?"

"Yes, ma'am. Though no one's admitting nothing, some-one's given this Tiger Development company the impression Rebel's not the united family company it once was, that's for damn sure."

Bingo, Teresa thought. Things were worse than Wells had let on. And if Durinda had tried to sell in the past, she might be the weak link now. Durinda's need for fast cash might all be adding up to one big scandal.

Teresa considered for a moment if a last discreet inquiry about Durinda's past spending habits would be appropriate, but before she could ask another question, Barron hiccuped, leaned his head back against the chair and fell asleep. His mouth slackened and his breath rattled around inside his mouth, the snores coming immediately. Teresa put down her glass and walked quietly outside, pulling the heavy door closed behind her.

She again had the feeling that she was in possession of all the crucial facts and just needed time to sift through them to understand the tale they told. Whatever it turned out to be, the center of it was probably money. Even in wealthy families, money and the fight to control it rooted most feuds.

Maybe Cecilia Joachim had stumbled on some information, or was acting as a go-between for someone—possibly the family member interested in selling stock—before she disappeared. Teresa realized she'd have to press further into trying to find out about the rumored sale of Rebel Chemicals, knowing that it would mean knocking heads with Wells. Regardless of the fact she'd been dismissed from the case, she had every intention of finding out what was going on with the Talmadges.

Most detectives, she'd found, were unable to let go of a stream of clues once they'd begun to sniff them out. And since she'd been beaten on the head by someone, she had more than a passing interest in finding Cecilia and discovering what the devil was going on.

Besides, she reasoned as she slid into the front seat of her car, Wells Talmadge was the first man in longer than she cared to admit who intrigued her on a personal level. Even if he was mad at her and she at him, it would be good to see him again.

Her car coughed and sputtered but finally started on the third try. She headed for Balboa Street but at the corner of Dauphin and Columbus decided to go left. She had wanted to see the place where Verastine was killed in the dark and judge for herself how probable the hit-and-run explanation was, and tonight was as good a time as any.

Teresa stopped a block down the street from the warehouse where the police had found Verastine, and killed the car lights. She reached for her purse, then remembered she didn't have her gun, so she threw her bag under the seat and let herself quietly out.

The evening was moonless and velvety dark, the smell of green mold, salt and wild lavender heady and very typical of Port Jackson. Columbus Street, lined with small commercial buildings, was deserted and, save for the omnipresent night rumbles of thunder over the bay, silent.

Teresa stood for a moment and got her bearings. There were no streetlights on Columbus Avenue, as Vergel Glenn had noted, and no lights at the high school football field across the way. She walked silently toward the building anchoring the street, keeping her eyes on the brick wall where the word *Grocer* was still visible.

Stopping across from the building, she looked both ways. A car was coming down Hope Avenue, but passed by without turning. Teresa spotted the alleyway beside the building and crossed the street quickly. She stood on the curb in the darkness, then slowly turned in a circle. If her memory served, the alley emptied onto Balboa behind the abandoned warehouse.

Verastine probably came from behind the building, past where she stood now, and was just crossing the street when she'd been struck, most likely by a car turning off Hope. Teresa stared into the street. It was wide and recently paved. Sidewalkless like most of revenue-poor Port Jackson, it offered plenty of room for a car to maneuver in order to avoid a pedestrian. Teresa looked up and then back at the road.

Even in the moonless dark it should be easy to see a person. Especially a person dressed in white.

She continued down the alley running parallel to the side of the warehouse. A dog was barking over on the next street, and she heard a siren toward downtown. None of it added up, Teresa thought. An accident should never have happened here, unless the driver's vision was somehow impaired.

She reached the end of the alley and looked both ways. The porch of the Wallace's house was visible from where she stood, as were the upper-story windows. Teresa felt chill bumps rise on her neck as she stared at the empty panes of glass, realizing someone could be looking back at her and she'd never know it.

Quickly she turned and walked the length of the warehouse. The back side was solid brick save for one loading dock completely covered by steel doors. At the far end she stopped and peered into another, much narrower alleyway. She gasped. Light streamed out of a small second-story window and bathed the building next to it with the outline of a window. Into the light intruded the silhouette of a person, a tall, broad-shouldered man, from the shape of him. Teresa stepped back against the building and felt her pulse speed up.

No one should be inside this building. It had been vacant for years. But if someone was there tonight, maybe they'd been there Monday night. Maybe they'd seen or heard what happened to Verastine.

Or maybe Verastine had seen or heard them, a little voice mumbled in her brain. Teresa touched the pocket of her dress and felt the hard outline of the small but powerful flashlight she was carrying. It wasn't really a decent weapon, but it was comforting to have something in her hand. Stealthily she hugged the side of the building and moved toward the window. If it was open, maybe she'd hear something. She noted the narrow aluminum door directly under the window and stopped, trying to focus her eyes.

Was it slightly ajar?

She continued to creep along a few feet, then stopped. If someone came out the door she'd have no place to hide. At that moment the light went out. Teresa stared in disbelief at the dark wall, then three seconds later she heard footsteps—terrifyingly they were not from the direction of the warehouse but from the alleyway behind the warehouse. Which meant she had to turn and confront an unknown person in the dark, or take her chances inside the warehouse, where someone else waited.

Teresa turned and ran for the door, pulled it open and slipped inside. The dark was thicker and blacker inside. For a moment she stood, then moved to her right where a bulky set of stairs shot up into the darkness. She continued past them to the side wall of the stairs, listening with all her concentration. The door she'd just come through groaned as it was opened and the footsteps stopped.

Above her the floor creaked. Teresa stood completely still, swallowed and clutched the flashlight. Whoever was there could not hear her breathing or her heart pounding, but both sounded abnormally loud to her own ears.

Tentatively she put her right hand against the stairwell and felt the outline of a doorknob. *There must be a small closet of some kind,* she thought. Too bad she hadn't discovered it earlier and had time to lock herself in.

Teresa pressed herself against the doorway, wincing as her hipbone reminded her of her fall the day before, and continued to listen. She heard the footsteps again as the person from the alleyway made progress across the room. Above her she heard nothing.

Suddenly she had the urge to cry out, to warn either the person upstairs or the person downstairs of the other's presence, for her intuition told her one of them was in grave danger. But she let the impulse pass and clamped her teeth together. She was in danger, too, and until she knew from whom, it wasn't worth her life to take the chance to warn a stranger.

She dared to move her head slightly toward the side of the stairwell, hoping to catch a glimpse of movement, but saw nothing. Her eyes were becoming more accustomed to the darkness, but she couldn't make out any human form, only ancient orange crates and several silver milk cans. Light, pale and intermittent from heat lightning miles over the bay, flashed in a window somewhere above.

Above, the floor creaked and Teresa shrank back into her hiding place. Then she heard footsteps again, coming across the floor near her. Despite the depiction of glamour and danger on television, real private detectives seldom had this kind of encounter. Even in her five years as a cop she'd never been in such a tight spot.

Teresa clutched the flashlight and tensed, but the person who'd come in behind her stopped and began to climb the steps. She decided to make a dash for the door once both people were upstairs. The footsteps, deliberate and even, stopped as if the person had read her thoughts. She heard an intake of breath, then a man's voice.

"What are you doing here? I thought I was going to meet your boss," he said.

"I guess I'm the boss," came a low female reply from farther up the stairs. "And I'm here to catch a rat. Come on up, then we'll talk about your plans to back out on our deal."

Their voices carried in the thick air, both full of tension and fear. The man's had a trace of an accent. Teresa's brain leaped to tie a name to it but couldn't.

"You must let me explain what happened," the man said.

"Come on up here first," the woman replied. "Did you bring the money?"

"Yes," the man answered.

"Where is it?"

Teresa caught a glimpse of a large, paper-wrapped parcel in the man's hands.

"Here," he said. "Did you bring the documents back?"

"Of course," the woman replied. "Where's your sister?"

"Leave her out of this. Your business is with me."

"I don't like loose ends," a second male voice said from the top landing. "Both of you come up here, now."

Teresa heard the Hispanic man swear then shout, "What in hell are you doing with a gun? For God's sake—"

The sound of a blast cut short the man's voice; a second and third shot paralyzed all of Teresa's reflexes for a few seconds while her instincts organized her body into motion. If she had still been a cop she would have gone after them. But she didn't have a gun, or a badge, or a partner.

So she ran away from them, around the stairwell and across the floor, slamming into a milk container and sending it flying with a wail of metallic banging. She reached for the doorknob as a bullet ricocheted off the concrete floor by her feet.

Teresa pulled open the door and ran down the alley. As she reached the end, her mind tumbling over where to go for the nearest phone, she ran full tilt into a man as he turned the corner. The collision sent her thudding into the side of the wall, and a scream of pain and surprise screeched from her lungs.

"What the hell's wrong!" the man cried out, grabbing her by the arms.

Teresa looked into the shocked eyes of Wells Talmadge. "Let me go. I've got to get the police."

"You're not going anywhere until you tell me why you're running like the hounds of hell are after you."

His fingers bit into the tender skin of her arms. Teresa stared at him, the possibility that he was involved, or even aligned, with the woman who'd just attempted to murder her rushing through her brain. "What are you doing here?"

"No more questions." Wells looked down the alleyway, then met her frightened eyes. "Come on with me. I want to see who, or what, you're running from."

Teresa inhaled, gambling on her intuition that Wells Talmadge was as decent a person as she'd originally judged. "Don't go in there. We need to call the police. Dear God, I think someone's been killed!"

"What?" He stopped and pulled her around the corner behind the warehouse. The silver Mercedes was parked up the alleyway a bit, hidden partially by the overhanging limbs of a magnolia tree.

"Do you have a phone in your car?" Teresa asked.

"Yes." He held her arm and they hurried toward it. "But tell me what happened. Are you saying someone attacked you in there?"

"Someone fired a gun at me. A woman, I think," Teresa said as Wells opened the door and reached for the phone. "Whoever it was shot someone else, Wells. We better call an ambulance now!"

Chapter Eleven

"What are you talking about?" Wells demanded. He grasped Teresa's arm more tightly.

"I—I heard a man scream inside the warehouse. And I heard shots...."

Wells pushed the phone into her hands. "Call for help. And stay here!"

His heart pounded and shock stiffened his muscles but Wells made his legs carry him back down the alleyway. He listened for a moment outside the closed door and heard nothing, then grasped the knob and yanked.

The door stayed closed fast. The night air hung thick but silent around him. He beat on the door with both fists. "Open the door!" he finally yelled, but after a silent few moments turned and ran back to the car. Teresa was standing, pale and tense, next to it.

"They're coming. Did you go inside?"

"The damn door's locked." He opened the trunk and pulled out the jack handle for the car. "I'm going to try to force it open."

"Shouldn't we wait for the police?"

"For God's sake, Teresa, I thought you were a professional detective—"

"You've seen too many television shows—"

"But if someone's been shot—"

"Exactly! If someone's been shot and the shooter is still inside we'd be nuts to go in. I don't have a gun! It's too dangerous." Her words did nothing to stop him. She ran behind him back to the warehouse, her legs shaking with nerves. In the distance a siren began to wail. Help would be here soon, though she wondered if it would be soon enough for the man inside.

"What happened?" Wells demanded again, shoving the jack handle in near the lock. "Tell me what went on in there."

"I saw a light and went in to investigate," Teresa began. "A woman I know, the one whose wake you and your family attended, was hit by a car and killed out in front a few nights ago. I'm looking into her death and needed to check out the scene. When I saw the light I thought the person might have seen what happened the other night."

Wells grunted and the jack slipped, clanging against the ground as it fell from his hands. The siren was louder now. The police would be here in a few seconds.

"You certainly have a knack for being in the wrong place at the wrong time," Wells said through clenched teeth. He inserted the edge of the jack again and pulled. Wood splintered and the metal hinge groaned. "Did you hear what was going on inside?"

"A little. It seemed to be a meeting of some kind." She didn't add that it sounded criminal, since Wells seemed intent on ignoring any danger. "A man with a Spanish accent asked a woman if she'd brought some documents. He said he had her money—"

Wells stopped as if he'd been struck. "The man had a Spanish accent?" The pulsing sense of dread sped up. "Did you recognize the woman's voice? Was she Hispanic, too?"

"What? No. I don't know, I don't think so. And of course I didn't recognize—" Teresa suddenly went silent. She was sharing all this information without regard. Shock had loosened her tongue. But suspicion, sharp and acidic, clenched inside her suddenly, and she took a deep breath in order to regain her control. "*Should* I have recognized her?"

"I don't know."

"Really?" Teresa took a step back from Wells and wrapped her fingers around the flashlight still in her pocket. "What were you doing here, anyway? I'm sure the police will want to know that."

"Actually, I was looking for you. I saw your car on the street and decided to see what you were doing." He glared at her and shoved the jack handle farther into the crack, then finally managed to spring open the door. He dropped the tool and pulled the door ajar. Squealing tires and the wail of the sirens told Teresa the police had arrived, but she followed Wells into the warehouse without waiting for them.

"Hello?" Wells yelled.

"Don't be stupid," Teresa said, grabbing his arm. "The gunman might still be here, too. Wait for the police."

"Let me go." Wells walked farther into the warehouse. "Where is the guy who was shot?" he asked Teresa.

"On the stairs, about halfway up."

Wells sprinted upstairs just as voices yelled out in the alleyway, "Come out with your hands up. This is the police!"

"Oh, my God," Wells yelled from the stairway. "Teresa, tell the police to get in here. Raoul is bleeding badly."

"Raoul," she whispered. Raoul could only be Raoul Joachim, the missing chemist, brother of the missing maid. She was suddenly sure Wells had suspected it was Raoul inside. How had he jumped to that conclusion, she asked herself? Had Wells come to meet him? Had he thought the other person was Cecilia Joachim?

Unable to put her thoughts into coherent order, Teresa turned and ran toward the door, then remembered her cop training and put her hands up. "Don't shoot. Civilian, and I'm unarmed," she yelled out. She was blinded by a spotlight and told to lean against the wall. The night erupted into shouts, grim faces and hard hands as a cop patted her down and told her not to move.

Remembering what she used to do to suspects who disobeyed, she didn't.

RAOUL JOACHIM WAS pronounced dead at the scene. There was no sign of the two other people Teresa had heard on the stairway, but the doorway leading to an outside fire escape on the front of the building was found open. It yielded no prints or clues, although a cigarette butt was found outside, crimson lipstick circling the filtered tip.

The gun that had killed Raoul with two shots to the chest was not recovered at the scene, but two bullets fired from the gun that had murdered him lay on the metal table inside the one interrogation room used by the Port Jackson police. Betts Vaut pointed to the silver .38 ammunition wrapped in a plastic bag and turned to where Teresa and Wells were huddled on hard wooden chairs against the wall.

Further ticking Betts off was Teresa's insistence on the fact that Raoul had had a parcel with him, though nothing was found at the scene.

"Now, Teresa, you're sure you didn't have your gun with you tonight inside that warehouse?"

It was the fifth time she'd been asked that question in the past three hours. She inhaled, trying to keep her antagonism to a minimum. She understood police procedure. Repetition was key to questioning a suspect. Even the best-rehearsed lies fell apart under repetition. "No, I did not."

"Where is your gun?"

"I have no idea. I assume whoever stole it from my house still has it."

"So whoever killed Mr. Joachim just happened to have the same caliber of gun."

"Come on, Betts. This is America. This is Alabama. Every other citizen on the street has a gun and a good percentage of them are .38s. Doesn't it figure?"

Betts ignored her speech. "But you never personally met Mr. Joachim?"

"No."

"*Never* met him? Think hard, now."

"No."

"Never met his sister, either?"

She grimaced. Betts had wasted no time putting together Raoul and Cecilia Joachim. "That's right."

"But you were looking for her the other day when you got yourself conked on the head at Barron Rinaud's place?"

Teresa made no reply for a moment. The connection between her, the Talmadge family and the missing Joachim brother and sister was glaring, but until she could make more sense of it than the cops she was going to keep quiet.

"No comment. My cases are private."

"Murder kind of overturns all that client privilege nonsense, don't it, girl? Who were you working for when you were trying to find that maid? Wells?"

She said nothing while the two men glared at each other like wet roosters.

"Honestly, Betts," Wells broke in. "You've been up this road a dozen times already. Let us go. You've got her statement and my statement. What more do you want?"

"Wells, I'm just a poor old country boy trying to understand how one of Port Jackson's leading citizens and an ex-policewoman came to be involved in a murder where the citizen's employee gets himself killed by the exact same kind of gun the ex-policewoman alleges was stolen the day before! Now I know you all are saying it's coincidental, but if there's one thing I don't like, it's coincidental situations that leave people dead.''

"So charge one of us or let us go home," Teresa replied. Meeting Betts's stare, she bent her cramped fingers, not liking the tight, dry feeling left from the chemicals they'd used to test her for gunpowder residue. She'd willingly submitted to the test, knew it was correct procedure, but still resented the fact that Betts had seen fit to do it. It had touched her that Wells had demanded to be tested also, though right now she'd give anything to be home, alone, free of them both.

Betts walked around the table and sat down. He picked up the typed statement Wells had given and frowned. "Now let me just get this real clear in my mind, Wells. You say you left your grandpa's house about six, headed to your office in Pensacola, but stopped halfway and came back because you wanted to talk with Miss Worth. You went to her house, found she was gone, and were driving back to Davis Circle when you noticed her car parked on Columbus." He looked up and smiled. "That's all correct?"

"For the tenth time, yes, that is my statement."

Betts put the papers down and folded his hands together. "And why did you want to see Miss Worth?"

It was a new question and seemed to surprise Wells. He sat back in the chair. Teresa cut her eyes to his fatigued face and saw his mouth pursed with tension. "I wanted her to do some work for me."

"Work? You mean detective work?"

"Yes. That's what she does for a living, isn't it?" he snapped. "We'd discussed her working on a case earlier and she'd decided not to accept the job, but I was going to go over and see if I could change her mind."

Betts nodded. "Mm-hmm. Yes, sir, that's what she does. Can you tell me any more about it than that?"

"No. I can't."

"I see." Betts stared at the paper again. "And Mr. Joachim was employed by your company for how long?"

"Three years."

"As a chemist?"

"Correct."

"Good employee, was he?"

Wells paused a moment then shook his head. "Betts, I've told you several times, yes, he was a fine employee. He was young, sharp and eager. The best."

"But wasn't there some problem lately with him? Didn't show up for work lately, I hear."

Wells narrowed his eyes. "I'm not going to discuss any business-related issues with you, Betts, unless my lawyer is here. Do I need to wake him up and get him down here or are we going to say good-night?"

"Now just hold on a minute and let me think." Betts rubbed his chin, doing his best impression of a slow-witted sheriff while all present knew he had a mind that worked like a well-oiled bear trap.

Wells turned to Teresa. "Can I give you a lift? I think your car is still in front of the warehouse."

"Yes. Thanks." She looked to Betts, knowing this dismissal ploy of Wells's would do no good until Betts was really ready to let them go. "Okay if we leave now, Betts?"

"Sure thing," the cop replied, suddenly as friendly as if they'd stopped by for a chat. He stood and reached his hand across the scratched table. "I'll be in touch, now. You all get some rest. I'm hearing we might have a hurricane in town soon, so everyone needs to catch up on their rest."

Wells shook hands but glared at Betts and opened the door. A minute later they were in the Mercedes, speeding down Government Street toward Teresa's house. The night was still and muggy, and a huge rainbow ring hugged the beginning of a moon. Teresa was so exhausted her bones hurt. Her head throbbed, and her stomach complained so loudly that she rested her hand against it self-consciously.

"Hungry?" Wells asked.

"Yes."

"Got any eggs at your place?"

She thought of the package of groceries she'd left unpacked on the counter hours ago. "Yes."

"Bread and coffee?"

"Yes."

"Good. I'll fix you breakfast before I leave, then walk over and get your car and drive it back."

She was too tired to eat, too tired to argue. "You don't have to do any of that."

"Yes, I do. You look like hell."

"Thanks." She managed a small grin. "You were really coming by to see me?"

"Yes. I acted like an ass today and I wanted to apologize." He grinned. "It seems I've been doing that since we met. I also wanted to tell you the truth about Raoul Joachim." He squeezed the steering wheel so tightly his knuckles shone white. "Damn sight too late now, I guess."

"How did you know it was him in the warehouse?"

"It's a long story," he replied.

"I'm ready to listen," she whispered softly.

"Thanks." His right hand left the steering wheel and squeezed her knee. "I owe you an explanation."

She looked at him, glad for the company, totally mystified by the emotional connection she felt forming between them, but ready to listen now that she was sure he was going to tell her the truth. "You look like hell, too."

He nodded his head in agreement. They didn't say another word the rest of the way home. She let him take her key and open the door, then left him alone in her wreck of a kitchen and took a five-minute scalding shower. She soaped her hair, not caring if it hurt the partially dissolved stitches, then wiggled her damp body into a navy blue cotton jumpsuit. The mirror showed fatigue and puffy eyes that begged for makeup. She rubbed lotion on her face, combed through her wet hair and switched off the bathroom light.

Teresa walked into the kitchen and sat down. Bacon was spitting and sizzling on the stove and the air was full of warm bread and coffee smells. Wells had cleaned off the mess she'd left earlier and set out place mats and silverware. Without a word he set a steaming mug in front of her.

"How do you like your eggs?"

"Over easy."

"Three or four?"

She chuckled and felt her spine relax for the first time in hours. "How about two? I've got good cholesterol and would hate to blow it all at once."

"Do you have grits?"

"No, I hate them. Sorry."

"I do, too." He threw her a smile and she found herself liking his face more than ever. His blue eyes were dark with fatigue, his blond hair was spiky and unkempt and his shirt bore a wide grease stain on the left arm, but Teresa liked what she saw. He seemed at ease and in charge, two things she'd never imagined she'd want in their relationship. Not that the series of confrontations and staredowns they'd had formed anything like a relationship, her mind quickly added.

"Here. Eat it all."

"Thanks." Teresa picked up the fork and ate. He sat beside her and ate twice as much in half the time, refilled their cups and looked off into space.

"That was some meal," she finally said to break the silence.

"You looked like you could use one. Why don't you hit the sheets and I'll go get your car?"

"There's really no reason for you to do that, Wells. I'll get it later. We can talk, or you can go on home and get some rest."

The tension was returning to Teresa's body. She wasn't sure, but it seemed to be related to being so close to Wells Talmadge, too close to his muscular arms and quick blue eyes. She picked up her mug as if to ward him off, took a sip and put it down so hard that it sloshed over her hand. Quickly Wells covered the spill with a napkin and held his hand over hers. She flinched as if to pull away but Wells held her hand in an embrace, staring at her, sopping up the coffee. She couldn't look away from the need she saw in his eyes.

This is insane, she told herself. But she felt it, too. She was suddenly embarrassed at her appearance and reached to fluff up her bangs. "God, don't I look a sight. I—"

"Don't," he said, moving his other hand to stroke her damp head. "Don't." He stood and pulled Teresa into his arms, his hand moving down from her hair to the small of her back, pressing her gently against him. Her mouth met his and she trembled, then returned the openmouthed kiss with a rush of desire and hunger that overwhelmed her.

Wells hugged her tighter to him, deepening the kiss, moaning as her breasts pressed against his chest.

After minutes passed he released her, placing both hands gently on her face. "Teresa, I—"

"Don't," she whispered, her voice shaky, her body unsteady and weak. She put her hands on his and moved them from her. "You don't have to explain, or apologize. It's been a bizarre day. People commonly reach out after things like this. It's shock. Believe me, I was a cop for several years. I understand."

Wells looked at her as though she'd lost her mind. "I had no intention of apologizing for kissing you, Teresa. I've wanted to before, every time we've been together, as a matter of fact. I'd like to kiss you again. And again, then carry you into your bedroom and kiss you some more and then make love to you. But it's not the right time, for either of us. Give me enough credit for knowing that.''

She was stung by his words and felt foolish. ''I'm sorry. Look, why don't you go on home? All this other stuff can wait. I'll talk with you later today.''

Teresa turned away and walked two steps toward the living room but he reached out and stopped her with a firm hand on her arm. ''I will. But first I have to tell you something.''

''What?''

''I lied to the police tonight.''

Teresa swallowed hard. She heard a humming in her ears as his words echoed but was too exhausted to feel any fear. ''What? What did you lie about?''

''About Raoul. He wasn't a good employee. He used to be, but two months ago he went to hell. Missed a lot of work. Was belligerent about the last pay raise, which wasn't much but was more than he deserved. I approved a salary advance for him, but that only seemed to make him worse. Then the rumors about Tiger Development started drifting in and Raoul began to act furtive. Working late without signing in. Logging some heavy usage on the computers. One of my senior chemists got worried that he was up to something. It seemed likely to me, too, though I hated to believe it of the kid. He'd worked hard, pulled himself up out of the Cuban barrio in Tampa and was a hell of a fine chemist.''

''That's some lie, Wells.'' Teresa walked across the dark living room and stood looking out the window. ''Betts is going to find this out, Wells. You'd better tell him the truth yourself.''

Wells shook his head and chewed on his lip. "I also lied about why I was at the warehouse tonight. I wasn't looking for you. I was there for another reason."

She waited, watching as sheets of heat lightning backlit the thick, overcast night, so far away she heard not a single clap of thunder.

"I was going to meet someone there."

Teresa's throat contracted as chill bumps skittered across her arms. She turned and faced him. "Raoul?"

He leaned his massive shoulders against the door frame and shook his head. "No. I was going to see his sister, Cecilia Joachim."

Teresa gasped and ran her hand through her hair as if she could untangle her thoughts along with the snarls. "How did you find her, Wells?"

"She found me. I was on my way to see you when I got a call about twenty minutes outside Port Jackson. It was Cecilia. She said she was in Raoul's car at a pay phone near the warehouse, and that she was worried Raoul was in danger. She said he was meeting the man he'd sold some stolen information from Rebel to, and she wanted me to come to the warehouse and confront them."

"Why didn't you call the police?"

"Because I was furious and couldn't wait to get a piece of these guys. It was a bad choice, I know, but Cecilia was nearly hysterical. She said Raoul had taken money to sabotage the company, but had a change of heart and was trying to back out of the deal. Raoul was meeting the person tonight, but Cecilia begged me to meet her out back and go with her to confront Raoul and his cohort." He made a snorting sound of self-disgust. "I never should have agreed without going to the police first, but I did."

"Mr. Impetuous. Is there nothing you won't do to protect Rebel Chemicals?" Teresa said sharply.

"To protect my family," Wells shot back. "We're on the verge of losing everything that's been built up for three generations, Teresa! All due to some damn corporate raider who has used every dirty trick in the book including playing my family against one another and waving money in front of a man too weak to turn it down. I've been hoping for a face-to-face with that scum bag for a long time. It was too good a chance to pass up."

"It could have been a setup."

"I thought of that. I didn't care. The banks turned down a major loan request earlier today, and I knew that news would send any chance I had of keeping Rebel's troubles quiet right up in smoke. I had to do something. To try to help my grandfather, yes, but also our company employs twelve hundred people, Teresa! All of them are going to be hurt unless I can do something."

"This is unbelievable, Wells." She sat on the chair beside the sofa and put her face in her hands. "So that's why you didn't want me looking for Cecilia. You were looking for her yourself, trying to get a lead on Raoul."

"Right. I knew if you scared her off, I'd lose Raoul, too."

A frisson of fear shook through Teresa. "What happened to her tonight? Where is she now?"

"I don't know. But she has my car phone number, and she can call the office in Pensacola. I'm hoping she'll get in touch."

"I'm hoping she's okay!"

"I'm sure she is. After all, the police were around there for hours. All that would have scared her back into hiding."

"So she doesn't know about her brother? Or if she does, she's alone?"

Wells hung his head. "I know. This whole situation is ripped. I'll tell the police about this tomorrow if she doesn't contact me first."

Several seconds of silence passed. "So now what?" Teresa finally asked.

"I want you to help me find Cecilia today," he replied. "We'll go see her together, find out what she knows about Raoul's blackmailer, and see if she knows anything about Tiger Development."

Teresa sat back and stared across the dark room. It was five in the morning and time had an unreal quality to it. She was suddenly beyond tired. For all his suffering tone, she suspected Wells Talmadge was still keeping something from her about this story.

Teresa moistened her suddenly dry lips. "A murder's been committed now, Wells. It's too big for you to handle privately. Besides, there's only one reason I can think of why you'd want to handle it yourself. And that reason isn't good enough."

He crossed his arms, his form filling most of the doorway as he turned to her. "What reason is that?"

"You're trying to protect someone."

"What?"

"You think someone in your family is behind Tiger Development, don't you? That someone you know bribed Raoul. And that someone in your family is a murderer."

There was a moment of complete quiet, then Wells gasped. He blinked his eyes at the horror of hearing the charge aloud, even though he'd had the same thought a hundred times the past hours. Teresa was right. He'd put his family above the law in an attempt to save them from themselves, maybe in an attempt to satisfy his need for a family to be proud of. But now all of that was changed. Teresa was right. If one of them was working with whoever shot Raoul, it was too late.

It was also too late to keep his last secret from Teresa. "I don't think anyone in my family would murder someone in cold blood. For any reason. I know I can't convince you of that, but I will tell you why I'm sure my family is not responsible for this. I got a lead this afternoon on an attorney in New Orleans who might be running this whole thing. An investigator I hired before you to research Tiger Development turned up an address in Fairhope."

Teresa nodded. "The guy associated with P. Verlaine?"

"How'd you know that?"

"I'm a good detective. But I only have a post office box registered to Tiger Development. You have a name?"

"Hey, I'm sure you'd have found this tomorrow." He smiled but Teresa was not in a mood to join in.

"What is the name?"

Wells reached into his pants pocket and pulled out his wallet. He removed a slip. "The property is on Dogwood, and the deed is registered to two men."

"Anyone I'd know?" she asked, unable to keep the sting of reproach from her voice.

Wells stared at her, a glint of reflected light shining from his eyes in the shadowy room. "This is the real reason I was coming to see you tonight, Teresa. I know what you've gone through these past few months, trying to find your daughter. Lots of people in town really admire you for all your efforts—"

Fear, hot and powerful, ran through her veins. Her hands began to tremble. "Cut the speech, Wells. What's this got to do with anything?"

He cleared his throat. "The names on the deed are Franklin Reynolds, a man who died about thirty-five years ago, and another man. DuBois Gaillard Beaulieu. It looks like your ex-husband may be involved somehow with Tiger Development."

"And murder," Teresa whispered. "Oh, my God."

Chapter Twelve

Teresa stared at Wells. She couldn't believe he'd actually said her ex-husband's name out loud. "Wait a minute. You found a piece of property with my ex-husband's name on the deed? In Fairhope?" Fairhope was a lovely, sleepy town across the bay from Port Jackson. Teresa had planned to move there with Katie once because the schools were so superior. "That's impossible. I've been investigating all his assets for months and I've never found that."

"My investigator is sending a copy of the deed, but he told me over the phone that until a couple of years ago it was owned by this Reynolds character. Then it was transferred to DuBois. The transaction was handled by the same attorney that sent the correspondence to Sissy."

Teresa fell onto the chair beside her and cradled her head in her hands. The facts were almost too much to take in. "Does this mean you think Doobie is involved somehow with Tiger Development?" Teresa lifted her face from her hands and stared at Wells.

"You said he was involved in things like this before—"

"But he doesn't have the money! You said Tiger had to be bankrolled by some major cash."

Wells shrugged. "So he has a partner. The leveraged deals depend on borrowing on *future* assets."

She frowned as a vague memory shifted from one part of her brain to another. "I can't believe all this."

Wells stood beside her and tenderly moved his arm around her shoulder. "We need to go check out this address in Fairhope. Maybe we can turn up a lead on your daughter. At this point, that would make both of us very happy."

The truth of what he said sent Teresa's pulse racing. "You're right. Where is it? What's the address?"

Wells saw pain and hope in her face. "I've got the information in my car. I'll get it and maybe we can drive out later—"

"I want to go now." She stood and looked around for her tennis shoes. "We'll go now! My daughter—" Teresa stopped herself and raised a shaky hand to her face. "DuBois took our daughter and disappeared several months ago. I thought for sure he was in Europe. But if he owns a place here—" Suddenly she noticed the flashing red light of the answering machine on the coffee table.

Like a sleepwalker Teresa walked to it and pressed the button on the machine. It clicked, clicked again, then clicked a third time. A fuzzy, crackling static filled the tape.

"Hi, honey. This is Zelda. It's nine-fifteen. I just wanted to let you know the lab called and said they'll have the results of the test on your mysterious bag of dirt by tomorrow at four if I drop it by first thing, so I'll do that for you. You can pick it up, then come have supper with me. Sorry you didn't make it over for gumbo, but I saved you some. Talk to you tomorrow."

Teresa saw Wells's puzzled expression but ignored him. She'd explain about the soil samples later. Now she had to listen. She was drawn to the tape as if by a magnet. The machine clicked again, then a whispered voice began to speak. Teresa began to shake and leaned over to touch the recorder as if she could reach through the steel to caress the face of the person whose voice filled their ears.

"This is Katie Elizabeth Beaulieu. I've just got back from a long trip." Several beats of silence passed but then the child continued. "I'm calling this number. Would whoever is living in this house please answer? I need to find the doctor who is taking care of my mother, Teresa Worth. If someone is there, please come to the phone."

The little girl waited in silence, the soft sounds of her breathing reverberating in the air. Then another voice, that of a man talking sharply in the background, prompted the child to speak hurriedly.

"I'm sorry," the dear, sweet voice Teresa had despaired of ever hearing again said, "I'll have to call back." Then there was a click of disconnection, a dial tone and the tape stopped.

Teresa quickly hit the Save button, tears streaming down her face. She felt drugged, hallucinatory, as if she were about to vomit. She hit the Play button once more and listened, then saved the message again. When the machine rewound, she removed the cassette, hugged it against her chest and collapsed onto the couch. Her girl was okay.

Her Katie had remembered the phone number.

Her sweet Katie-bug was looking for her mother. "That bastard," she murmured.

"Teresa?"

Wells's voice pierced through her anguish and she turned to him.

He walked around the coffee table and sat next to her on the couch, reaching out to move a strand of wet hair from her mouth. "Go ahead and cry. I'll be here when you're done. I'll help you."

She saw tears of compassion glimmering in his eyes and then completely lost control. The fear, the hysteria, the sadness she'd tried to keep at arm's length for months spilled from every pore.

In response, Wells took her into his arms and let her cry, rocking her, his big hand cradling the side of her face as she spilled out the whole story of Katie's disappearance, the frustrated police efforts, the unsympathetic judges and overburdened court system, the fear of leaving the house any night at eight, the wrenching hole in her life that threatened to suck all the joy of being alive out of her, leaving nothing but hollow bones and motion.

Finally, when she was empty, she lay against Wells's chest for a moment, then forced herself to sit up. She accepted the box of tissue he silently offered, excused herself and washed her face. When she returned several minutes later he had washed the dishes and was putting on his jacket.

The early-morning light slipped through the windows, casting the room in pink and gray light. "You ready to go?" he asked.

She was grateful beyond words for his help. Teresa picked up her purse. "Yes."

"You know there's a better than even chance she won't be there."

"I've got to see," Teresa replied.

"I know." Wells nodded and took her arm. "Here we go, out to rescue our families. Together. I should have hired you months ago."

"You didn't know me months ago."

"I should have," he said. The look of naked sincerity on his face was nearly too much to bear.

THE CAUSEWAY WAS EMPTY of cars. A fog blanket hovered just above their heads, blocking the sky. The pavement gleamed with dew that shimmered just like the light reflected off the flat black mirror of the gulf.

Teresa stared at the water and thought of Katie, wondering how much she'd grown, aching to put her arms around her.

"Think we're going to get that hurricane? My grandfather's cook says it's coming," Wells said.

"I don't know," Teresa replied. "Maybe."

The miles clicked off and the silence stretched around them. Wells patted her leg, and she felt the tension in his touch. "We'll be there soon," he said.

Teresa sighed and closed her eyes. She thought about the kiss she and Wells had shared, about the things she'd thought of him, the conversations they'd had this past week. The attraction she'd felt for him had been immediate but, as always during the three years she'd been divorced from DuBois, it had been denied and pushed aside.

But pushing this man aside was going to be much harder to do from this point on, she decided, both because of Wells's tenacious nature and her own needs. She felt safe with Wells Talmadge, safe and hopeful. Cutting her eyes toward him, she caught his glance.

"Planning ways to keep me away now?" he asked.

Teresa laughed and rested her hand on his thigh. "Maybe you should be the detective."

"Well, if that's your intention I'd better be direct. I don't plan to listen to any reasons for why you won't see me," he replied.

"I can't promise to have much to give right now, Wells. My daughter—"

Her voice caught. Wells remained silent, respecting her need to control herself. It was a contradiction in his behavior she found very appealing. Though consistently impetuous, he responded with compassion to other people's emotions.

Teresa swallowed hard and went on. "It's just that I don't know what DuBois told her. She seems to think I've been sick. It's going to take a while, and a lot of attention, to get her settled."

Wells squeezed her hand. "I understand that, Teresa. I'm willing to take it real slow from here on. Slow, but steady."

"Thank you, Wells," she mumbled. They drove on, both more relaxed now that a tenuous agreement had been reached. Fifteen minutes later the Mercedes was creeping down the center of Fairhope's business district. All the shops were closed, and no pedestrians were about except for a woman in a white uniform and blue sweater hurrying from a twenty-year-old, hubcapless Chevrolet Impala parked in front of a large Colonial house.

Teresa had a sudden memory of Verastine getting out of a car in front of the house once when she'd sprained her knee and had one of her church friends bring her to work. Remorse for the lack of attention she'd spent on Vergel's case skittered through her, but she shook it off. She'd get back to that this afternoon, she told herself. Unless she found Katie—then it would have to wait a bit. Everything would have to wait while she caught up on her girl. Tears welled in her eyes and she hurriedly slapped at them, refusing to hope, but unable not to.

"The address is sixteen Dogwood Lane," Wells said. "Do you know exactly where that is?"

"Past the Grand Hotel, I think," Teresa said. "It's probably one of those narrow older streets that wind down to the bay, then back out to the highway. They all have flower names."

"Where all the little summer houses are?"

"Little summer houses" was the term the wealthy always used to describe the mansions their ancestors had built along the secluded beaches. In spite of her turmoil Teresa grinned. While Wells was nothing like the arrogant social snob her ex-husband was, he was obviously from the same background. "Right. All the little two-story, ten-bedroom summer houses."

Wells laughed, understanding the gentle rib immediately. "My grandparents have a place on Azalea, but it doesn't have a number. I think some legitimately smaller ones are over on that street that cuts behind where that developer wanted to build condominiums."

They continued on, meeting a few cars and joggers, finally locating Dogwood Lane. It was little more than a dirt road, the signpost faded and barely legible. Wells turned the Mercedes and proceeded carefully, but they bucked and rocked along the gouged roadway. A quarter mile down the road they found two houses on a thickly forested lot. Through the drooping leaves Teresa made out that the smaller house was boarded up, but the main house appeared occupied. It was freshly painted and sported ferns in large pots hanging over a wide front porch.

An old pickup full of wire cages sat in the driveway, and chickens ran over the patchy grass that managed to grow in the shaded yard.

The hum of locusts and buzz of mosquitoes was thick and the air smelled like low tide. Wells stopped the car and Teresa leaped out before he could open the door for her. There were no numbers on either of the houses, and the mailbox had Harper painted on it in thick black letters. Despite the tension stiffening her muscles, Teresa willed herself to stay calm.

She looked around carefully and couldn't imagine her exhusband hiding out here. "Are you sure the address you found out for Tiger Development was on Dogwood Lane in Fairhope, Alabama?"

"Yeah. The attorney had several pieces of correspondence. All to the same address."

Teresa looked around, wondering if they were being watched from the inside. Wells had parked the car directly behind the truck, and no other form of transportation was in sight. If DuBois and Katie were inside, they'd be hard-pressed to get away without her seeing them.

"You want me to go ask if this is the right address while you wait here?"

"No," Teresa answered, slapping a mosquito against her arm. "Let's both go."

They walked like soldiers to the door, stiff and in sync. Wells lifted the pitted brass door knocker and let it fall while Teresa held the screen. They stepped back and listened. No one answered.

"Now what?" Wells said.

Teresa used the door knocker this time, putting her entire strength into it, then stood back again.

Still no one answered the door. But somewhere close by, a child laughed. The light, giggling sound floated on the heavy air.

"Did you hear that?" Teresa said in a whisper, gripping Wells's arm.

"Out back, I think."

They crept off the porch and around the side of the house. The pine and dogwood trees were dense at the sides, and Teresa slapped at some more bugs as Wells pushed an over-turned wheelbarrow out of their way. Teresa noticed for the first time that there was a fenced backyard. Over the weathered wooden barrier drooped an ancient magnolia tree. The tree was dying, its limbs black and gray and scaly. A handful of creamy, opulent flowers grew on the one branch that still sprouted the waxy leaves, and piles of blackened blossoms lay on the ground.

Teresa thought of the trees in Barron Rinaud's backyard, but before she could decide if there could be some logical connection, a young girl shrieked and giggled with joy, just on the other side of the fence.

"Get it, Rocky. Get that stick!"

Teresa and Wells raced to the fence. Standing on her toes she peeked over, while Wells nervously held her arm. The backyard was huge and overgrown. A swing set, rusted and peeling green paint, drew her eyes. A girl in a pink-flowered playsuit sat on the swings, while a brown hound dog with one white foot gnawed on a stick.

The girl was Katie's size and looked about Katie's age.

But it wasn't her daughter.

Teresa's eyes welled for a moment, but she raised her chin and called out, "Hi, there. Is anyone else home with you?"

The girl stopped pumping her legs and pointed to the house. "My granny's inside. You want I should get her for you?"

"Please do," Wells hollered back. "We'll go back to the front door."

The young black child jumped off the swing, the tiny neat braids on top of her head flying, and ran toward the house. Wells put his arm around Teresa's shoulder and gave her a fierce hug. "Come on. Let's go talk to Granny."

Teresa didn't trust herself to speak, but allowed him to guide her along. Her mind churned with disappointment and a hundred fragments of memory.

"Look at all those trees," Wells said. "I've never seen so many dead magnolias."

The backyard was full of dead magnolia trees like the one by the gate. *Like the ones at Barron Rinaud's,* Teresa found a part of her brain offering for a second time. She tried to focus on why that seemed important to her, but she couldn't. She could only think of Katie and the raw, taunting terror that she might never find her.

They made their way back to the porch and waited. The door opened and the little girl gave them a big grin. "My granny will be right here. You folks want to come in?"

"Mary, you run out to play now. And you keep that dog from coming in. I just done mopped that kitchen floor," a woman hollered from the interior of the house.

Little Mary grinned, and a moment later the woman appeared. She was round-shouldered and bosomy, with coffee-colored skin. Her high cheekbones were elegant, and on the left side of her face were sprinkled five freckles that made a perfect half circle under her eye.

"Miss Teresa! What you doing all the ways out here?" the woman said.

Wells looked at Teresa with a shocked expression. "Do you know this woman?"

"Yes," Teresa answered, her own surprise clear on her face. "This is Sister Hanks Harper. She used to work for my husband's family."

"You all come on in now. I'll get you some coffee and breakfast." Sister Hanks smiled at Wells, but didn't meet Teresa's glance.

They followed her inviting sweep of arm and went into the cool house. Teresa decided the woman seemed nervous to see her. It could be because she'd heard Teresa was investigating Verastine's death, or because of DuBois. Teresa had seen to it that the story of DuBois's abduction of Katie was in the papers, but even without newspaper coverage word would have gotten around.

"This is Wells Talmadge, Sister," Teresa said after they'd followed the elderly black woman into the small kitchen.

"Mrs. Harper," Wells said.

"How are you, Mr. Talmadge?" Sister said. She hurried over with a cup of black coffee. "You Miss Sissy's grandson, ain't you?"

"Yes," Wells replied. He looked to Teresa, allowing her to take the lead. He read fatigue and despair on her face, but she was calm and had the sharp, focused look in her eyes he'd become familiar with. If Wells was any judge, Teresa

Worth would not leave this kitchen until she had some answers they would both benefit from.

Teresa and Sister Hanks chatted back and forth. Mary was Sister's only granddaughter. Mary's mother was at work in Fairhope and Sister minded the child during the day.

"I like having that child around me," Sister said as she stood at the stove. "She's a character, that one. Reads real good, too. Reads the paper to me at night."

"Don't make any food for us," Teresa replied. "We ate a while ago."

"I ain't doing nothing special, child. You just sit down and have your coffee." Like most Southern women, Sister ignored her guests' protests about food and set enough sausage and bacon and biscuits on the table for six people before turning to get eggs and more coffee and gravy. Teresa dished up a plate for Wells and put a piece of ham on her own plate, but her stomach churned and tightened at the smell of so much food.

So she bided her time and watched as Wells and Sister and Mary ate. The child chatted about her dog and Sister got up and down three times for more food. Teresa caught Wells studying her anxiously several times, but she knew it was wiser to bide her time and let the scene play out naturally. That was the way it worked best with Port Jackson people. Hurry up and wait until they were ready.

Sister Hanks was a decent soul. She wouldn't lie if they asked her direct questions, but Teresa knew the old woman would do much better with the kind of questions they had after she'd shown them some hospitality.

"Granny says a hurricane is coming," Mary offered when the breakfast was at last over. "I never been in no hurricane."

"Really?" Wells replied. "Is that so, Sister Hanks? I heard on the radio there's a storm out in the Bahamas but it's not expected to make it over to the gulf."

"Yes, sir, Mr. Talmadge. It's coming. Three, four days at most, I say. Mary, honey, you go out and spread some feed for those chickens now."

The three adults watched the child run outside, then lapsed into silence. "You good at predicting hurricanes, Sister?" Teresa asked.

"I ain't never wrong. I knew Frederick was coming two days afore he hit this place. Had all my windows boarded up, too. We lost lots of trees in Frederick, but no windows. Not this house."

"Did a storm kill those magnolia trees?" Teresa asked softly.

"No, ma'am. I don't rightly know what's ailing them trees. Think it might been that Mexican man what come out last month and sprayed them a couple of times. But whatever it is, I hope it don't get into my chickens."

Wells cleared his throat. "This is your house, Sister?"

Sister stared at Wells and folded her hands together, then looked directly at Teresa. "Your husband done gave me this house when his mama died. Said I could live here in the summer instead of in Port Jackson, where I have to pay so dearly for my air conditioner. He knew my daughter worked out here and said his mama would've wanted him to take care of me. I know he done a terrible thing to you, Miss Teresa, taking that baby of yours. I hopes you don't blame me for any of that. I'd never allow such a thing, had I known about it. Miss India's turning in her grave, I bet, that Mr. DuBois done such a thing to a good woman like you."

"I know that, Sister," Teresa said, "and I want to thank you for saying so. But I need to ask, do you know where DuBois is now?"

Sister immediately shook her head. "No, I don't. I ain't heard from young Mr. Beaulieu for over a year now. If I did, I would've done told the police. Verastine used to ask me about him all the time, scolding me to tell if I knew something 'bout him. Poor Verastine like to died blaming herself about him taking that baby." The old woman wiped fat tears from her eyes with the edge of her apron. "And now poor old Verastine's dead, too. Nothing but bad things been happening lately."

"Have you ever heard about a company called Tiger Development?" Wells asked.

Sister stopped crying and stood. She peeked through the back windows at her granddaughter, then turned to get the coffeepot. "Tiger Development? Yes, yes, I gets a package now and then in the mail with that name on it. Nothing to do with me, though."

Teresa's spirits, beaten down in the past few minutes, began to lift. "What do you do with the packages, Sister?"

"What Mr. Beaulieu said do, put them away. He used to come get them ever so often, said it was business he didn't want to be bothered with. I've got a big box of them in the other room." She poured Teresa more coffee, looking as though she were near tears again.

"Can I have a look at those parcels, Sister? They might tell me something about where DuBois has taken Katie."

Sister moved around the table and poured Wells more coffee, then put the pot back on the stove. She stared out at the backyard. "Yes, sir, there's a hurricane coming. That's for sure."

Wells reached across and squeezed Teresa's hand. She looked at him, then back at the woman at the window. "I know I'm asking a lot, Sister, but . . ."

"Your little one's about the same age as Mary, ain't she?"

"She's seven," Teresa whispered.

"Uh-huh. Same as my little Mary." After a moment Sister Hanks turned and faced them. "I'll get them letters for you, Miss Teresa, but I sure don't know what's going to happen when Mr. DuBois comes looking for them."

"I'll handle him," Teresa said. "I promise I won't let him give you any grief about this, Sister."

"Ain't grief for me I'm worrying about," Sister said and looked at Wells. "You know Miss Teresa's husband, sir?"

"No, I don't, Sister."

"He's a man don't care much for other people's feelings about things," Sister replied. "Been like that since he was a little boy. His daddy died when he was real small, and his mama was too sick to take much care of him. My husband and I tried, but Mr. Doobie didn't take much to us telling him to be considerate of other folks. I was hoping he'd change when he came back from California with Miss Teresa, but I guess he didn't."

Wells nodded. "It's hard for people to change, Sister."

"Don't I know that." After a moment she shook her head and walked off toward the other room.

She returned several minutes later with a cardboard box. It contained six manila envelopes, all of which bore French postmarks. Teresa reached for the top one, but before she opened it little Mary came rushing in the back door.

"Granny, Granny. That man's car is ringing!"

"Ringing?" Sister said.

"My car phone," Wells said. "Thanks, Mary," he added and rushed outside.

Teresa helped Sister clear off the table, battling the mists of defeat that swirled around her.

"Don't worry so, Miss Teresa," Sister finally said. "You'll find that baby. I just know it."

Teresa squeezed Sister's arm. "I hope so."

Wells returned at that moment, a grim look in his eyes.

"We've got to go, Teresa," he said.

"Why? What's wrong?" She'd opened the first envelope and found stock investment statements and a brief letter from an attorney. Teresa waved her hand at the papers. "We need to go through these—"

"There's no time. Sister Hanks, thanks for your help and for breakfast. We'll get these back to you soon."

"Don't got nothing to do with me," she said, her eyes bright and fearful.

"Wells, what's going on?" Teresa demanded.

"We've got to go meet someone."

"Now? You go, I'll finish with these and—"

"No. You need to come with me."

Something in his voice frightened her. "Who are we going to meet?" Teresa asked.

Wells picked up the box and patted Mary on the head. "Cecilia Joachim. She's agreed to go see Betts Vaut at the police station."

"God. Did you tell her about her brother?"

"She knows. Which is why we need to get there, Teresa. Cecilia says she got a good look at the two people who ran out of the warehouse. She said she'd never seen them before, but would surely pick them out now until the day she died. Let's go."

Chapter Thirteen

Wells made the hour trip from Fairhope to Port Jackson in forty minutes. Their ride was silent as Teresa fought to regain her composure and recover from her shattered expectations about Katie, and to keep the strands of mysteries surrounding her daughter from knotting together completely.

Wells was more than preoccupied with wondering who Cecilia Joachim was about to identify as the people she'd seen leaving the warehouse after her brother's murder.

"Did Cecilia say anything more about who she saw?" Teresa asked as he pulled the car into the police parking lot.

"No. And I asked her outright for names. She sounded really scared, though."

"Scared?" *Of you?* Teresa's mind whispered.

"Yeah, petrified. She said she slept in the car last night because she was too afraid to go back to the place Raoul had rented."

"Does she think the people saw her?"

"I think so." Wells slammed the door behind Teresa and took her arm. "She said she didn't know if Raoul had been arrested or what, but when she heard about the murder on the news she called Bay's house looking for me."

"She thinks you can help her more than the police can?" Teresa replied.

"She's not thinking clearly at all, Teresa. I think she was working on adrenaline, not common sense."

As Wells pushed open the heavy inner door of the police station, the frigid air made Teresa shiver. She understood Cecilia's reaching out to Wells for help instead of an anonymous police officer. The first person she'd called when she discovered DuBois had kidnapped Katie was Zelda. "I'm glad you got her to meet you here, Wells. She may be able to tell us everything."

"Let's hope," he replied tersely. "Is Betts Vaut here?" Wells asked the man at the front desk.

"He's busy right now," the uniformed officer replied. "Hello, Miss Worth. Your gun turn up?"

Teresa stared at the man, then realized it was the cop who'd come to her house to take the theft report. "No. Thanks for remembering, though. Is Betts with a young Hispanic woman? We told her we'd meet her here. I'm sure he'd want to know we've arrived."

The policeman looked doubtful and divulged no information, but he did pick up the phone.

Wells and Teresa sat and waited. Five minutes later they were told to go back to interrogation room one.

Wells knocked, then opened the door at the shouted "Come in." His hands were sweating with nerves. Coming face-to-face with Raoul's sister, while informative, held the possibility of ruin for his family if it turned out one of them had been in any way involved in Raoul's death.

But he could manage damage control over the Tiger Development scandal only so far. Now that someone had been murdered, he'd have to weather the publicity he'd tried so hard to avoid.

The door swung open. Betts Vaut was sitting at the table, papers spread out in front of him.

He was alone. "Hello, Wells, Teresa. What's going on?"

"She's not here?" Teresa replied.

"Who's not here?" Betts answered.

"Cecilia Joachim," Wells and Teresa replied in unison.

Betts put down his pen and folded his arms. "No, she's not. Should she be?"

Teresa and Wells looked at each other in growing alarm. "I don't understand," Wells began. "She said she was ten minutes away." He looked at his wristwatch. "That was nearly an hour ago."

"You two aren't making yourselves too clear," Betts said. "You saw Cecilia Joachim and talked with her?"

"No. She called me." Wells walked quickly across the room and peered through the barred and slate-covered window. "I don't understand this."

"Why was she coming here?" Betts demanded.

"She was at the warehouse last night," Teresa said. "She said she was waiting in Raoul's car for him and saw two people leave."

"You mean to tell me she was there? Why didn't you call me so we could go pick her up?" Betts thundered. He stood and pounded his fist down on the tabletop. "Damn it to hell! You private citizens who think you can take on the police officer's duties without totally screwing things up—"

"Now calm down," Wells yelled back. "I told her to come see you so she could give you a statement."

"But she didn't, did she?"

"Maybe she still will," Teresa offered lamely. "Why don't you two sit down and cool off?"

"And let her get out of the state before she tells us what she knows? No, thanks." Betts grabbed the phone. "I'm going to put out a bulletin and have her picked up. What kind of car is she driving?"

"What kind of car did Raoul drive?" Teresa asked.

"I don't know," Wells replied.

Betts said a few choice words about interfering private detectives and citizens who stuck their noses where they didn't belong, then put a call in to another officer. "Call DMV and have them check the records for the dead man. Find out what car was registered to him. As soon as that comes up, put out a bulletin to pick up that car! Should be a young woman driving, his sister. Cecilia. Just a minute." Betts looked at Teresa. "What's this girl look like?"

Briefly Teresa described the woman from the picture she'd been given, then she and Wells listened until Betts was finished.

"Okay, now tell me what she said on the phone."

Wells repeated the conversation while Betts took notes, twice. "But she didn't give you any names?" Betts demanded again. "Nothing about what they looked like or anything?"

"No. That's it."

"Did she say she had the money?"

It really bothered Betts that the package of money Teresa thought she saw Raoul with hadn't turned up. "No," Wells said.

"And you didn't talk to her?" Betts asked Teresa suspiciously. "I thought you were the one looking for her. You two join up or something?"

Teresa ignored the implication in Betts's voice. "I didn't speak to her, Betts. Now, can we go? I've got a lot to do today."

"Fine. Go on, then. But both of you leave numbers at the front desk where I can reach you!"

Ten minutes later they were back in the Mercedes, heading to Teresa's. "I don't like this," she said. "Why would she agree to meet us, then not do it?"

"You tell me," Wells answered. "Something spooked her."

He pulled into Teresa's driveway and put the car in Park. "I better go home to change and let them all know I'm still around. Will you be okay?"

"Yes. I'm going over to the office. It's Saturday, so I can't reach anyone at the utility companies, but I want to get letters out to them requesting information on Sister Hanks's house. I'll bet DuBois never changed all those billings over when he gave her the house, so the business applications might have another address." A long sigh escaped her as she thought of the leads she'd run down to dead ends about Verastine. She mentally made a list of people to ask more about the pyramid parties. The housemaids would probably be scared to talk, but she was determined to find out more about who had planned to attend that night. One of them might have been in the area and seen a car, or a person.

"What are you going to do?" she asked Wells.

"Tal has demanded that we have a big family powwow tonight. I think he's found out more about the tender offer from Tiger Development."

"You need to lay out this whole thing, Wells. You can't carry it all on your shoulders anymore."

Wells made a face that was one part determination, one part refusal. "Did your ex-husband ever get involved in buying other companies out in the past?"

Teresa thought for a moment. "DuBois never said much about what he did. He had an office downtown that he went to every day once we moved here, but I had the impression he basically invested the profits from holdings he'd inherited." Teresa turned to Wells. "I know it sounds stupid in this day and age that I knew little of how my husband made his money. When I met DuBois in California I fell for his charm and old-style manners. We married quickly, too quickly, as it turned out, then I got pregnant the first month we were married. It was clear fairly soon that Doobie was a lot more complicated in certain ways than I'd bargained for."

"Complicated?"

"He was an only child of an older couple whose fortunes were on the decline. Though he said he wanted to earn his way in the world, he never really got past looking for the easy way to hit it big. For a while I think he was trying to change himself. He joined the police force, talked about having a career 'serving the needs of the community,' like his grandfather had done. But it wasn't to be. He got busted in an internal affairs sting of his precinct. He was lucky to stay out of jail for theft." Teresa felt her stomach tremble at the memory of Doobie being led away from their small apartment in cuffs.

Wells nervously rubbed his hands on the knees of his pants. "This is hard for me to ask, but I have to. Did DuBois have the kind of character that would..." His voice died out while he tried to temper the words he wanted to use to describe the despicable methods of Tiger Development.

"The kind of character that would bribe and hide and manipulate behind the scenes?" Teresa finished for him. "I'd say any man who'd kidnap his own daughter was capable of about anything, wouldn't you?"

"I'm sorry, Teresa. I'm sorry this is hitting so close to home."

"It's not your doing, Wells," she said, her voice harsher than she'd intended. "Look, let me go back to the office now. I have a couple of other cases I need to get to today but I'll try to run down that French attorney again."

He grasped her hand and gave her a searching look. "How's that head? Are you sure you're okay?"

"I'll be fine."

Wells squeezed her arm and gave her a brief kiss. "How about if I come by at five or so and take you to dinner? My meeting isn't until later."

"No, I need about twenty-four hours of sleep. And I have to be here at eight, so that doesn't give me much time in the office."

"Eight?" he asked softly. "Oh, right. Katie might call again."

"Right."

"Okay. Well, I'll call you later. Maybe I could come by and cook for you again?"

She smiled. "Do that, Wells. And thanks."

"For what?"

Teresa remembered how gently he'd held her in his arms, how he'd let her cry and pour out her story of loss in the early-morning hours. "For understanding about Katie, and about the pain I went through with Doobie."

"You're welcome."

Teresa let herself out of the car and walked toward the door. Wells honked and drove off. Teresa let herself into the cool house and tossed her purse onto the couch. She sat and picked up the answering-machine cassette tape, aching to hear Katie's voice again. She loaded the tape inside but before she could press the Play button, her front doorbell rang.

Teresa peeked out through the window, hoping it was something she could ignore. It wasn't. Vergel Glenn Johnson was standing there, an expectant look on his face.

"Vergel! Come in," Teresa said, pushing the screen door wide. "It's good to see you. How are things going?"

"They're going okay, Miss Teresa. I just came by to ask you if anything's come up about Mama."

"Not yet, Vergel. Nothing except I discovered that your mama wasn't called to go out by Miss Wallace. It seems there was a party she was interested in going to, but she didn't want anyone to know about it."

"What kind of party, Miss Teresa?"

Briefly Teresa filled him in on the pyramid-party gossip Mazie had told her about. "You never heard her talk about that?"

"No, I didn't. But it sounds like something Mama would go to, to get more money for us." The young man shook his head. "Explains why she had her pay with her, too, I guess."

"Maybe," Teresa replied. "I'm not ready to say anything just yet, Vergel. I've still got some things I'm checking on, and Betts Vaut has two men working on this case, too. They're still checking with body shops and car dealers in the area to see if they can match that paint they found on your mama's clothes. I think we'll find who did this."

"Okay. Well, I appreciate it, Miss Teresa." He rose and wiped his hands against his chest. He was wearing a faded orange sweatshirt that had Auburn University printed across the front. When he turned to leave, Teresa stared at the face of a ferocious tiger displayed on the back of the shirt.

Auburn University's football team was called the Tigers. DuBois had graduated from Auburn and was very active with the alumni, if she remembered right, and followed the teams closely.

Could that be the key to Tiger Development's name?

Someone else she'd run across lately had mentioned Auburn. But who? A piece of a conversation spun in Teresa's mind as a name surfaced, then disappeared into the fog of fatigue. She couldn't remember now. But she would.

It was time for a shower and a nap, she decided. Then she would go back to work. The name would come to her later if she stopped trying to force it.

BARRON RINAUD nervously peeked through the window of the tiny apartment over the garage at the driveway below. It was empty. *Where is that woman?* he said to himself, his hand fidgeting with the cheap drapery.

He turned and peered closely at the person lying on the open sofa bed behind him. She looked peaceful, as if she were napping. In fact she was in a deep, drug-induced sleep. The frosted glass in which he'd administered the potion of gin and ground-up sleeping pills lay on its side on the floor beside her. The iced tea ran in a tiny stream toward him, the lemon wedge he'd wrapped in cheesecloth a soppy lump beside the glass.

He turned away, frantic suddenly that Cecilia Joachim would wake up and be ill, and that he'd have to deal with it. "Where are you?" he wailed aloud, peering outside again.

As if in answer to his plea, a dark blue Cadillac with Florida plates pulled into the driveway and came to a stop below. Barron scurried to the door and pulled it open. His small eyes swept the surrounding area. But there were no witnesses; only the dead magnolias along the driveway watched as the blond woman in dark glasses hurried up the stairway and joined him.

"Thank God y'all got here! I was so afraid she'd wake up and then I'd—"

"Be quiet, Barron," the woman said, raising her hand as she would to a child. She removed the dark glasses and stared at Cecilia Joachim. "I can't believe our luck. She just came to you...."

"I nearly fainted when I saw her sneak in here this morning. When I came up she didn't answer for a minute, but finally she opened the door. She's real scared, what with her brother and all, but when I brought her something to eat she just broke down and told me everything."

"I can imagine," the woman replied. A sudden thought creased her brow. "Did you hide the money her brother brought the other night?"

Barron stopped trembling and nodded. "Yes. You want me to tell you where? It's the best place. Even if Betts Vaut and those old boys show up with a search warrant they'd never think to look under—"

"I don't care, Barron. As long as you took care of it." She placed a slim hand on his face and caressed him. "You're always so good about taking care of things for me."

He put his dry, bony hand over hers and kissed her palm. "You know I'd do anything for you."

"I know you would, darling. When you called I wasn't afraid. I knew I could count on you. Now be a love and tell me again what Cecilia said about seeing the people leave the warehouse."

Barron took a deep breath and let the woman withdraw her hand. "She said she was sitting in the car, real low in the back seat, waiting for her brother to come. But after a while he didn't come. She was fixing to get out and look for Raoul when she saw a man and a woman come down the front fire escape. They ran by the car. She didn't get a good look at the woman except to say she was wearing dark glasses and a scarf, and was tall and blond haired. But she saw the man all right."

The tall blond woman stared at Barron. "Did she know him?"

"No. But she described him down to the mole on his face and his diamond pinkie ring. She never met him, since he ran off before she hit town, but there's no doubt in my mind she'll identify him to the police if those boys show her the right pictures."

"And now that Teresa Worth's snooping around, I've no doubt his will be the first picture she'd suggest Betts Vaut show her," the woman said sharply. The woman began to pace, threw a glance down at the unconscious girl, then paced some more. "I should never have picked him to help us with this. I should have stuck to family."

"Now, now. Don't go sounding all down in the mouth, darling. We're almost there. You got the whole damn board of directors in an uproar. Half of them are ready to sell out to Tiger Development. Before you know it, we'll own the whole thing."

The woman's gaze became foggy and she sat on the bed beside Cecilia. Her hand found her neck. "Where is it?"

Barron knew what she meant without asking. He tiptoed past the prone form of the girl, picked up the purse lying on the arm of the couch, then tiptoed back and handed it to the woman. "Here you go."

The woman snapped open the small silver evening bag and peered inside. She smiled, then clicked the purse closed.

"Can you believe she came back just to bring that," Barron said, his nervousness returning in a rush. "She was worried when she heard about that private detective. So I guess your telling Jordan to hire Teresa Worth to find her worked, after all."

"That it did," the woman replied. She reached into her pocket and brought out a package of cigarettes and a lighter, lit herself one, then resumed her pacing. Her intelligent and agile mind was running through the options as her crimson lipstick melted around the filter tip. None of the plans pleased her. She swore aloud softly, then kicked the glass lying on the floor against the wall, where it exploded into a hundred shards of tinkling sound.

Barron gasped and jumped, but he didn't protest. He couldn't take his eyes off the blond woman. He watched her the way an insect might watch a spider spinning a web, impressed by the mastery though fearful of his possible place in it.

"Go down and call him at the summer house. Tell him we're bringing Cecilia Joachim to him. Tell him to be sure to send the help away. Then come back up and help me get her into the car."

"Bringing *her?*" Barron stared at Cecilia. She was lying so still he was afraid she might be dead. "But that—that's kidnapping." Trembling moved from his hands to his arms and up to his shoulders. Barron felt feverish and jittery, as if he had influenza, as if his very bones would start shaking next. "You said no one was going to get hurt when we started this. Now two people have been killed and you're fixing to get involved in kidnapping! I can't do this." He collapsed against the door frame, then slid down into a heap on the floor and buried his face in his hands. "I can't!"

"You damn well better, Barron. You've been in this from the first! You want Bay Davis Talmadge ruined as much as I do, and you know it! So stop this poor, weak-kneed poet routine and run down and make that call or I swear I'll kill you!"

Barron removed his hands from his face and stared up at the blond woman he'd loved for so long. She had a leaden, frozen look in her eyes that he'd seen for the first time last week when she had panicked and hit the gas instead of the brakes in the unfamiliar car. The maid's body had been thrown like a plastic highway cone. Neither he nor the man riding in the rear of the car had been able to get her to stop the car.

Slowly Barron rose, the hairs on the back of his neck standing out in fear that he'd be equally impotent in trying to save Cecilia Joachim.

He stumbled down the creaking stairs and ran into the cluttered kitchen. For several frantic seconds he couldn't find the telephone number, but finally remembered that he'd hidden it in the Ladies Auxiliary Cookbook. With hands that felt ice-cold and stiff, Barron Rinaud dialed the number.

After four rings a young girl answered.

"Hello?"

"Hello, darling. This is Uncle Barron. Is your daddy there?"

"Yes, sir, he is. When are you coming to see us?"

"Soon, Katie, real soon. Now run get your daddy."

"Okay. Be right back."

DuBois Beaulieu was not pleased with Barron's message. "Is she out of her mind?" he hissed. "I can't have this! I *won't* have this! My daughter's here, for God's sake."

"Now calm down, DuBois. And don't worry about Katie. We won't be out there till well after dark, so you can just tuck her in and we'll be quiet."

"No. I won't consider it. I'll come to Port Jackson. You two stay put and we'll decide what to do when I get there."

"Doobie, I'm only the messenger here. You best do as she says." Barron knew the reason DuBois had gotten involved in the first place. It wasn't love and greed, as it was with him. It was fear. As the blond woman's number-one point man, Barron thought now might be the right time to remind him of that fear. "You send the maids away, Doobie, and get Katie her dinner, or I'll guarantee the district attorney is going to get an anonymous call about where you're staying now and where you'll be staying if you leave."

DuBois sucked in his breath. "You're as sick as she is, do you know that? She's a murderer, for God's sake! You can't trust her."

"I don't see as I have a choice, DuBois. And neither do you, if you want to stay out of prison."

"You rotten little bast—"

Barron hung up the phone before DuBois was finished. He knew what the man was going to say.

But words couldn't hurt him.

The only person who could hurt him was waiting upstairs. With a sigh Barron took a nip directly from the gin bottle on the counter, stuck a sprig of mint in his mouth and chewed. He hoped no one would happen down the driveway before they got Cecilia Joachim into that car.

Barron looked up at the sky and shuddered. It was blue and cloudless. Spooky weather for August. Maybe the old folks were right and a hurricane was coming.

"Just my luck," he said aloud, staring at the line of dying magnolias, then raced back up the stairs.

Chapter Fourteen

Teresa woke to the sound of bells in the midst of a dream that she was drowning. She sat bolt upright, straining for a breath, her heart beating fast. Nearly falling from the bed, she pulled herself up on shaky knees and peered out the bedroom window, then hurried to the front door.

"Hey, baby girl, how are you?" Zelda asked, a smile lighting up her face. She shook a white envelope in front of Teresa's eyes. "I knew you were anxious for that soil report, so I decided to bring it by and see with my own eyes that you're among the living."

"You're a dear, Zelda," Teresa replied. "Come on in." The sky caught Teresa's eye as Zelda hurried past, and the detective stood for a moment and stared at it. It was blue, too bright a blue for a gulf coast sky. The color looked thin and painted on. Something about the shade made Teresa think suddenly of Jordan Morisette's eyes, and she felt a chill.

She took a step outside and looked around. There wasn't a cloud in sight and, equally unusual, the humidity, which hung like a wet sweater around one's shoulders in Port Jackson during August, was nonexistent.

"What's wrong?" Zelda called from the living room.

Teresa let the screen slam behind her as she returned inside. She ran her hands along her arms to quell the chill bumps that had formed. "Nothing. I was just looking at the sky. It's so weird out there. If I didn't know better, I'd think I was in California, it's so dry and clear."

"If you were in California it might be dry but it sure wouldn't be clear," Zelda retorted. "I've heard that smog looks like a coal fire most days of the summer."

"You're right. But when it rains or the winds blow, nothing is as pretty."

"Well, it ain't going to be pretty around here very long, according to the cleaning woman at Dr. Smithson's. She says it's fixing to blow up a hurricane."

Teresa raised her eyebrows and sat on the couch, her eyes darting to the answering machine. The red light shone steadily, reassuring her that she'd missed no calls during her nap. "I've been hearing that. What does the weatherman say?"

"That it'll miss Alabama by a hundred miles."

"Then I guess we'd better get worried," Teresa said as they shared a laugh. "What time is it? I need to go to the office for a while."

"It's three-thirty, honey. And from the looks of you, I'd say hurricane or no hurricane what you need is to go back to bed. Where were you so early this morning? I stopped by to see if you wanted lunch but you were already gone." Zelda frowned. "Where's your car, anyway?"

"Oh, my car." She'd forgotten that it was still parked on Columbus, in front of the warehouse. It seemed like a month ago that she'd stopped over there. "It's a couple of blocks away. I'll get it later." Casually she slit open the envelope and removed the report while Zelda began a non-stop monologue about a girl who had just had a breast implant. "Don't tell me those aren't store-bought titties," Zelda said with a giggle before Teresa's attention was diverted to the document in her hands.

The toxicologist's report was brief. It gave a fourteen-entry breakdown of the chemical composition of the material, but the lab technician had circled one of the components. That entry read, "Lead, 0575 parts per hundred thousand." He'd then scrawled, "This is well above standards. Suggest you call the EPA if this was from residential area."

Teresa held up her hand to attract Zelda's attention. "This report says the lead content is way beyond normal."

"What is it?"

"Five hundred and seventy-five parts per hundred thousand."

Zelda whistled. "I'll say. God, even those little kids that ate the peeled-off paint in that apartment downtown didn't show that high a reading. Where'd that dirt you gave me come from?"

"A house on Dauphin Street," Teresa replied. Her mind began to whir away as she tried to fit this piece of information into the puzzle of Tiger Development and the dead chemist.

"Well, I'd tell them not to eat anything in that house until they have someone from the EPA get readings. They'll wind up poisoning themselves."

"Lead is that bad? Does it affect vegetation, too?"

"Sure it does. That stuff gets rid of everything in its path quicker than a batch of weed killer." Zelda stood. "Well, I've got to run. I'm going to a potluck over at the church. You want to come along? Jasey Fly is making barbecue and hush puppies."

"No, you go on, Zelda." She gave her friend a quick hug and decided not to tell her about DuBois until she was sure her lead was a strong one. Teresa had found that those around her suffered nearly as much as she did over Katie, once for the child and a second time for the mother.

"Thanks for bringing this by, Zelda. I'll talk to you tomorrow."

After Zelda had gone, Teresa showered and made a plan for the rest of the day. She wanted to get the lab report to Wells. While he had been worried about Raoul Joachim's theft of the formulas for some of the pesticides, Teresa had a sudden fear that Raoul's espionage might have had more sinister consequences. The memory of the dead magnolias, both at Barron Rinaud's and in Sister Hanks's backyard, flashed through Teresa's mind as she speculated on what a major accident with lethal pesticides would do to Rebel Chemicals' reputation and balance sheet.

Teresa shuddered when she thought of Sister's little granddaughter playing in that yard.

Hurrying into her bedroom, she chose her green silk dress. It was the nicest dress she owned, though she didn't allow herself to look too closely into why she wanted Wells to see her looking her best. She added gold earrings and pulled her hair back with combs, smiled at her elegant and somewhat somber appearance, then hurried out into the strange, cool weather.

She would walk over to get the car, then stop and see Wells before she went into the office. And if the opportunity arose, maybe she'd have a little private chat with Durinda Talmadge. The more she mulled over Barron Rinaud's conversation last night, the more she thought there was probably some link between Wells's green-eyed mother who needed money and Tiger Development's inroads at Rebel Chemicals.

A half hour later she pulled onto Davis Circle. The silver Mercedes was parked near the front door. She pulled in behind Wells's car and smoothed down her skirt, hoping she didn't look as worn down as she felt, and walked to the door. Before she could knock, the door opened.

"Evening, Miss Teresa."

"Mazie! Hello, what are you doing over here?"

"I'm just helping Jesse and Margaret out. There's a whole lot of folks coming for dinner, so Miss Durinda sent me."

Teresa read the anxiety in the girl's glance and gave her arm a quick squeeze. "Don't worry about what you told me the other night. I won't mention it to anyone."

"Thank you, Miss Worth. Jesse said she was told there weren't going to be any more of those parties I told you about."

"There aren't?" Teresa replied. "Do you know who told Jesse there weren't going to be?" Her pulse picked up. If Tal or Jordan had told the cook that, it might be a clear link to the scam, and possibly to Verastine's death.

"No, Jesse didn't say. But we all hear things in this town, and most of us really couldn't say from where if you asked us."

Teresa met Mazie's gaze, understanding the wisdom of her remark. "Well, thank you again for letting me know you called Verastine. Now, could you go ask Wells Talmadge if I could see him for a few minutes?"

"Yes, ma'am." Mazie gave her a brilliant and relieved smile, then led her to the same parlor she'd waited in once before.

Barely a minute passed before Wells hurried into the room. "Teresa! This is a lovely surprise. Did you get your nap in?"

"I did." She studied him, liking too much the way he looked in the cool white shirt and beige linen trousers. His blond hair was still damp from a shower, and he had a tiny cut on his chin where he'd scraped it with a razor. "When I got up I was given something I wanted to show you. How about you? Did you go to Pensacola?" She raised her hand to touch the nick on his chin as she spoke. "You look like you were in a hurry when you shaved."

He didn't answer but instead stepped closer and put his hand on her arm. "I'm not doing real good. I keep thinking about this morning." His grip tightened. "I realize my timing is rotten, Teresa, but I want you to know I meant it when I said I wasn't lost in a fit of compassion when I kissed you."

"You don't have to explain, Wells. I wanted you to kiss me. Timing or not, I wanted you to."

Suddenly he stepped closer and folded her into an embrace. Teresa met his mouth, not intending to return his kiss, but did with a hunger that surprised and even shamed her. She opened her mouth onto Wells's and kissed him again, then pulled her face away and rested it breathlessly against his white shirt.

Wells held her fast. "Okay, now that we've agreed on that, what is it you wanted to tell me?" he finally asked.

"I can't do this and think clearly."

Gently he moved her away from him and looked directly into her face. "Is it so bad to lose control sometimes?"

"No." She bit the bottom of her swollen lip. "No."

Wells kissed her again, this time with a nakedness of emotion that shook Teresa's remaining resolve to keep her distance. She held him to her as hard as she could, wishing she could show him the full extent to which she could lose her control. With her hands against his chest she finally broke the kiss. "We'd better stop this now. Your whole family's in the other room."

"I'll lock the door," he said, his voice husky and needy. He nipped at her chin, then trailed a kiss down the side of her neck. His fingers cradled the underside of her breasts, and she felt the delicious, hot stirrings of her body.

"That would keep them out. But not from hearing," she murmured.

She kissed him fully again, hugging him to her, loving the way his hands roamed over the silk of her dress, pressing and urging her. When they separated she kissed his mouth while he stared, his blue eyes hooded, waiting for her to make the final move. She raised her finger and touched the imperfection on the corner of his lip, which seemed more noticeable in the fading evening light. "I like this," she said softly.

"I want you, Teresa," he answered. "Let's leave, go back to your house. Right now."

The words thrilled her but she managed to step out of his arms and fell onto the chaise. "You have an important meeting in a couple of hours, remember?"

"I'll postpone it," he said with a laugh, though his voice told her he could not.

"I have to go to the office, too."

"Is that a no?"

"That's a 'we'll discuss this another time,'" Teresa answered. "And I hope it's another time soon."

Wells's aggravated expression mellowed. "Very soon. Can I get you a drink?"

"Yes. Something soft, though. I'm going to the office."

Wells ran his palms down his thighs, then walked across the room and poured her a ginger ale and himself a whiskey from the decanter on the table. "Okay. What's up?" He handed her the drink then sat beside her on the couch.

"Look at this and tell me what you think." Teresa unfolded the toxicologist's report and handed it to him.

Wells studied it for a moment, then set his drink down with a bang. "Where did you get this?"

"From a lab."

"I mean the sample. What did you send them?"

"A bag of soil I found in Cecilia's apartment the other day. It was labeled *M.* I didn't make much of it until I ran across another one stuck inside a rubber boot. I think it might explain why Tiger Development hired Raoul Joachim to work with them."

"Good God...." With a grim expression Wells read the report again. "I'm no chemist, but I'm fairly sure this is a breakdown of the ingredients in our liquid fertilizer, with the addition of the lead. What the hell...."

"How much damage would it do to you and your grandfather's leadership if there were an industrial accident now? Would it make it easier for Tiger Development?"

"We'd be fish in a barrel. If one of our commercial accounts put this on their crops, it would wipe the crop out and pollute the soil for a hundred years!"

"And you'd get smacked with a lawsuit?"

"Hmmph. We'd probably get slammed with a temporary restraining order by the government not to do business. This is incredible."

"Do you think Raoul already altered the formula on the computers? If he did—"

"We're thinking alike, Teresa. If this stuff was mixed it could already be ready to ship out." Wells stood. "I'm going to call the plant and have them freeze all shipping until we can spot test every batch." He yanked open the door but then stopped short, spun around and pulled Teresa back into his arms. "I'm sorry, I'm ready to jump back into work and leave you sitting here. Can you wait a few minutes and let me come with you to your office? I want to help you get the ball rolling on following up on Katie. We could even drive over to New Orleans, if you want to try to see that lawyer who handled the paperwork on the property Sister Hanks is living on."

"No. You go ahead and make your calls. I'll finish my drink and then go to the office."

"I'm going to take your advice and let the family know everything that's gone on. But I'm not looking forward to laying out everything we've discovered about Tiger Development, especially to my grandfather. I called his doctor today and told him the meeting was going to be stressful. He said Bay was strong, but now with this…" He glared at the report in his hand and shook his head.

"I understand how you must feel, Wells. But your family trusts you. When the chips are down, they'll pull together."

"I'm not so sure, Teresa. One or more of them may have sold out already. Look, let me run and make that call. My aunt and my mother and grandmother are out on the back veranda. Come sit and visit with them, then I'll walk you out to the car."

The opportunity to talk to Durinda was too appealing to pass up. "Okay," Teresa replied. "I've got time for that."

BAY AND SISSY TALMADGE sat on the swing, not talking, both staring off into the strange, dry coolness of the night. Eugenie was absent, and so was Jordan. Tal Morisette sat by himself on the settee across from his grandparents and Durinda was polishing her fingernails at the small table opposite him, a bizarre thing, Teresa thought, since the woman lived somewhere else.

"You all remember Miss Worth. I'm going to leave her with you folks for a few minutes while I make a call."

"Hello, everyone," Teresa murmured, sitting beside the senior Talmadges. They nodded and said good evening, although Tal ignored her. Durinda smiled as she stood and gave Wells a kiss before he left, then gave Teresa a head-to-toe appraisal before returning to her grooming.

Sissy smiled. "How nice to see you again, dear. You're Jordan's friend, aren't you?"

"She's not a friend, Grandmother," Tal muttered. "Miss Worth is a detective. She was working for Jordan."

"Jordan hired her?" Bay yelped, then glared at his wife. "Did that boy say Jordan hired a detective? What in God's name for?"

Tal returned to his drink without answering, but Durinda answered before Teresa could. "Something about that little housemaid, I think. She ran off with a piece of jewelry of Gens's and Jordan tried to handle it herself instead of going to the police. You know how fond our family is of managing little scandals like that, don't you, Daddy?"

Bay's face reddened and he leaned forward on his cane. "Tal! Go get that sister of yours. I want to talk to her," he yelled, stamping the heel of the cane on the floor.

"She's indisposed, Grandfather," Tal retorted. "One of her beaux up and died so she's in mourning. At least until dinner," he added, bitterness and booze obviously in control of his tongue. "After dinner I'm sure she'll want to go out and get a replacement for him."

"I'm sorry," Teresa began, her mind rushing to Raoul's death. Before she could think of a tactful way to extract a name from Tal, his grandmother cut her off.

"Tal Morisette!" Sissy gasped. "Don't you talk that way about your sister. My goodness, what will our guest be thinking about us?" Sissy smiled at Teresa nervously. "Can I get you another drink, dear? Don't pay any mind to this family of mine. Everyone's out of sorts because of the weather. Jesse, that's our cook, she says there's a hurricane coming."

"I said go fetch Jordan," Bay interrupted, pointing his cane at Tal. "Right now, boy! I want this aired out before this damn meeting tonight!"

"Someday I'm going to have enough money not to have to do your bidding, old man." Tal stood unsteadily and walked out of the room.

"Tal! Don't you ever—"

"Quiet, Sissy," Bay interrupted. "He's just blowing off steam."

Teresa looked after Tal and felt compassion for the young man despite his behaviour. It was the first time she'd seen him without Jordan, and he seemed more than ever a shadow person, lost without his vibrant mirror image.

"Don't ever be rich, Miss Teresa," Bay said. "It don't bring any happiness. Just look at my family. Rich and miserable."

"Daddy, really," Durinda said. "I'm not miserable."

"'Course you're not, darling. You're like me. You make people miserable. Not me, of course, because I pay your bills. Speaking of which, I heard Tal say yesterday that you're planning a trip to Hawaii. How in damnation do you think you're going to pay for that?"

"Now, you shush, Bay. Don't go making a scene," Sissy said.

"Don't you go shushing me," Bay shouted. "Miss Worth, I want you to explain again exactly what it was my granddaughter thinks she hired you to do."

"I can't do that, Mr. Talmadge," Teresa said. She cast a look at Durinda, hoping for some kind of support in this awkward situation, but saw that Durinda was enjoying the discomfiture the Talmadge cocktail hour was suffering. "But if it'll put your mind at rest, I'm not working for Jordan anymore."

"No? You mean you found the housemaid?"

All eyes were suddenly on her and Teresa swallowed. "No. But Jordan decided not to pursue the issue any further. And that's really all I can say."

"It must be interesting work that you do, dear," Sissy said hurriedly, hoping to settle things a bit. "How does one become a detective?"

"Most of us are ex-cops," Teresa replied. "We all use the same techniques."

"Oh?" Durinda chortled. "I thought private detectives got to do fun things, like break and enter, and all those kinds of things."

"No. We follow the law. More than most people."

Durinda gave her a piercing look, trying to determine if she'd been insulted. Teresa decided that this was as good a time as any to make her escape.

"Thank you for the drink, Mrs. Talmadge. I'm going to go on ahead and leave now. Please tell Wells good-night for me. I'll see myself out."

"Don't rush off, dear," Sissy began.

"Let her go," Durinda said. "The girl's busy, what with all the work she's not doing for Jordan."

Teresa let the dig drop and headed down the cool hallway, looking both ways for a sign of Wells, but he wasn't anywhere she looked. Neither was Tal, though she thought she caught the sound of Jordan crying somewhere upstairs. She opened the front door just as a dark blue Cadillac with Florida plates careered into the driveway.

It parked beside the other cars, and Eugenie Wallace got out. Teresa was shocked to see her driving herself, and more surprised as she tossed a smoking cigarette into the azalea beds.

Eugenie rushed blindly toward the door, clutching a long silver chain hanging on the front of her blouse. When she was a couple of feet away, Teresa spoke.

"Evening, Miss Eugenie."

Eugenie stopped short, grasping the pillar beside her. Her necklace, a lovely filigree locket, swung free. "Oh. Hello, dear. Good evening."

"That's a lovely car," Teresa said, nodding at the sedan.

"Do you like it? Wells gave it to his mother. I find it too big and too fast."

"I know what you mean," Teresa replied. Suddenly she remembered the day she'd seen Wells at Verastine's wake. He'd been picked up in this car, probably by Durinda.

Eugenie smiled vacantly then hurried past Teresa and into the house.

Teresa wasted no time. She walked around the sedan, noticing a small dent on the front right bumper. The panel underneath was crimped, with rust already setting in where the paint was chipped. Quickly Teresa reached in her purse for a plastic bag, scraped a piece of paint off with her nail, and hurried off to her own car.

She was filled with dread over the possibility of having to tell Wells she suspected his mother in the hit-and-run accident, and sicker still to think Durinda Talmadge was that cold-blooded.

A half hour later she dropped the sample by the police station and asked one of the men on the case to compare the paint sample with what they'd taken from Verastine. Surprisingly the cop didn't give her the third degree about how she'd come by it, and even agreed to call her with the results.

Teresa then went to her office. She made three calls and drafted two letters. Her search for the registered owner of the utilities at the property inhabited by Sister Hanks promised to be a long, drawn-out affair, but she was used to that in her efforts to find DuBois.

When she finished that task, she picked up Wells's file and opened it to add her notes about Tiger Development and the lab report on the soil sample. She sat for several minutes, going over the likely suspects to have been involved inside the family with the takeover attempt, and kept coming back to Tal and Jordan. She had to clarify why they had been looking for Cecilia. While her instincts told her it was to find Raoul and silence him, her brain again had trouble imagining those two as cold-blooded murderers. Plus, in the warehouse that night, the overheard female voice was familiar, but it was the man's that had been most haunting, and she was sure it wasn't Tal's.

Sighing, Teresa added the name Franklin Reynolds with a question mark to the page of things to do.

When she wrote the name she had a sudden memory of seeing it before Wells had mentioned it. But where? She picked up the phone book and found no local listing for the name. Turning quickly, she dropped the book and knocked over a stack of paperbacks she'd never gotten around to reading. They tumbled to the floor.

Leaning to pick them up she had a sudden flash of memory. She was in Cecilia's apartment. The old textbooks by the drafting table had been inscribed "F. Reynolds—Auburn University" along with a year. But what year? She'd have to go back and check that out, she thought with excitement.

Her rising spirits triggered another idea. She made a call to directory assistance in Auburn, then surprised herself by reaching the alumni association president by phone. Mr. Walter Mornay was courteous and pleasant. When she told him she was looking for relatives who attended Auburn, he was more than willing to help. She asked for current mailing information on DuBois Beaulieu, Franklin Reynolds, Durinda Talmadge and Barron Rinaud, the four people in the midst of her puzzle who attended Auburn and might be involved in Tiger Development.

Mr. Mornay promised to call her back.

Teresa leaned back and decided she'd had a good day, after all. It was seven-fifteen, so she resolved to go home. She stood, but the ringing phone made her turn back to her desk. Maybe it was Wells, she found herself thinking with excitement. She couldn't wait to tell him about the headway she'd made.

"Hello. Worth Investigations."

There was a pause, then a timid, elderly voice spoke. "Miss Teresa? Is that you?"

"Yes. Who is this?"

"This is Sister Hanks Harper, Miss Teresa. I come into Port Jackson on account of the storm that's coming, and

Vergel Glenn gave me your office number. Can you talk with me for a minute?''

"Of course, Sister. I'm glad you called. If you're worried about that box of stuff I took this morning, I told you—"

"No, ma'am, I ain't worried about that none. I told you, it's nothing to do with me. No, I'm calling you on account of something else."

"Yes?"

"I seen him."

Teresa's heartbeat sped up and she swallowed. "You saw him? Who, Sister?"

"Mr. DuBois. I seen him today at a house in Fairhope."

"My God. Was Katie with him?"

"No. Not that I saw, Miss Teresa. I just saw him. Same old tall, skinny boy. Nice clothes but needing a haircut. He was in the backyard of a house over on Azalea. My daughter Jewel works next door to it."

"Where exactly in Fairhope, Sister?"

"I don't know its number, but I think it belongs to the Talmadges. Big old house not used much."

Teresa's hands began to shake. She couldn't believe her quest to get Katie back might finally be over. But if DuBois was at the Talmadge place, what did that mean? The obvious answer was that one of the Talmadges, like it or not, wasn't just spoiled, but also rotten and capable of murder. "Thank you, Sister. Thank you so much for calling me."

"Don't thank me none, Miss Teresa. I'm just keeping a promise to poor old Verastine, is all. I'm done with it now."

Teresa hung up the phone, then ran from the room. *She* wasn't done with it. Not by a long shot.

Chapter Fifteen

Teresa yanked the green silk dress over her head and dropped it in a heap at her feet. She didn't stop to pick it up but pulled on black cotton slacks, a purple T-shirt and dark running shoes. She pocketed her flashlight and a lock-picking kit she'd kept since her days as a cop on the street.

She'd taken the kit off a burglary suspect who'd shot her partner with his own gun and escaped, partially because she'd gone out for coffee without double-checking that the man was locked in his cuffs. It had been the worst night of her life as a cop, and had convinced her to give in to Doobie's pleas that she quit the force and come to Port Jackson with him for a fresh start.

She'd kept the picks as a reminder to never underestimate what cornered people are capable of, never dreaming that the cornered person might some day be her own husband.

"Damn, I should have bought another gun," she said aloud, but shrugged off her anxiety about being unarmed. She couldn't picture a real need for pulling a gun on Du-Bois, anyway, especially in front of Katie. Teresa's heart lurched at the thought of her daughter and the burning excitement that she might have her back as soon as tonight. She stopped in the kitchen to grab an apple to quiet her complaining stomach and had just picked up her bag when the phone rang.

Teresa glanced into the living room. It was exactly eight. She walked to the coffee table and stared down at the phone. The answering machine clicked and she held her breath.

"Teresa, this is Wells. My grandfather had another heart attack a few minutes ago. Jordan and my mother just left with Sissy and the ambulance. I'm following with the others. Meet me at the hospital if you can." His voice lowered and was muffled, as if he was covering the receiver so as not to be overheard. "The police are looking for you, Teresa. Betts Vaut was here a few minutes ago. He said the ballistics report has come back and the bullets that killed Raoul are the type your gun used. They're also mad as hell about some paint sample you dropped by. Said it's from the car that hit Verastine Johnson. Betts is pretty nervous, Teresa. I didn't tell them about DuBois."

Teresa swallowed and reached for the phone but the line disconnected and the tape whirred. She felt a sickening rush of fear. Had someone crept into her house and stolen her gun, planning all along to set her up for a fall?

Were Tal and Jordan cold-blooded enough for that? Her brain said no, although she thought they were gullible enough to be led by someone cold-blooded. Someone like Durinda Talmadge, who had dated DuBois and who knew Teresa was an ex-cop who owned a gun? Or even DuBois himself? The fact that Doobie had been spotted at the Talmadge summer place pointed even more strongly to Durinda being the rotten apple in the barrel of Talmadges.

"God, what a family," Teresa said, picturing the Talmadge clan. She recalled how fragile and scared Eugenie had looked, grabbing at her necklace, rushing to the family meeting that had ended tragically with Bay's heart attack.

Suddenly a piece of the puzzle snuggled into place inside her brain. "The necklace," Teresa gasped. Jordan had said she wanted Cecilia found because of the necklace inside the purse the maid had stolen. "It's a silver locket, with heavy scrolled filigree work. Aunt Eugenie's mad for it," Tal had said.

Wasn't Eugenie wearing that necklace tonight? If she was, it meant someone had seen Cecilia and recovered it. But who?

Teresa stood stock-still, letting the fragments of the two cases she was immersed in become a single picture. Suddenly she knew what was going on.

DuBois would have to wait a little longer for the verbal justice she intended to dish out to him, she decided. She knew Katie was safe. First she had to check out her hunch while she could still prevent more blood from being spilled.

TERESA PARKED on the block behind Dauphin, next to a foreign compact with Florida plates. She jimmied the lock and found the car was registered to Raoul Joachim.

With any luck she was sure she was going to find Cecilia Joachim back in her little apartment. What better place for the housemaid to hide than in plain sight? No one would think to look there, except perhaps Durinda Talmadge, who lived right around the corner.

Barron Rinaud's house was completely dark as Teresa crept by. If he had attended the Talmadge family meeting tonight, he was probably with the clan at the hospital. She stopped under the dead magnolia trees and stared at the apartment. A dim light shone from somewhere inside, and it appeared that the door was open a crack. She worried about getting up the squeaky wooden stairs without attracting attention. While she didn't fear any bodily harm from Cecilia Joachim, she wanted to get a look at what was going on in there before she made her presence known.

The wind was picking up and the darkening sky was now full of clouds. It was a complete change from the earlier balminess, for the air was heavy and ominous. Heat lightning flashed from the south, and a few scattered drops of rain splashed in Teresa's face.

She took a step away and her foot hit something solid. Teresa leaned down under the magnolia tree and flashed her light. It looked as though the area had been freshly dug up. She kicked with her foot, then leaned down and used a stick to dig around. In a few seconds she hit something hard. Only a couple of inches down she uncovered a metal container. A label on it read Rebel Chemicals. Teresa recoiled in horror. God, had the chemist buried his altered poison here?

Making a mental note to have someone from the EPA come out first thing tomorrow, she pushed the dirt back and brushed her hands off. She needed to wash, but first she hurried to the side of the building and walked around to the back. The curtains on the windows were open, but she saw no way of getting up that high. Then she spotted the ladder. The same one she'd seen, no doubt, the day she'd been attacked.

Had it been there all the time without Betts Vaut's boys ever seeing it? "So much for police work," she mumbled, then tugged at the ladder. She could manage it, she thought, if she could just keep it from crashing against the house. After five minutes of negotiating she leaned the ladder against the back side of the apartment and then stood back and watched the window. No one looked outside. Though she'd heard no sounds from the room, her instincts told her someone was inside.

Gingerly she began to climb the ladder. The wind was picking up by the second and she knew she had to do this now or risk getting blown off. One of the rungs was broken, but Teresa managed to get to the window. Holding her breath, she raised her head and peeked in.

The light that was on came from the bathroom. The door was closed. Cecilia Joachim was lying on her side on the open sofa bed, sleeping. Nothing looked amiss.

Okay, Teresa thought. I'll climb down, go to the door and pay Cecilia a visit. Ask her about Durinda Talmadge and some floating pyramid games and if she could identify Durinda from the night of the killing. She began to negotiate downward. While she was in there, she was also going to ask Cecilia about the old chemistry books with "F. Reynolds" written inside. Somehow she still thought they might be important, though how she couldn't imagine.

"Hold it right there, honey. Step down nice and easy."

Teresa froze, three steps from the ground, and turned slowly. Barron Rinaud stood a foot away from the ladder. He was wearing a white suit and a blue-striped shirt with a yellow bow tie.

"Mr. Rinaud."

"Just go ahead and step down, darling. Watch out for that broken rung, now. We wouldn't want you to get hurt."

It was then that she noticed the weapon he aimed at her. Silver glinted in the moonlight. If she wasn't mistaken, it was her own gun.

"I think that's my pistol, Mr. Rinaud. Where did you find it?"

That made him smile, but only with his mouth.

"You going to shoot me for trespassing, Mr. Rinaud?" she added.

The wind took Teresa's words and swallowed them. She couldn't tell if he'd heard her, but she could tell one thing. He wasn't kidding. Slowly she stepped down to the ground.

"I think I should say 'put your hands up.'" Rinaud cackled. "Always wanted to say that to someone, but never got the chance. You come on along with me now upstairs."

"Great. I wanted to talk to Cecilia, anyway."

"Oh, Cecilia ain't in any shape to be talking, honey, but y'all come up, anyways."

His words sent a chill of fear skittering down her neck, but she kept her hands up and continued walking. When they got around to the side of the building, she saw headlights coming down the driveway. She glanced at Barron Rinaud, but he didn't seem the least bit concerned that in five seconds he was going to have an audience.

She stepped forward slowly, nearing the steps, then saw the car. It was the silver Mercedes. Suddenly Teresa whirled around and kicked at Barron Rinaud. Her foot found the gun, which went flying out of his hands into the weeds. He made a choking sound. Teresa slugged him in the stomach, then turned and ran toward the car.

"Wells, watch out!" Teresa grabbed for the door as it opened, then looked into the dead, cold eyes of Eugenie Wallace.

"Oh, Miss Wallace—" she gasped.

Without a word Eugenie raised her hand. She held a tire iron in her blue-veined fist. Before Teresa could duck, Eugenie hit her on the side of the head.

Teresa felt consciousness rush away and fell to the ground as the first raindrops began to fall from the sky.

SHE WAS BLEEDING. Not badly, but enough to feel faint and shaky. Teresa tried to sit up, but she couldn't manage it.

With a deep breath she closed her eyes and marshaled her strength. After a moment she opened her eyes again, the dizziness abating a bit. As far as she could make out, she was in a dark, black-dark, confined space, like a large closet. Her hands were tied behind her. She moved her legs and found that her feet were also bound.

"Damn," she said aloud, then quieted. Outside she heard noises. Nature noises. The wind was howling in gusts.

Somewhere close by, the sea was pounding against rocks. She was near the gulf. Very near. She could smell the salt.

Slowly she brought her legs up to her chest and rolled on her back. A crack of light shone through the wood above her, and in the dimness she made out the shape of a rope handle. A door above? She was in some kind of a bin, she decided. Like a sack of potatoes!

Her anger and frustration began to resurface, but only made her head throb. She felt the tightness of torn skin when she moved her eyes, so the blow Eugenie Wallace had landed must have opened her scalp. She was lucky she had such a hard head.

Teresa rolled back onto her side. Something was jabbing her on the hipbone. With a glimmer of hope she remembered her burglar's kit. Six thin screwdrivers and four files. If she could only wiggle them out.

For what she was sure was an hour, Teresa worked to push the small plastic pouch from her pocket. Finally she managed to maneuver them to the top, but she could not reach her fingers around far enough to pull them from her pocket without dislocating her shoulder. She laid her head down and felt the sting of tears against her eyelids, but bit her lip and made herself stop.

"Think, Teresa," she scolded. The gold hoop earring she'd put on earlier brushed against her cheek and an idea formed. Pushing with her shoulder and her chin, she managed to pin the earring against her face, then stuck her tongue over the hoop. After several tries she managed to grab the earring with her teeth.

Shutting her eyes against the anticipated pain, Teresa pulled, jerking the ring open and through her ear. The bauble spun away, pinging against the concrete floor and rolling away in the dark. Her earlobe stung, but she didn't think she'd hurt herself too badly. The memory suddenly of Katie as an infant pulling her earring off that way made her smile and gave her the strength to go on.

She scooted across the floor and found the earring, then used it as a kind of hook to finally pull the screwdriver kit from her pocket. When she felt it slide out she nearly cried aloud, though she managed to keep quiet. Despite the howling wind and storm outside, she was worried about who might be in the room above.

After her escapade with the ladder, Teresa had learned not to mistake silence for safety.

The rope was tight but not thick, and the file proved blessedly sharp. After about fifteen minutes of sawing with her cramping right thumb and index finger, she felt the rope snap, then tumble off. She sat up with a sigh, her shoulders aching and complaining, and rubbed her arms to restore the circulation. The wound on the side of her head seemed small, and she realized the comb she'd worn to look nice for Wells had probably broken the blow. She found one of the plastic teeth in her hair and thought ironically how vanity had played a part in saving her from more serious injury.

She should have picked up the phone and talked to Wells, she realized. If he had been with her, she probably wouldn't have been ambushed by Rinaud.

Pushing a surge of self-pity aside, Teresa attacked the ropes on her feet. A minute later she was free. She stood as far as she could and rolled her head and shoulders around. The tiny black space spun a bit, but with more deep breaths she overcame the dizziness. Slowly she explored the area. It was about six feet square, but just a little more than five feet tall. The rope handle brushed against her hair, so she ducked down. If someone was on watch on the other side, she didn't want to give them any reason to open the door until she was ready.

She leaned against the wall. It was concrete, like the floor, and very cold and damp to the touch. Wet, in fact. She rubbed the moisture off her fingers. Water was seeping in slowly from somewhere.

Teresa glanced again at the wooden door above her. Besides her bent earring and the pouch of burglary tools, there wasn't another thing in this hole to help her defend herself, or get out once she was ready to try the door. She felt her other pocket for the flashlight, but it was gone. Barron and Eugenie must have taken it before they'd tossed her down here. Thinking of them made her madder. What had happened to Cecilia? she wondered. The memory of the young girl lying on the bed pushed Teresa into action.

It was time to get out of here, to take another risk. She removed the thickest and sharpest of the screwdrivers from her pouch and curled her fingers around it. As weapons went, it was puny, but it might give her an element of surprise. With a deep breath she gently pushed against the door.

The thick wooden partition didn't move.

She pushed harder.

It stayed firm.

Exasperated, and unable to locate any kind of lock or bolt on the face of the door, Teresa stood directly under the center of it and put her weight into a hearty shove. The wood creaked and gave, then popped open. After hours in the darkness, Teresa's eyes ached at the light and she had to blink to make them focus.

She was in a garage!

The silver Mercedes was parked a few feet away. She leaned on her shoulder and pulled herself up and out of the hole, then closed the lid and looked around.

On the other side of the car was another door exactly like the one she'd been stored behind. Was Cecilia in there? Teresa wondered. Slowly she made her way around the car. Rusty gasoline cans and paint cans lined one wall, and below them gardening tools were heaped in a pile. Teresa's eyes searched through the tools, looking for a better weapon than she had, but a spade or even a pair of pruning shears didn't offer much improvement.

She continued to clutch the screwdriver and moved slowly toward the garage door. Three glass windows were built into the door, but the glass was broken out and the openings were covered with plywood. She looked through a crack and saw the back of a huge, sprawling house. Lights were on, but she didn't see anyone inside.

Quickly she hurried to the other storage bin. With both hands she grabbed the frayed rope handle and pulled. It creaked open and she peered inside. Cecilia Joachim lay facedown on the pavement, bound in the same fashion Teresa had been.

"Cecilia," Teresa called. The girl didn't move. Despite her racing heart, Teresa lowered herself into the pit beside the prone girl. Her pulse was very slow and she felt cold. Teresa's anger at Barron Rinaud and Eugenie Wallace increased. She removed the light jacket she'd thrown over her T-shirt and covered Cecilia, then cut the ropes. She needed to get her out of the hole, for this one was even damper than the one she'd been held in.

But with Cecilia unconscious, she didn't see how that was possible. Teresa knew she couldn't lift the girl over her head. She was going to need help to get her out.

Slowly she rubbed her hands up and down Cecilia's bare arms and gently slapped her face. The girl moaned, but her eyes didn't so much as flutter. Teresa struggled to wrap the jacket around her, lifting her onto her lap. When she did she felt something fall to the floor. Teresa reached over and picked up the metallic object.

It was a silver filigreed locket. She held it close to her face, then turned it over. On the back was inscribed "To Eugenie Talmadge love Franklin Reynolds, 12/25/47." Teresa snapped open the locket and found a man's picture inside. The name seemed hauntingly familiar.

"Who the hell is Franklin Reynolds?" Teresa whispered. And how did he tie Eugenie to Doobie's property, Tiger Development and murder?

Gently she laid Cecilia back on the floor. She had to get some help or this girl was going to die, of that she was sure. Teresa pulled herself out of the bin and walked back to the Mercedes. Maybe she could use the screwdriver to break inside. But could she start the car? Her days as a cop had taught her how crooks hot-wire cars, but this one was a diesel and she wasn't sure if ignition systems all worked the same. Besides, if the car had an alarm . . .

She turned to the garage door. It would be safer if she went out and called for help. Teresa bent down and tried to lift the door. It wouldn't budge. She looked through the crack and still saw no one inside, but the visibility was markedly worse than a few minutes before. Rain lashed the earth at a driving speed, and the wind howled steadily. She felt the wooden slats of the garage creak around her and wondered suddenly if the Port Jackson natives who had predicted a hurricane had been right.

"Just what I need," Teresa muttered. She picked up the pruning shears and approached the boarded-up windows. Tired and more scared with each minute, Teresa was ready to try something reckless. If she pried off the wood she could wiggle through, then seek help from a neighbor. She stuck the pruning shears in the crack, then the lights went off. For a moment she stood completely still, choking on panic.

Finally she realized that no one had thrown a switch; the electricity had gone out because of the storm. She pushed the shears through the crack and struggled to break the board. It gave way with a crash and the rain poured in, but she put her head down, heaved herself up and pushed her shoulders through the opening. A jagged piece of glass scraped her arm but she ignored the wound and pushed the hair out of her eyes.

Rain was falling in a torrent. She could barely make out the porch of the house, and knew she had to hurry or someone could be upon her before she ever saw them.

Teresa turned to the left and ran parallel to the house. About fifty yards from the garage she came to a brick wall at least eight feet high. Another car, a black Cadillac with Florida plates, was parked there. "Damn," she said aloud. Who else was here with Rinaud and Eugenie?

The car was locked. She knelt beside it and tried to look inside but in the dark and the rain she couldn't see anything but the gold-etched initials on the driver's side door. "D.G.B." glimmered in ornate script.

Teresa stood, feeling as if her heart would pound right out of her chest. DuBois Gaillard Beaulieu. "My God, I'm at the Talmadge house Sister told me about," she said aloud, though no sound escaped in the storm.

Which meant Katie, her darling girl, could be inside.

Teresa clutched the screwdriver and ran back toward the house. Her mothering instinct overruled her police training and any fear for her own or Cecilia Joachim's safety. If Katie was in there with Eugenie and Barron Rinaud, she might be in trouble. Teresa ran faster despite the danger, for where Katie was concerned, there was no contest.

EUGENIE LIT THE CANDLE and placed it on the table.

"You're not going anywhere, DuBois. Stop being fool-ish," she snapped.

The slim, angular-faced man with the red-gold hair sat across from her. He glared at Barron Rinaud, who stood in the doorway with the silver pistol gripped in his hands. "You are absolutely out of your mind, Eugenie. You're not going to get away with this. You ruined everything when you shot that chemist!''

"He was backing out of our deal,'' she said simply. "I'm enough of a Talmadge to never allow that. Besides, I'm not the only one with blood on my hands,'' she added.

"What are you implying? I never hurt anyone. . . .''

"Don't forget about that poor maid what was killed,'' Barron drawled from the doorway. "Poor old Verastine.''

"Eugenie was driving when the car hit her,'' DuBois shouted. "I told you all to go for help when we stopped, but you wouldn't.''

"You know that was impossible. She saw you! She opened her eyes and we all realized she recognized you. Or don't you remember about that?''

DuBois clenched his jaw, his small, pale eyes darting nervously around the room. "Look, I agreed to find a lawyer to front for Tiger Development. And I went to Paris and made the arrangements for the phony company. But I sure as hell never agreed to go around killing people just so you could finally humiliate your brother.''

"I never planned to merely humiliate Bay Talmadge, my dear, I planned to ruin him. And I nearly have. So don't go pretending I'm the criminal and you're an angel.'' Eugenie tapped her fingernails against her teeth, then pointed at DuBois. "The only reason you came in on this deal was greed. Just like two years ago, when you bought that property that was left to me by Franklin because you'd heard it was up for development. You tried to take advantage of me, Doobie, and now I'm taking advantage of you. Only I promised you a tenfold return on your money and you're going to get it. I got Tal and Jordan and Winton Smithson to give me proxies for their stock and I now control the biggest share. In a matter of days I'm going to call a meeting of the board, get rid of Bay and Wells and sell the company to the highest bidder. It's all working out like we planned last year. It's no time to panic, DuBois. You'll have enough money to go back to Europe with your daughter for good."

"For God's sake, Eugenie. You've got the police looking for a murderer now! And if you think your nephew and your brother are going to sit still once you've played your hand, your grasp of reality is even more tenuous that I thought. I'm out of this deal now." He stood. "You fired the gun that killed Raoul Joachim, Eugenie. Not me."

Eugenie waved her hand in the air as if to swat a bug. "Sit down, DuBois. You stole that gun from your poor little old ex-wife's house to implicate her in a crime one of your sleazy friends was planning. Don't you think the police are going to find that interesting?"

"How do you know—" DuBois stopped himself too late and sat. He ran his hands through his hair, shaking his head as if he couldn't believe he was being bested by the two people before him. "Look, I stole that gun as a way to get her off my back in the custody battle. She would have never done any time. My plan would have worked, too, except that you had to send Tal and Jordan Morisette out to get her involved in finding your damn necklace!"

"I'll thank you not to refer to my engagement present that way." Eugenie clutched the bodice of her dress and gave out a little cry. "My locket! Where is it?"

"Don't worry, darling. I'll find it for you," Barron said, walking closer to the table where she and DuBois were seated. "But first we have to decide what we're going to do now."

"You're in no position to decide anything, Barron," DuBois said. "Everything you've planned so far has backfired."

"I think not," Barron said, pointing the gun at him. "I think my suggestion to Eugenie that Jordan hire your wife was a good way to keep an eye on you. Besides, with Wells running around after Miss Worth, it gave us all a little breathing room."

DuBois raised his hand as if to strike out at Barron, but Eugenie stood and slapped her hand against the table. In the soft light her face was lined and haggard; her blond hair frizzed around her face. "Stop it, the both of you. We have to think what we're going to do now. Cecilia Joachim knows too much. I say we need to get rid of her."

DuBois stared at Eugenie, but Barron kept his eyes on the gun. "We could shoot her with Miss Teresa's little piece of business here," Rinaud said in a strangely flat voice. "'Cause little Miss Detective a little more trouble that way."

"You two better not involve Teresa in this any further," DuBois yelled. "My God, she's no fool! If you keep pulling her into this, she's going to figure it all out!"

"You scared of your ex-wife, Doobie? Don't be. She might figure it out," Barron retorted, "but she ain't in no position to tell anyone about it."

"What do you mean?" DuBois demanded, his arrogant bravado slipping back to show fear. "What have you done now, Eugenie?"

"Shut up," Eugenie said sharply. "Don't talk to me like that, DuBois! Franklin won't have anyone speaking to me in that tone."

Doobie stood and leaned over the table to whisper to Barron. "Look at her! She's losing it. She thinks her dead lover is back. We've got to get the Joachim girl out of here. When she wakes up we'll pay her not to talk, we'll explain that her brother was killed by accident. If we don't panic, by this time next week we'll both be rich."

Barron shifted his eyes nervously toward Eugenie. While the chance to finally be off the stingy dole of Bay Davis Talmadge had been the chief motivation in his turning against his family, Barron's deepest allegiance was to Eugenie. She might be nuts, but she was the only one who'd treated him with any concern at all through the years. Even so, she didn't look well, he had to admit.

"You okay, darling?" he asked. "Maybe Doobie here is onto the right thing. After all, isn't this what you wanted? To own Rebel Chemicals? To pay your brother back for sending Franklin Reynolds away, and into the arms of another woman?"

"Yes," Eugenie murmured in a strangled voice. Her hand clutched again at her throat. "Where is my necklace, Barron? Do you have it?" Her eyes glowed as she reached out for Barron's shoulder. "It's the only thing I have left of his, Barron. When Bay forced me to marry Gerald Wallace, he threw out all my letters and pictures. Said Franklin was only after our money, and that I needed to settle down and forget about the business and concentrate on Gerald. Well, just look at how it all turned out, darling. Now Franklin and you and me will have all Bay's money. Maybe now Bay will know how all us poor relations have felt all these years."

The venom in her voice seeped through the air like poison smoke.

"You're right, darling," Barron said. "Sit down, DuBois. We're not done here yet."

Doobie slumped into his chair while Eugenie began fanning herself with her hand. "It's warm, but I feel so calm. I'm sure it's because Franklin will be here soon. I've waited so long to be with him again."

"Can't you see?" DuBois hissed in Barron's ear. "She's mad. We've got to handle this!"

Eugenie snapped her head around to glare at DuBois and rested her hand gently on Barron's shoulder. "Shoot him, Barron. We don't need him anymore. We'll bring in his wife and leave them both here. The police will think it was a lovers' quarrel. They're so common among the young. Do you remember being young, Barron?"

IN THE HALLWAY OUTSIDE the candlelit room Teresa gasped, then covered her frozen lips with her wet hand. She was dripping wet and shaking, but unable to move. The sight of her ex-husband sitting in the other room had riveted her to the spot for the past several moments, just as the tale of hate and destruction she'd overheard had.

Solving cases in the past had always brought with them great satisfaction, but this night's revelations about who killed Verastine Johnson and Raoul Joachim and why, as well as the reasons for Tiger Development's formation seemed only frightening. Everything was so unnecessary that she felt nothing but sick.

The story was going to devastate Wells, Teresa realized. But she'd have to deal with that later. Now it was time for some action, or more death would follow.

After she'd broken in the back door she'd searched upstairs and found no trace of Katie. She prayed DuBois had sent the child away before the storm had worsened, but knew she couldn't count on it. Teresa was going to have to show herself and ask him, then trust that she and DuBois together could stem the murderous course Eugenie was lucid enough to be plotting.

The walls shook around Teresa and the wind howled against the doors. Somewhere outside she heard a tree snap and crash into the side of the house.

"I said shoot him," Eugenie demanded. "I want him gone before Franklin arrives."

Teresa stared into the room as Barron raised the gun. "Don't shoot!" she yelled, hurling her wet shoes at the center of the table, praying she could distract them by knocking the candle aside.

The flame sputtered and the shoes crashed against the floor. A second later the gun went off and Teresa dived into the room behind the couch. Eugenie was screaming, an eerie, mad wail, while Barron fired wildly.

Two shots. Three shots. Four shots.

In the murky, lightning-lit gloom, Teresa saw Eugenie collapse in a heap. Then, save for the wind and the rain and the impotent clicking of an empty gun, the huge old room was silent. When Teresa finally stood, she realized one of the candles still burned on the floor in the center of the room. It cast its light onto her face.

"It's you!" Barron shouted, and ran out into the storm.

"DuBois, where is Katie?" Teresa demanded.

Her ex-husband got up from behind the chair where he'd been hiding. He was trembling and wan. He'd aged years in his months in hiding, grown thinner and more stoop shouldered. At that moment she couldn't imagine what had ever held her to him for five years. But then she thought of Katie. "Where's my daughter?"

DuBois looked at her in shock, as if she were a specter. "Teresa? But how?"

"There's no time for that now. Where is Katie?"

"She's—she's with the maid. In Port Jackson." He looked around, then gasped. "My God!"

Teresa turned to where he was looking and saw Eugenie. She was propped against the wall, eyes open, a neat round hole in the center of her forehead. Barron's errant shot, Teresa realized, had killed her.

She pushed aside hysteria and spoke with force. "You've got to help me get Cecilia Joachim into the car. The tide's rising fast. We've got to get out of Fairhope before the roads are washed out."

"I can't." DuBois wrapped his arms around his body. "I can't, Teresa."

"Nobody's leaving," a voice called out.

Teresa whirled around.

Barron Rinaud stood in the doorway holding an antique shotgun. Teresa knew from the look of terror and pain in his eyes that it wasn't a good time to ask him if it was loaded.

Chapter Sixteen

"Mr. Talmadge?"

Wells turned toward the soft female voice. The hospital waiting room was crammed full of people consoling his newly widowed grandmother. He had sat in shock and grief for the past few minutes, unable to accept that Bay was dead. He looked numbly at the young black woman speaking to him.

It was Eugenie's maid, Mazie. "Yes?"

"I'm real sorry about your grandpa, Mr. Talmadge. And I hate to bother you while you're with your folks. But Sister Hanks called me and asked me to come down and give you a message."

"It's okay, Mazie," Wells said, forcing himself to stand and escort the young woman out into the hospital hallway. He had a fleeting instant of hope that he'd find Teresa outside, but there was no sign of her. He turned his tired eyes to Mazie. "What's the message?"

"Sister said she told Miss Worth that she saw her ex-husband out in Fairhope this morning, and now she's worried that Miss Worth will be stuck out there in this storm. Sister wanted me to tell you, so's you could help."

"What? Where in Fairhope did Sister send her?"

"Out to a summer house owned by your family, Sister said."

Wells reeled back in surprise. "My family? When was this?"

"Earlier, Mr. Talmadge. Sister said she called Miss Worth at about seven o'clock."

"Thank you, Mazie," Wells said, then hurried out into the parking lot. He couldn't help his family anymore tonight, and he couldn't honestly say he wanted to after the hateful verbal attack on Bay by the others at the meeting earlier.

But he could honestly say that Teresa Worth's safety did matter, and hurricane or no hurricane, he was going to get to Fairhope if he had to swim there.

BARRON HAD TIED HER HANDS behind her back and her legs to the legs of the chair. DuBois was similarly bound, and they sat in gagged silence watching Barron obliterate his pain with a bottle of twenty-year-old brandy beside the dead, staring body of Eugenie Wallace.

Outside the hurricane roared and Teresa felt herself choke on the rage boiling inside her. To think she had come this close to finding Katie, this close to finding love with Wells, only to be cheated out of it by two people's greed and madness. With all her pent-up fury she banged her feet against the floor and, gag or no gag, screamed at Barron to let her go. But he was oblivious to her and Doobie. He sat and drank, one hand on Eugenie's knee, while the storm howled and Teresa glared.

"Think, Teresa, think," she lectured herself, squeezing her eyes closed to concentrate. She could feel the shape of the lock-picking tools in the back pocket of her slacks. If she could just reach them . . .

The sound of glass breaking made her open her eyes. The storm sounded louder now. Nearly simultaneous curtains of lightning and volleys of thunder rocked and echoed off the roof, while rain beat against the windows, blown sideways by the hundred-mile-an-hour winds.

The lack of air pressure was making her feel dizzy, and her hair and skin buzzed from the electricity in the air. In addition, she realized that her feet were wet. God, there was an inch of water on the floor, which meant one of the doors had broken open! The storm was a killer. She had to get out!

Teresa turned her eyes toward Doobie only to find him staring fearfully at the doorway. Glancing quickly in that direction, Teresa was grateful for her gag. For if she'd been able to speak, she would have yelled with joy. Wells Talmadge, tall, gorgeous and soaked to the skin, stood just outside the room in the hallway, his face grim and intense as he perused the shotgun leaning against Barron Rinaud's side.

He looked toward her and she smiled and thanked him and begged him to be careful with a single glance. He nodded, then ran into the room with a shout.

His ruse worked beautifully. Barron fell backward off his chair, knocking Eugenie's body sideways and the gun to the floor.

"What in God's name—" he squeaked.

Wells grabbed the man roughly by his shirtfront. "You worthless bag of bones! What the hell is going on here? Are you insane?"

"Don't hit me, Wells. I didn't mean for this to happen. I've lost sweet Gens. What am I going to do without Eugenie?" Barron was raving drunk, sobbing with fear and grief.

In disgust Wells let his cousin loose, then bent over and felt the side of his great-aunt's neck for a pulse.

"I didn't mean to kill her, Wells! You've got to believe I'd never hurt Eugenie. You know I loved her."

"Shut up!" Wells hollered. "Sit there and don't move."

He lifted the shotgun gingerly from the floor and walked toward Teresa.

"It ain't even loaded, Wells," Barron sobbed, clutching at Eugenie's dress.

Wells leaned down and hugged Teresa, ignoring Doobie as he took a knife from the table and cut her legs and arms free. Teresa pulled the gag from her mouth and fell into his arms. "Oh, God, Wells. Katie isn't here. She's in Port Jackson. Can we get back in before the hurricane comes ashore?"

"Take it easy, Teresa. Katie will be fine if she's in Port Jackson. I don't know if we can get out of here." He looked down at the floor where there was now two inches of water. "But we'd better at least try."

Suddenly Teresa remembered Cecilia. "Oh, God! Cecilia! She's in the garage! Untie Doobie so we can get out of here."

Wells cast his eyes on her ex-husband. "You sure you want me to cut him loose?"

Teresa hugged his arm and stood, nearly falling because of cramps in her legs. "Yes. Hurry. We'll take Barron with us." She looked quickly toward the doorway and froze. "Wells, where did he go?"

Wells spun around, the knife blade glimmering as a terrifying sheet of lightning slammed against the night, illuminating the empty space where Barron and Eugenie's body had been.

"He's gone." He handed Teresa the shotgun. "Hold on to this just in case. Let me cut Doobie's ropes and we'll go outside and get Cecilia. We'll put her in the car and you two can drive her out. I'll look for him then."

"There isn't time!" Teresa wailed, clutching Wells's arm as an explosion like a small bomb being dropped echoed off the bay.

Doobie stood without a word and the three of them faced each other for an instant. "Come on," Wells ordered, "let's get Cecilia."

Doobie followed Teresa and Wells through the house like a sleepwalker. There was no sign of Barron, but without a weapon, and with as much liquor in him as she'd watched him consume, Teresa didn't worry about the little man anymore.

Two minutes later the three of them pulled the still-unconscious Cecilia out of the storage hold and into the back seat of the Mercedes. The keys, to Teresa's fleeting disgust, were on the floor of the car. DuBois started the car and backed it up. "How did you get here?" he asked.

"Your friends brought me," she shot back.

"There's no time for this now," Wells interrupted. "Doobie, head out to the old farm route beyond the town. It's higher and you won't have to go near the causeway."

"I'm not leaving you here," Teresa interrupted, resisting the push Wells was trying to guide her into the car with.

"Yes, you are. Your daughter's waiting for you in Port Jackson, Teresa."

Her eyes filled with tears and her throat burned. She knew he was right, but she couldn't bear to leave him behind. "Come with us, Wells."

"Barron's a scoundrel of the first order, Teresa, but he's family. I've got to at least try to get him out."

"It'd serve him right to drown out there," Doobie said suddenly.

Wells leaned into the car, a look of pure animal hate on his face. "I'd say you're the last person to judge that. Just make sure you get these two women out of here or you'll wish you'd drowned yourself out in the bay."

Turning back to Teresa, Wells pulled her to him and kissed her hard. "I'll follow in my car. Don't worry." He pushed her into the car and slammed the door before she could reply.

Doobie put the car in reverse. It hydroplaned and fish-tailed on the water-covered pavement, then settled down on the crushed rock. Silently Teresa sat in the dark as the car crept down the driveway and out to the road. Several inches of water parted on either side, and it still fell in sheets from the black sky.

At the main road the car died. Teresa opened her door and found a rushing torrent of water. "We're going to have to carry Cecilia. There should be emergency people up the road."

"You're crazy," DuBois shouted back. "I'm going back to the house. It's safer!"

"Don't be a fool," Teresa argued. "It's right on the water. If the tide rises, the walls will give way." She looked across the dim light of the car into Doobie's face but saw no one that she knew. No one that she'd ever known, she realized at that moment. DuBois Beaulieu was not the man he pretended to be, not even to himself.

"I'm sorry, Teresa, but you'll have to go alone. Do what you want. Maybe I can get a ride with your boyfriend," he said, then disappeared into the storm.

Teresa pulled Cecilia out of the car, slung her arm over her shoulder and began to drag her. Her body screamed with fatigue and strain, and she tasted the sweet, sick taste of blood in her mouth.

Her head wound had opened up, Teresa realized. But she had to keep walking. "Come on, Cecilia," she moaned. "Help me!"

They fell. She pulled the sopping girl up into her arms.

A second time they fell, and Teresa was horrified to realize the water was well above their ankles. Cecilia, miraculously, came to. She was in shock and crying, but at least she moved.

Teresa stayed in the middle of the road, trying to follow the broken lines. She tried not to think of Katie, or Wells, or the storm lashing the house he searched for his family in.

Teresa heard a rushing sound in her ears. She was afraid she was going to pass out, afraid she already had. The scene of madness, the sounds of the empty revolver clicking, kept replaying itself as she dragged Cecilia toward the lights ahead. The gun held six bullets, and she always carried ten. Ten bullets had been taken from her purse. Eugenie had fired three times in the warehouse, and hit Raoul twice. That left three bullets.

But Barron after had fired four times tonight; he'd run out of ammunition. Right? It didn't add up, Teresa's brain cried. She blinked and tried to focus. What if it wasn't out of bullets? What if the gun had only jammed? That meant Wells, and now DuBois, had gone back to a house where Barron Rinaud waited, with a gun, her gun, that could still kill.

"No!" Teresa yelled. She turned with the half-drowned Cecilia.

"Teresa!" a voice shouted. "Thank God!" Strong arms were around her, squeezing her.

"Wells? How?" Teresa started to cry. "You've got to send help. To your house. Barron. DuBois."

"I couldn't find him anywhere," Wells shouted.

The loss of blood, the fear and fatigue finally took their toll. Teresa fainted and for the first time in eight months let go of her worries.

Epilogue

"They buried Eugenie and Bay Talmadge on the same day," Zelda said, her voice low and somber. "Don't know when Barron Rinaud's funeral was. No one much wanted to talk about that."

"I don't, either," Teresa said from her hospital bed. "Is Betts coming back today, did he say? I know the paperwork is driving him crazy."

"I told him to leave you alone till tomorrow. Katie's coming back later with Mazie and that child don't need to see Betts Vaut in here with her mama any more than she has already. Besides, after those boys from the EPA dug up all that money Barron had hidden under those dead magnolia trees and it blew over half the town, he's got his hands full."

Despite the sorrow and grief surrounding them, Zelda and Teresa shared a laugh at the thought of Betts Vaut and the Port Jackson police department chasing down one hundred thousand dollars blowing in the wind.

Finally Teresa put her hands against her cheeks. "I can't laugh, Zelda. It makes my head hurt."

"It should hurt. Concussions make your brain swell. Soon as they let you out of here I'm going to make you some stuffed peppers. Peppers are good for swelling. Will Katie-bug eat peppers, you think?"

At the mention of her daughter's name Teresa's heart expanded with a joy she hadn't felt for eight months. "I don't know. We'll ask her." She turned a searching look on Zelda. "She's okay, don't you think? She looks fine, doesn't she, Zelda?"

"She's gorgeous, just like her mama." Zelda looked serious for a moment. "Katie's a strong, sweet child, darling. She's following your lead on this. As long as you stay calm, she will. How'd she take the news her daddy is going to be away for a while?"

DuBois had miraculously survived Hurricane Olivia inside the Talmadge mansion where Barron Rinaud had fallen or jumped down the stairs to his death. Teresa shook her head gently to dislodge the image of Barron with his hand on a dead woman's knee. "Not too badly. She didn't see him much the past few months—I guess he did a lot of traveling. But I think she'll be okay, Zelda. I'll have to tell her someday about DuBois's part in all this, but that can wait. With all his lawyers, he'll be out of prison by the time she's ready to discuss it."

"I still can't believe him throwing in with Eugenie and Barron. Even to make money, he had to see those two were insane with revenge."

"He told me he was trying to change, and hoped to give Katie a happy life. He even said he had planned to let me know where she was in a few months, once they were settled in Europe so I couldn't get her back."

"He's a bastard," Zelda said strongly.

"He's weak, Zelda. But he does love his daughter."

"If that's love, I don't know what you'd call cruelty," her friend retorted.

"Families can be snake pits," Teresa said softly. "At least to some. I gather Doobie's wasn't very warm or caring. And look at the Talmadges. Bay Talmadge was a great businessman and leader, but he wreaked a lot of havoc on the ones he loved most.''

''Hey, pretty lady. Up for some more company?''

Teresa smiled and looked up, glad to be interrupted. With a wave she beckoned to Wells, who stood in the doorway with a single yellow rose in waxed paper as well as a small, covered parcel. ''Yes, but I told you yesterday, no more flowers. You've got this place looking like a florist's already.'' She gestured toward the line of bulging vases against the hospital-room windows.

''This isn't for you. It's for Katie. I told her I'd bring her one of her own yesterday. And I'm a man of my word.''

''Well, I'm going to run off now,'' Zelda chimed in. ''Good to see you again, Wells.''

''You, too, Miss Zelda.'' Wells leaned over and kissed Teresa softly. Her new line of stitches ran down the side of her face, but that didn't detract from her beauty in his eyes. ''How you doing this morning?''

''I'm good. Finally slept last night. How's Cecilia?''

His blue eyes darkened. Teresa saw guilt and anguish in his face and longed to chase it away, but she knew a proud man like Wells Talmadge would never completely shake the shame over what his family had done. He could, however, put it behind him and go on to live without looking back too often.

''She's good,'' Wells answered. ''She flew out to California this morning to be with her family. I'm having her brother's body shipped there for burial. She won't have to come back until DuBois's trial.''

He squeezed Teresa's hand. ''I'm sorry you and Katie are going to have to endure all that.''

''We'll get through it. How's your grandmother holding up?''

''Sissy is a strong woman. She's actually risen to all this. Got Jordan into counseling. Tal's being charged with fraud in their little pyramid scam, but I think they'll go easy on him because of Bay's connections." He laughed ruefully. "Even dead, my grandfather is trying to run the show."

Teresa patted his hand. "And how are you doing? Things quieted down at the plant?"

"I'm trying to get things settled. I've decided to sell my shares to Glomar Plastics, though. They say they want me to stay on as president, but I think I'm going to look for something else."

"Really?" Teresa was stunned to hear Wells speak so casually of walking away from his family's business. She squeezed his hand in support. "Well, whatever you want is fine with me, Wells. I hope you know that."

"I do, baby. I do. Maybe both of us need to think about making someplace other than the gulf coast our home." He kissed her softly. "Sissy says we have to stick together, 'cause that's what families do in hard times."

"I agree," Teresa said quietly.

"Me, too." He walked to the window and peered out as the sunshine streamed through the blinds. "The town's in good shape. Nothing much got damaged. Lost a few trees. Nothing like Frederick."

"How about the summer house? Zelda told me Fairhope took the brunt of the hurricane."

"Water damage is all." He turned back to Teresa. "You saved us the real damage, you know, by not letting me off the hook or backing down in your search for Cecilia."

"I'm glad we found her."

"*You* found her," he said with a smile. "Her and those damn dead magnolias. The whole plot was under our noses the whole time. Raoul must have been testing the mixture when he came to see Jordan so he could report to Eugenie. Such a waste."

"It wasn't your fault, Wells. I hope you understand that."

"I know. But it's all so senseless. Just like my aunt Eugenie's hatred. She lived the last forty years to take what my grandfather loved most, because she thought he'd done that to her. Then they both died the same night, and neither ever knew the truth about the other...." Wells turned his back again and fought for his composure.

"Come here," Teresa said. "Come here and let me remind you that they didn't ruin the important things."

Wells sat beside her and hugged her for a long moment. He kissed her hair gently, then turned Teresa's face to his. "I'm glad you see how important you are to me."

"I do."

"I love you, Teresa, and that's a phrase I want you to hear again in a few months, in a more official setting."

Teresa smiled. "I love you, too, Wells." She felt tears spring into her eyes. She wrapped her arms around Wells's neck and kissed his face. "You're a dear, and I can't wait to be with you forever. But you know Katie and I need some time...."

"I'll give you whatever you need, sweetheart. Time included. I promise you that."

"And you're a man of your word, right?"

"Right. Now come here and let me give you a little physical therapy."

With a smile Teresa went back into his arms.

A few seconds later a small female voice called from the doorway. "Did you remember my rose, Mr. Talmadge?"

Teresa felt a dizzying surge of joy at the familiar voice. "Come see your mama, Katie."

The blond child, all flying legs and hair, threw herself against Teresa. "Hi, Mama! How are you feeling today? Can you come home yet?"

"Tomorrow, little miss," Wells broke in, moving down to allow Katie to sit between him and Teresa. He handed her the flower with a flourish.

"As I promised," he said.

"Thank you very much," Katie said, snuggling into her mother's lap.

"You're welcome," Wells said, then stood. "I'm going to run now, ladies. But how about if I come back around five and bring some shrimp from Mama's for supper?"

"Yes, yes," Teresa and Katie said in unison. "Be sure and ask her to grill it," Katie added. "Mama hates it when people ask her that."

The three of them giggled and Wells blew Teresa a kiss.

"Thank you, Wells," Teresa called.

"Don't thank me," he said. "Just be happy to see me when I get back. Oh—" He looked down at the parcel he'd set on the dresser. "I almost forgot, Miss Katie. I got you something else." Wells pulled the brown paper off the box and opened it. Inside was a handful of ears and soft brown fur.

"Another bunny! Oh, thank you, Mr. Talmadge. Mama, look. He's little, like Gussie was when we got him."

Teresa's eyes brimmed with tears. "Thank you, Wells. For everything." She draped an arm around the warm, dear body of her child and threw a kiss to the man who meant so much to her. "You'll find us here. Waiting for you."

"I'm counting on that," he whispered with a smile.

"Do," Teresa said. "Do."